THE WORLD ACCORDING TO VINCE

a romantic comedy

STUART REARDON
JANE HARVEY-BERRICK

Stuart Reardon Publishing

CONTENTS

The World According to Vince

Copyright © 2020 Stuart Reardon & Jane Harvey-Berrick

Editing by Tonya Allen

Cover photographs by Stuart Reardon & Shutterstock
Cover models: Stu Reardon and Vincent Azzopardi
Cover design by Sybil Wilson / Pop Kitty Designs

MEET VINCE

What readers said about Vince when they met him in 'Gym or Chocolate?'

PLEASEEEEEE tell me there's going to be a book 2... Vin NEEDS to be hog tied and dragged to my book shelf! #VinIsMine

The secondary characters: Vin, Rick's best friend who is a top male model and Cady's best friend Grace, a solicitor, make an interesting pair and I bet these two would make a hilarious partnership. I hope they get to have their story, too.

I loved Rick's best friend, Vin, and will be watching out for his book.

Rick's best mate, Vin, had me in fits, swears like a trooper and dishes out dodgy advice like hotcakes, and Grace, Cady's bestie is lovely.

Add in secondary characters like Vin ('fooker' seems to be his favourite word) and Grace (as elegant and as spirited as her name) to round out the craziness that is this story.

There are other delightful friends included in the narrative, Vin and Grace, the besties.

Speaking of panty melting ... the athlete turned model that is Rick's friend, Vin. He's goofy, irreverent and hot! And then there's Cady's lovely friend, Grace. The gals have a wonderful friendship much like Rick and Vin's. I can't wait for Vin and Grace's story.

Although he's not a main character, I also found myself really enjoying Vin! He's hysterical in his lack of giving a care and softens and warms your heart with how sweet he can be (I love the animals, too, Vin, so I feel ya!).

This book was so funny from beginning to end. Loved the secondary characters. Can't wait for Vin's story.

DEDICATION

To Pip, Rocket and Winnie—and all our four-legged families.

PROLOGUE

GRACE

It was close to midnight when my cell phone rang. I'd already worked another 14-hour day in the office plus two more at home, and I was wearing my pajamas, cocoa in hand, ready to call it a night and crawl into my enormous and comfortable bed. So when I saw the name 'Knob-head' flashing up on my phone, I let it roll over to voicemail. But then he rang again and again and again, and on the fifth ring, against my better judgment, I answered.

"Faith ... I mean, Grace! Don't hang up!"

Ugh, knob-head! The stupid British guy never could get my name right. Why had I answered? Oh yes, because he was the best friend of *my* best friend's fiancé.

"It's late, Vincent," I said sharply.

At least I was able to remember that his given name was 'Vincent' and not 'Knob-head'.

"What do you want?"

"I've been arrested. I need a lawyer."

"What? Oh my God, what?! You got yourself arrested three weeks before Cady and Rick's wedding! What did you do?"

1

I may have panicked slightly, but Vince's voice was annoyingly calm.

"Yeah, I know. Fookin' bummer. I told the policewomen that, but they were hard arses. They said they had to take me in, asked for a couple of selfies and booked me anyway. They let me use my phone though—cheers, girls!"

I heard a woman laughing in the background and wondered if this was one of Vince's stupid pranks.

"What have you've been arrested for?" I asked skeptically.

"That don't matter but..."

"It really *does* matter, Vince! It kind of matters a lot."

"Um, hang on," he mumbled, *"I've got a list somewhere."*

I could hear rustling and in the background drunks were yelling. My stomach sank—this wasn't a prank, which had been my first guess and fervent hope. Then Vincent's voice came back on the line.

"Alright, yeah: burglary and larceny, whatever that is. I think that's everything."

My eyes bulged. It sounded serious.

"I know a couple of criminal lawyers who can..."

"No! I need you, Fa— Grace. Please! I'm at the 20th Precinct police station, but they'll be moving me to Central Booking and then the Tombs. Fook me! I don't like the sound of that!"

"Vince, I'm a corporate lawyer. I do mergers and acquisitions. I'm not a criminal lawyer. I can't help you."

"Yeah, but I'm not a criminal, so that's okay."

"Vince, no! Listen to me for once! You need..."

"Please, Grace! For Rick's sake! For Cady's sake! For the sake of puppies and kittens—especially the puppies. Please! You're my only hope!"

He made it sound as though he was about to be taken away and locked up for a hundred years, which might have saved the world a lot of angst.

I heaved out a long-suffering sigh.

"Fine. I'll come. I'll do what I can ... just ... don't talk to anyone. Don't say anything. Don't even comment on the weather."

"Is it a nice evening?"

"Shut up, Vince!" I took a deep, calming breath. It didn't work. "Anything else you want to tell me?"

My question was sarcastic, but I should have known better.

"Yeah, ta. Could you go to my flat and let me dogs out for a slash." He paused. *"And if they've shit on the floor, could you chuck it in the back garden."*

"What?!"

"Cheers, Gracie. You're a mate."

He hung up.

I really, really couldn't stand Vince Azzo.

CHAPTER ONE

GRACE

I really, really couldn't stand Vince Azzo. Wait, let me back up and I'll start at the beginning.

My best friend in the whole entire world is a superb human being named Cady Callahan. She's kind, clever, funny as hell, and last year she ran the New York City marathon raising a ton of money for veterans' charities. Seriously, my girl is awesome. She's also the top radio breakfast host on the Atlantic seaboard and happens to be engaged to the almost equally awesome Rick Roberts, who owns the number one gym in Manhattan and used to be a professional athlete. He's British, too, a little on the reserved side and quiet, like me. And to be fair, Cady creates enough noise and chaos for both of us.

It was almost perfect, as perfect as life can be, that is. We all got along great and I was really excited to be Cady's Maid of Honour at their wedding in three weeks.

I did say *almost perfect*. Except for one thing—the proverbial fly in the ointment, the bump in the road, the pain in the ass that was Vincent Azzo—Rick's best friend.

The trouble was, he thought the world revolved around him—the world according to Vince. Well, I had plenty to say about Mr. Vincent I'm-always-right Azzo.

First, he's a jerk.

Second, he makes me so mad because he never listens.

Third, he's a douche.

Fourth, he can never get my name right.

Fifth, he's a knob-head.

He just doesn't listen to me—and I'm his lawyer and OMG how on earth did that happen?!

Well, I'll tell you, but you're not going to believe me—Vince was a law unto himself and I was supposed to uphold the law. He made it so darn hard. That man ... that *jerk* made me crazy.

He's an opinionated, rude, crude, knob-head, whose every-other word is 'fook', 'fooking' or 'fooker'. Yes, that's what he is—a giant knob-head. And a manwhore, don't forget that. Tinder was invented with him in mind. His Tinder account includes 'dates' with dozens of models, actresses, A-, B-, and C-list celebrities.

'Dates'? Yeah, that's a euphemism for 'slept with' which is a euphemism for 'brought to a screaming orgasm'—allegedly. He's the one alleging, obviously, so the evidence is circumstantial, subjective and therefore to be struck from the record. I'd call it a mistrial. He'd call it, "'avin' a laff". Because he's a stupid British knob-head. Case dismissed. Or so I thought.

Any redeeming characteristics, Your Honor?

He's kind to animals. And that's where this story starts. With a dog. Seventeen dogs, to be precise. You kind of had to be there. Seeing is believing, right? And that sums up Vince—he had to be seen to be believed, and then you had to look again to make sure you weren't having a daytime nightmare, and that he really was that much of an jerk.

You needed the full surround-sound 360° version to really understand the extreme level of his knob-headishness. That's his word of choice to describe himself, by the way, but my gosh, it fits him!

Oh, what does he look like? Well, 6'4" with abs that you could use for a ladder. It pains me to say it, but he's gorgeous, a former Armani catwalk model (yes, really). But when he opens his mouth, which he invariably does at exactly the wrong moment, his personality screams knob-head.

Mostly, I just ignore him—or try to—but right now, he's my problem.

He'd been arrested on serious charges, and I knew for a fact that he was supposed to be having a suit-fitting with Rick at Armani's Fifth Avenue store tomorrow afternoon for their wedding suits— and they didn't reschedule appointments for anyone.

The clock was a-ticking and I hurried to dress.

It was cold out, the temperature dropping like a stone as a freezing wind howled down from the Arctic threatening snow, and I was not relishing a hike across the city at this time of night, checking on his unruly hounds, then schlepping back to the Manhattan Detention Centre on White Street.

Although the possibility of snow was the least of my worries. Besides, as a kid from the mid-West, snow was just a fact of life for four months of the year.

 *Fascinating factoid: Minnesota averages 110 days of snow annually.*

I was just as happy driving with chains on a truck as tires. I'd even driven a snowplow the winter I'd dated Paul Lund.

But in New York City, it's different. Sleet, snow and puddles outside; Savannah-heat on the Subway and in buildings; and the next Polar-vortex could arrive anytime through April.

In short: it was ass-freezing cold.

I bundled up with layers, pulled on my trusty Ugg boots and slid on a quilted down coat that was more duvet than item of clothing. A knitted hat and gloves came next, but it was my Maxwell Scott chestnut tan briefcase that completed my ensemble—and screamed *lawyer*. No, it hadn't been a gift from my parents when I graduated law school a decade ago because although I received hugs and good wishes, they would have thought spending that sort of money on a bag as frivolous. I agreed, but still enjoyed the frisson of guilty pleasure every time I touched the butter soft leather. It was a man's briefcase, or so the saleswoman had told me when I'd bought it for myself.

"But, madam, 'The Lorenzo' is a briefcase for a gentleman!"

Which made me love it even more, and now it went with me everywhere—and especially to chilly police stations in the middle of the night. It was part of my armour, my shield of justice ... and I say that with just a hint of irony.

I'd never wanted to work in criminal law—it was too messy, too unpredictable, too ugly. I preferred corporate law where I understood the intricacies, the loopholes, the ways another lawyer would try to trip me up during a deal, poring over wordy contracts hundreds of pages long, due diligence reviews an inch thick. I had a large, comfortable office, with a large corporate Cherrywood desk and three assistants. It suited me.

Traipsing around New York City at one in the morning to see the Knob-head did *not* suit me.

"You owe me for this, Cady," I grumbled to myself as I jumped in a yellow cab.

Vince had only recently relocated from Los Angeles and now rented a tiny basement condo with attached yard in Brooklyn Heights, not far from the Transit Museum.

My cab driver only agreed to wait for me when I promised him a tip of fifty bucks—half now and half when I came out again.

I punched in the access code and woke the dogs as the door swung open. I like dogs, I do, but I wasn't keen on being slobbered all over or having them jump up and try to lick my face.

At least I knew what to expect as I'd met them once before in a park, so thank goodness they knew me and didn't try to bite. If anything, they seemed desperately pleased to see me, whining and crying, then charging for the backdoor and begging to be let out. It took me a few seconds to undo all the bolts, by which time, they were almost frantic, scrabbling at the polished wood and leaving claw marks.

"Alright, you guys!" I snapped. "Take it down a notch—you don't want to wake the neighbors."

I was surprised when they seemed to listen to me and stopped yelping, but as soon as the door was open a crack, they squeezed through, Tap being the last, which didn't surprise me.

They all took long and satisfying pees, and I was as relieved as they were when I couldn't see any puddles or mess anywhere in Vince's shiny, white kitchen.

Tap was the first to return, shivering from the cold. She was a scrawny little thing with three legs, but very affectionate as she nuzzled against me, peering up with her big beautiful eyes and no doubt asking me why I was here and not Vince.

"I'm going to try and save your dad," I said to her, rubbing her soft ears. "Mostly, I'm trying to save him from himself. Wish me luck."

The other two dogs spent longer snuffling around outside, and eventually I had to call them in.

Tyson was a large mutt of indeterminate heritage whose long, pink tongue was always hanging out the side of his mouth like he was grinning at you. But he was tall, with heavy shoulders and very strong, and without such a sweet personality, he would have been intimidating.

Zeus was the one in charge—a tiny Yorkshire terrier with a loud, high pitched yip, who could have sat comfortably in the palm of both hands, but seemed convinced that he was a Rottweiler. But then again, he did have Tyson to back him up.

He eyed me warily, then pointedly stared at his empty food bowl.

Vince hadn't said anything about feeding them, so I hoped there was nothing complicated about their diets as I carefully placed a Milk-Bone into each of the empty dishes, and filled up the communal water bowl.

I swear the dogs' faces fell when I relocked the backdoor, and Tap tried to follow me as I left, but I gently pushed her back inside the kitchen, feeling horrible as her soft whines reached me outside.

I gave the cab driver the rest of his tip, then sat back with my eyes closed while we re-crossed the river to Manhattan.

'The Tombs' was what New Yorkers named the towering, gray Manhattan Detention Complex, a building so depressing that it could have been designed during the Soviet era.

Considering it was now nearly three in the morning, it was surprisingly busy. The entrance teemed with law officers in their navy-blue uniforms, all armed, all with the look on their faces that they'd seen it all, experienced every aspect of humanity and society's failings. I wasn't sure where Vince fit into that.

I presented myself to the Desk Sergeant who was polite and efficient, and handed me Vince's charge sheet which I read with disbelief as my eyes grew wider.

I glanced up at the Desk Sergeant who was obviously holding onto a smile. He raised his eyebrows and nodded. My eyebrows had already scaled the heights and were approaching lift-off.

I sat down heavily on one of the plastic visitor seats, sweating as I peeled off layers one at a time, until I was taken to meet my 'client' in an airless, windowless room, furnished with a table and two chairs bolted to the floor.

Vince swaggered into the room escorted by a woman police officer whose happy demeanor and flirty smile seemed at odds with the whole, bizarre situation.

The other surprising thing was that Vince wore a well-cut suit and crisp white shirt, both of which were now covered in dog hair and paw marks.

"Gracie!" shouted Vince, crushing me in a huge bear-hug. "You came!"

"Good luck with that one!" laughed the police officer, and she left the room, shaking her head.

"Hmpfh!" I groaned in a muffled voice, trying to free myself from Vince's iron grip. "Put me down! Now!"

I'd learned that Vince responded best if you spoke to him like his dogs—with clear commands in short sentences.

He beamed at me. "You look nice. Your cheeks are all pink—it suits you."

I ignored his comment, grit my teeth, then pulled out a notepad and pencil from my briefcase.

"Why don't you start at the beginning?"

CHAPTER TWO

VINCE

She'd come! Gracie had come! I couldn't believe me fookin' luck! I'd been certain she'd have phoned Rick and sent him instead. He was me best mate, but he weren't no lawyer. And I'd got meself in a right pile of shite this time. Even with a couple of sexy birds arresting me, I hadn't been able to talk my way out of this one.

But there she sat, in the middle of the night, cool as a cucumber, her soft hazel eyes trying to look annoyed. But she wasn't fooling me.

Grace *cared*. I knew that she tried very hard to hide that fact at the firm of sharks where she worked, but she couldn't hide it from her friends.

I reached across the table and held her hand.

"How are me dogs?"

She gave a small, reluctant smile as she tugged her hand free.

"Well, they'd all been very good—no accidents—but they were busting to go out. Tap came straight back in, but Zeus and Tyson had a good snuffle around outside. I, um, gave them a Milk-Bone each, I hope that's okay? I wasn't sure if they had allergies or anything. And I refilled the water bowl."

She looked so worried and anxious that I wanted to kiss a smile right back onto her pretty lips, but I knew that would just earn me a slap—which wouldn't be the first time. No one kissed Gracie without her permission.

"They're good dogs," I nodded. "How was Tap?"

All three were rescue dogs and I loved them, but Tap was special. I'd found her wandering around a building site when I'd been on a photoshoot in Dubai. Her back left leg had a huge, manky cut and I could tell that she was in a lot of pain. So I'd tempted her out with a few veggie crisps and took her to a local vet. He couldn't save the leg and it took me four months to sort the paperwork to bring her home. She got nervous if I left her alone too long, but had the sweetest temperament. She liked to tap me with her front paw when she wanted a cuddle, which is how she got her name from. She was my special girl.

Gracie's smile faded. "Tap was more anxious than the others. I felt really bad leaving her again. But I'll drop in on my way to work in the morning and feed them—just tell me what they eat."

I gave her a puzzled look. "That's alright, Gracie, I'll do that meself."

She gave her trademark irritated stare.

"Vincent," she said slowly and clearly like I was five years old. "Vincent, you've been charged with two felonies—there's a very real chance that the prosecutor will push for prison time. The only place you'll be going right now is to your arraignment, and they might not even post bail because you're a Brit and potentially a flight risk. At the very least, you'll have to surrender your passport."

I leaned back in my chair, frowning. "So, the police are a bit upset with me?"

She rubbed her forehead. "Yes, Vincent. The police are upset with you. So is the director of the animal shelter." She glared at me and tapped her pencil against her blank notepad. "Now then, just so tonight isn't a complete waste of my time, why don't you tell me *exactly* what happened when you left your apartment this evening? Don't leave out *anything.*"

"Are you sure?"

Her lips thinned in irritation. It was kind of weird how much she turned me on when she did that.

"Right," I said, adjusting my pants as my trouser-snake sat up and took notice of Grace's sweet face and glorious little titties.

"Stop staring at my chest!" she said crossly.

"Oh, yeah, sorry. It's force of habit."

She rubbed her forehead again. I hoped she didn't have a headache.

"What time did you leave your condo?"

"Eight o'clock."

She sighed and stared at the ceiling, before scratching a note on her legal pad. "And where did you go?"

"I was meeting this woman off Tinder at her hotel about 8.30pm. So we chatted for a bit, had a few drinks, did the business —twice—I had a quick shower and left."

Grace stabbed at her notepad, leaving black squiggles all over it. Maybe lawyers were like doctors with their terrible handwriting.

"What time did you leave the hotel?"

"Nine o'clock."

Her mouth dropped open. "You had sex twice and left the hotel half-an-hour after you arrived? Can anyone confirm that?"

I grinned at her. "Roxy could confirm it—she was counting her orgasms. Had to use both hands. To count, I mean."

Grace tapped the pencil on the table in a fast, annoyed rhythm.

"And *I* mean, can anyone other than *Roxy* confirm what time you left the hotel?"

"Oh right, yeah. I asked the doorman about vegan restaurants in the area and he suggested a couple so I tipped him a twenty. He'll remember me."

She made a note of that, too, then looked up.

"And when you left the hotel, where did you go next?"

"Well, I was starving so I was going to check out one of the places the bloke at the hotel suggested, but I never got there."

"Why was that?"

The anger reared up inside me again as I remembered what happened next.

"I was walking past this building and I could hear dogs barking, like really crying and upset. Turned out the place was an animal shelter but it's not staffed at night. There was a notice on the door saying that they needed to re-home five of the dogs or they were going to be euthanized in 72 hours! That's the fookin' word they used, *euthanized*, like it wasn't really murder. And all I could think was that those dogs needed to be saved! So I legged it over the wall, kicked open the door and started letting them out of their cages. That's when the cops turned up."

Grace stared at me, then looked down at my charge sheet.

"It says here that you'd gotten leashes on five of the dogs and had six puppies stuffed in the pockets of your jacket."

"They were cold," I said, leaning forward. "They were only little bugs, too small to put on leads."

Grace's lips moved like she wanted to say something, but the words didn't come. Finally, she sighed.

"Vincent, what were you going to do with eleven adult dogs and six puppies?"

"Take them home with me," I grinned at her.

She blinked several times. "And then what?"

"Ah, well, I hadn't quite worked out that part, but I'm sure I could have re-homed them. Everyone loves dogs, right? Every family should have one—you can learn a lot from animals."

She shook her head but I didn't think she was disagreeing with me.

"Did you have any intention of selling them?"

"Course not!" I said, somewhat insulted. "I just wanted them to have a proper home, not live their lives in cages. It's not right—they

STUART REARDON & JANE HARVEY-BERRICK

haven't done anything wrong." I had to swallow the lump in my throat. "It's not their fault they got born at the wrong time in the wrong place."

Grace's eyes glistened.

"So, shall I tell the Judge that and he'll let me go?" I asked.

Grace sighed again. "Oh, Vincent," she said.

"That's me name, don't wear it out!" I grinned.

Grace didn't smile. I wished she would—she had a smashing smile.

"Okay, here's what's going to happen. Tomorrow morning, you'll be brought before a magistrate judge for an initial hearing. I'll be there as your attorney, God help me. This is the arraignment and it's when the judge decides if you'll be held in prison or released on bail. You'll also be asked to plead guilty or not guilty to the charges. I suggest, given the evidence, that you plead guilty to burglary and not guilty to larceny. The judge will post bail—we hope—and you walk out of there. The prosecutor won't want his or her time tied up in court on this, so we'll try to get it all down to plea bargaining. That means I try to persuade him or her of a lesser sentence, like a fine or court-ordered community service."

I frowned, trying to follow what she was telling me. "So, I can go home after I meet the judge tomorrow morning?"

"Let's hope so. Just stick to the facts ... and Vincent, try to say as little as possible."

"Maybe the judge is a dog-lover?" I said hopefully. "He'll be on my side!"

"The judge is on the side of the law," she said severely. "Now, let's talk money. Bail could be between $5,000 and say $10,000, but maybe less if the judge is an animal-lover," and she smirked at me when she said that. "And you should know that I bill at $750 an hour."

I grinned at her. "Really?"

"Yes."

"Good for you! That's fookin' fab!"

"Thank you."

"I don't have any money."

Her eyebrows rocketed. "You expect me to do this *pro bono?*"

"What's the singer of *U2* got to do with it?"

"*Pro bono*, not Bono! It means 'for free'.

"Cheers! You're a love."

"Wait! That was a question!" She stared at me. "Oh, never mind."

I winked.

"And how are you going to post bail?" she asked faintly.

"Could you phone Rick for me? He'll see me right."

She nodded and scratched a note in her teeny tiny spidery writing.

"Is there anything else you want to tell me?" she asked tiredly.

"I didn't have any supper," I said, hoping she'd take the hint. "I'm so hungry, if I weren't vegan, I'd probably chew off me own leg."

She gave a short, stiff nod. "I think the vending machine has chips and crackers; maybe some fruit."

"Cheers!" I grinned at her. "Lots, please! Don't forget I'm a growing lad."

She stuffed her notebook back in her briefcase like she was trying to choke it.

"I'll see you tomorrow," she said. "And behave!"

I leaned back in the hard chair and winked at her, smiling as she huffed impatiently and told the copper outside that she was done.

I was taken back to the grotty cell, but a few minutes later a carrier bag full of crisps, crackers, apples, oranges and a jar of peanut butter was delivered to me.

I tucked in hungrily, scoffing it all down then wondering if I should have saved something for breakfast. The police in this place were pretty decent, although so far they hadn't been able to find me anything vegan to eat. But my Gracie, she'd come through for me.

I wished again that she was *my* Gracie, even though she was completely out of my league. Then a thought occurred to me: I was fairly confident that given enough time, she'd succumb to my lad-about-town charms. But in the nine months since I'd first met her, she'd avoided me as much as possible, which was strange. Birds usually flocked to the call of a mating Vince.

Maybe all I needed to do was stuff up the court case enough so that she'd have to spend more time with me; but not stuff it up so much that I spent any more time in clink.

Whatever Gracie thought of me right now, I knew that she'd never abandon a friend in need. And even though I was Rick's friend rather than her friend or Cady's friend, I still qualified for the title. Rick and me were best mates; Cady was cool; and Grace? Well, she was fook hot.

CHAPTER THREE

GRACE

I lay on my bed with my eyes wide open. No matter how much I tried to force myself to sleep (which never works, as insomniacs all around the world know only too well), I couldn't make my body relax or my brain stop whirring.

My job with Kryll Group was 99% office lawyer: it was rare that cases went to court and when they did, I was never lead counsel. The partners took those cases and I definitely wasn't considered to be a trial lawyer. I'd always wondered if they were right. But more importantly given the current context, I'd never defended a criminal case in my life and never expected to. I was fairly confident I knew enough to help the giant knob-head who'd gotten himself into this mess, but twinges of self-doubt had me shooting upright and making notes on the pad by my bedside table instead of sleeping.

In the end, I gave up the fight and staggered out of bed. I prepared in my usual methodical way, checking and re-checking facts, statutes and precedents on one of the several legal databases that I had access to. It was unlikely that I'd need that level of detail at an arraignment but I couldn't *not* prepare to the nth degree—that was the way I was wired.

I sat at my small breakfast bar, staring out at the snow swirling against the grainy darkness of the night. It was too wet to settle, but it was going to be a cold and cheerless day. As I waited for the thin light of morning to filter through my tenth floor window, I'd already left a message with my personal assistant, Gary, to let him know that I was taking the morning off for personal time but to pick up my lunchtime deli sandwich as usual, please.

The American Bar Association recommended that all lawyers offer 50 hours *pro bono* each year, and it had been made a requirement of any new lawyers who wanted to be admitted to the ABA. It looked like I'd be getting my hours in early this year.

By 5.30am, I decided that Rick needed to share in my misery. Anyway, Cady would have left for work an hour ago and would be starting her breakfast show shortly. It was 50/50 whether Rick would have gone back to bed or gone to the gym.

I called his cell phone and his grumpy voice was slightly breathless when he answered. I guessed he was on a treadmill, and shuddered at the thought. I took a hot yoga class once a week to de-stress, but treadmills, gyms and weights were anathema to me; and even though Rick had gifted me a lifetime membership to his gym, hot yoga had been the only class that could tempt me. This was New York in January, and when Rick had said the word 'hot', he'd said enough.

"Grace, you alright, luv?"

"Just peachy, Rick. It's your knob-head friend who's in trouble."

I heard Rick groan. "What's the idiot done now?"

"Only gotten himself arrested."

"What?!"

"Two felonies and an arraignment in five hours. He broke into an animal shelter and tried to dognap all the inmates. He had six puppies stuffed in his jacket pockets when the police caught him. He says you'll post bail."

For a moment there was silence and I checked that the call hadn't dropped.

"Rick? Hello?"

"Sorry ... I just ... bloody hell! He did what?! I can't believe he'd be so stup— actually, I can. That soppy bugger. Okay, what do you need me to do?"

"The arraignment will be at the New York City Criminal Court on Center Street. Can you be there by ten? We might have to wait around until they call Vince's case and I don't know how long that will be. Bring your credit card."

"Crap! Yeah, okay. Um, how much do you think bail will be, Grace? I'm happy—sort of—to pay it, but what with the wedding and all, funds are a bit tight."

I held back a sigh. No one was getting out of this unscathed.

"I honestly don't know, Rick, but the figure I have in my head is $5,000. It could be less, it could be more. But just tell me this: he says he's never been arrested for anything before—is he telling me the truth, the whole truth and nothing but the truth? Because if I find out he's been economical with the aforesaid truth..."

"Nah, you're alright there, Grace. He doesn't even have a parking ticket. The tight bugger doesn't own a car and walks everywhere."

"Good, that helps. The judge will be more lenient on a first offense." I let out the breath I'd been holding. "Okay, I'll see you at ten."

We said goodbye and I felt a small weight lift. Knowing that Rick would be there to support me in all his formidable sternness was a relief.

Rick tended to overthink everything which made him the complete opposite of Vince, and of Cady, too, for that matter. If anything, Cady and Vince seemed like a better fit from an outsider's point of view as both had a free-wheeling attitude to life. Rick and I were the thinkers and planners. But maybe opposites attract. Although not in my case. Not the knob-head.

I dressed in my favorite charcoal gray pantsuit with cerise silk blouse. I always felt confident in that outfit: powerful *and* feminine. I dropped a pair of pumps into my briefcase and pulled on my comfortable Uggs, thick coat, scarf, gloves and woollen beanie.

Hat hair was an inevitable part of city life in the winter.

First stop was Vince's apartment again.

He'd given me strict instructions on what and how much to feed his dogs, and asked—or rather begged—that I spend ten minutes throwing a ball for Tyson in the back yard. I agreed: as long as the hairy beast didn't slobber all over me. He had a lot in common with Vince.

Traffic moved like treacle, and with tired eyes I watched the taxi's meter tick steadily upwards. Although I'd promised myself to go through my notes one more time on the ride over, the heater was making me sleepy.

I jolted awake when the taxi jerked to a stop outside Vince's apartment, and I staggered out, bleary-eyed, without having read a single page.

Predictably, the dogs were delirious with excitement, and bounded around like they were on springs. Tap whined and cried, telling me what a terrible night she'd had worrying about Vince.

"Me, too," I sighed as I let them out to do their business. "I've hardly slept, but with a pinch of luck and a great attorney—that would be me—your dad will be home soon. Just hang on in there, sweet pea."

I filled their food bowls according to Vince's detailed instructions, Zeus's bowl toy-sized next to Tyson's trough.

While they wolfed down their food, I stepped into Vince's bedroom, my nerves jangling. I don't know what I'd expected to find—a mirrored ceiling, whips and bondage implements, silk sheets, framed photographs of himself—but it was all very single-man-about-town normal. Except, perhaps, for the three dog beds next to his, arranged by size.

The only photographs on his dresser were of the dogs. I'd

expected to see a legacy wall of Vince's time in the fashion industry, but the walls were bare and painted a soft, dove gray. Realizing I was dawdling, I opened the door to his walk-in closet ... his *enormous* walk-in closet filled with dozens of beautiful, hand-crafted suits in fine wools, cottons, linens and even silk. I half expected a blaze of holy light and angels to start singing, it was *that* incredible.

I found his passport at the back of his closet, shoved into his underwear drawer with a roll of twenty-pound notes thick enough to choke a Vince. *Tempting.*

Starting my day searching Vince's underwear drawer hadn't been on my to-do list. *Ever.*

Then had five minutes playtime before I had to get going. The traffic wouldn't have gotten any lighter in the last half-hour.

Once again, Tap tried to come with me, and once again I felt like a worm as I pushed her gently back inside.

I tried not to wince when I saw the triple figures on the taxi's meter, especially since I couldn't bill it anywhere. Oh well, this would be my good deed ... for the rest of the year.

I arrived at court early, and sat waiting for Rick to arrive. I prayed that Vince looked presentable, rather than like the kind of idiot who thought rescuing 17 dogs with no onward plan was a good idea.

I changed into my pumps and stowed my faithful Uggs, then studied the notes, making sure I knew exactly what I was going to say to the judge (as little as possible), and what Vince would say to the judge (less than that).

When I felt a dark presence looming over me, I glanced up.

"Thank goodness you're here, Rick!"

I gave him the quick, awkward, one-armed hug that seemed appropriate for the boyfriend of my best friend, then upgraded with a quick kiss on his cheek, seeing as he was now Cady's fiancé and had strayed into uncharted but 'trusted male' territory.

The only other man I kissed on the cheek was my dad.

"I brought my credit card," he sighed. "I can't believe the dickhead has done this. What was he thinking?"

"Vince? Thinking? I know not of what you speak."

He grimaced. "Yeah, that's the problem. How serious is this?"

"Worst case scenario would involve a custodial sentence, but as it's a first offense, I'm confident to plea-bargain down to court-ordered community service and a fine. I just need Vince to *not speak*, and we should be okay."

"Shall I offer to thump him?" Rick asked earnestly.

"Tempting, but no. Because then I'll have both of you before the judge, plus a seriously pissed-off Cady, and no one wants that."

We sat in silence watching the comings and goings of suited attorneys, uniformed police and other state officials including a game warden (or conservation officer as they were now designated in Minnesota), and a wide mix of clientele.

Just before court was in session, ushers led us into Courtroom Three. Rick sat near the back and I joined the bench with a weary bunch of state-appointed defenders.

Judge Herschel was a woman in her late fifties, with dark, all-knowing eyes—the kind that stared right through you. She reminded me of my scariest college professor, and I automatically straightened my spine when her sweeping gaze paused on me and she gave a small frown over her glasses.

Was it the suit? The briefcase? Or the fact that she didn't recognize me as one of the defense attorneys? I scanned my notes again although I could have repeated them verbatim by now.

She read through the docket, and I knew I could have a long wait because Vince was third on the list. In fact, the judge was pretty darn fast. Was that a good thing?

The first case was a repeat DUI who was seven times over the limit.

 Fascinating factoid: the record for blood-alcohol-content is 32 times over the limit, which was achieved by a sheep rustler

in South Africa. He was caught driving a Mercedes, and his passengers included a woman, five boys and 15 sheep.

Mr. Seven-times-over-the-limit frowned at the usher who was helping him cross the courtroom. I wasn't even sure how he'd been able to stand with that much alcohol in him, let alone drive. He didn't seem entirely sober now.

Bail was requested and refused.

The second case was a woman who'd been caught dealing meth —also a repeat offense.

Bail was requested and refused.

I shut down any expression on my face and glanced toward the door where Vince was being brought into the courtroom in handcuffs by the Deputy Sheriff.

He wore an orange jumpsuit and prison sandals, but his height and handsome face made him stand apart. The stubble on his face looked deliberate and just added to the raw glamor.

He saw Rick first and gave him a wide smile and a double-thumbs up, then noticed me and winked. The judge saw it too, and raised her eyebrows.

I wanted to slap the smile right off of Vince's face.

"The State of New York versus Vincent Alexander Azzo on the charge of burglary and larceny," said Judge Herschel.

"Yeah, but they was only little bugs," Vince said seriously.

"Bugs?" the judge said, glancing up and frowning. "You stole bugs?"

"Ah, I'm Mr. Azzo's attorney," I interrupted, leaping to my feet.

"Then please restrain the defendant," said Judge Herschel.

"I would if I had a muzzle," I muttered to myself.

"Do you have something to say, Counselor?" the judge asked in a warning tone.

"No, your Honor. My apology." *My client makes me crazy.*

Vince was asked to confirm his name, date of birth and address, agreeing that he'd only lived at his present residence a month. I knew this was a demerit in the judge's eyes.

The judge then read the charge sheet, making the same astonished face that everyone had so far, while the prosecutor hunched in his chair, clearly uninterested.

"The defendant attempted to steal *seventeen dogs?* By *himself?* On *foot?*"

"An attempt to re-home dogs from an animal shelter that the defendant now recognizes was ill advised," I said firmly.

"You see the thing is, M'Lud," Vince interrupted. "Three of them was about to be murdered and I couldn't walk past and not do nothing. I'll look after them and..."

"Mr. Azzo," the judge said sharply. "Do you wear spectacles?"

"Um, no, M'Lud," Vince said earnestly. "Perfect 20/20 vision, me."

"Then you may have noticed the woman standing in front of you who claims to be your attorney?"

"Yes!" Vince said happily. "That's Gracie. She's me mate!"

From the corner of my twitching eye I saw Rick drop his head into his hands. He looked like he had a headache. I know I did.

The judge threw Vince a frosty, unamused look.

"She's paid to talk for you. I strongly suggest you let her."

"Ah, gotcha! Shut up, Vin!" he laughed good-naturedly.

The prosecutor handling the whole docket had finally woken up and was gaping at the show going on in front of him.

"Counselor, please approach the bench," Judge Herschel said to me.

Feeling trepidation to the soles of my stylish shoes, I walked up to stand in front of her so she could address me privately.

"Is the defendant mentally competent to understand the arraignment and plea process, Ms. Cooper?" she asked in a clipped tone.

Oh, so many ways to answer that question.

I sighed heavily. "Yes, your Honor—he's just ... different. And British."

"Not another word from him or contempt of court will be added to his charge sheet. Do you understand?"

"Yes, your Honor."

"Can you make the defendant understand?"

I nodded firmly, trying to look competent, confident and professional.

"Hmm," she said, her gimlet gaze making me want to squirm like a bug under a microscope.

I approached Vince at the podium and leaned forwards. He smelled surprisingly good after a night in the cells. Maybe it was the whiff of expensive cologne that clung to his skin. I wanted to grab him by his orange jump suit, crush it in my fists, then slap that silly smile off of his face.

Vincent Azzo brought out my inner Alexa Bliss, and the man in front of me was heading for a smack-down.

I laid my palms flat on either side of him on the podium, and spoke slowly and clearly.

"Do not speak. Nod if you understand me."

Looking confused, Vince nodded.

"That nice lady sitting up there is a judge. Right now, she's considering including contempt of court to the collection of felonies you've already acquired. Without speaking, nod if you understand."

Comprehension dawned and a chagrined look passed across his face.

"For the rest of this arraignment, do not speak to me, do not speak to Rick, do not speak to the courtroom deputy sheriff, and especially do *not* speak to the judge *unless I tell you to*. Nod if you understand."

Vince's big blue eyes looked wounded, but he did as requested and nodded.

I took a deep breath.

"When you speak, you make things worse. Do you understand?"

He nodded again, his pouty lips pulling down.

"Good. Leave the talking to me. Okay?"

He leaned forward so the judge couldn't see him. "Are you mad at me, Gracie?"

I breathed in through my nose and out through my mouth three times before I answered.

"Yes, I'm mad at you."

"Sorry."

"Vincent?"

"Yes?"

"Shut up."

He gave a small smile and mimed zipping his lips shut.

If only.

It was at that moment that his stomach growled so loudly, it was like having another person in the room.

"Sorry, me Lud," Vince said, a serious look on his face. "Breakfast were a bit scarce."

Fiery sparks shot from my eyes as he smiled at Judge Herschel and I mimed a slashing motion across my throat.

Vince got the message and shut up.

We got through the rest of the arraignment without further incident, although the growling stomach was a continuous acoustic backdrop. There was another slightly sticky moment when Judge Herschel queried Vince's residential status, but I was able to confirm that prior to moving to New York, he'd lived in California for five years.

Then we got to the section where Vince had to plead.

He stood, straight-backed, towering over me and the prosecuting attorney.

"Mr. Azzo," said the judge, "to the charge of burglary, how do you plead?"

"Guilty, M'Lud, um, me Lady, um, your Honor."

The judge's lips thinned but it looked to me as if she was holding back a smile.

"To the charge of larceny, how do you plead?"

"Not guilty, Your Honor."

Judge Herschel glanced at the prosecutor who simply nodded.

Mollified, she ordered that Vince's passport was retained.

"I'm not a flight risk," Vince said out of the corner of his mouth.

"You'd better not be," I muttered. "I'll handcuff you to the radiator if I have to."

"That's a bit kinky, Grace. Game on!"

"Shut up!"

The bond was set at ten thousand dollars.

I thought Rick was going to cry, but Vince just smiled and looked like he was about to speak. I made another throat-slicing movement with my hand. Vince took the hint and winked at me instead.

We all reconvened at the prisoners' entrance where Vince appeared in a rumpled designer suit covered in paw marks and dog fur, and wrestled me into a bear hug that I most definitely did not want.

"You were fab!" he crowed. "I thought that Judge Hershey was going to send me to the galleys."

"You thought she wanted you to cook for her?" I asked confused.

"He means galleys like a Roman ship," Rick sighed. "He's been watching too many episodes of *Spartacus*."

Vince raised his fist in the air and yelled loudly. "*I am Spartacus!*"

I jumped and everyone turned to stare.

"Shut up, Vince!" I hissed, grabbing his arm and hustling him toward the elevator.

"Fookin' great film that," he grinned goofily.

When we found the bondsman, Rick handed over his credit card looking a little green as he was given a receipt for ten thousand dollars.

"Cheers, mate!" Vince said, clapping him on the shoulder. "I'll pay you back."

I sighed again. I sounded like a leaky tire around this incredibly annoying man-child.

"Vincent, this isn't a fine. Providing you return to court for sentencing on the date required, Rick will get his money back."

"Oh, coolio!" he smiled at his friend.

"Although there's every chance that in the future you'll be fined and have to pay costs, but you'll be given a reasonable time so to do. Understand?"

He nodded. "You know you're fookin' hot when you go all lawyer on me."

I shook my head and turned to Rick. "He's all yours. Don't let him get into any more trouble."

But of course, this was Vince we were talking about.

As we descended the steps from the Supreme Court, there were two news crews setting up at the bottom. I don't know who they were waiting for, but they got Vince.

"I want to make a statement," he announced in a loud, carrying voice with a stern look in his eyes.

The journalists turned to stare, and even though they had no clue who he was, the cameramen started to record. Maybe it was the way Vince's voice commanded attention, or the way he held himself in his designer suit, or that fact that he was 6'4" and looked like he was *someone*.

"What's he doing?" I hissed at Rick.

"No clue," he whispered back.

Vince waited until every eye was watching him. He looked handsome and serious, and I had no idea what was going to happen next.

"Right now, in our city," he said, his voice clear and full of purpose, "animals are being murdered. Dogs and cats, our family pets are being 'euthanized'," and he curled his lip as he spat the word out. "They're on death row through no fault of their own. Within 24 hours, five of the sweetest dogs you'll ever meet are going to be murdered by a lethal injection. Five beasties who could bring joy and pleasure to your home. This is happening in our city right now!" he boomed. "Because there aren't enough animal shelters, because not enough people care. Do you care?" he challenged the people watching him, eyeballing each of them in turn. "Do you?"

My jaw was on the floor, and I watched as he mesmerized his audience with his passion and compelling delivery.

"Across this city, our furry friends are dying in cramped, overcrowded shelters where diseases like kennel cough run rampant. And who cares? Not the city officials, that's for sure. If they cared, they'd have honored the law that the City Council passed in 2000 to put a shelter in every borough of the city. But have they done that? Have they bollocks! And because they've broken their promises, animals are suffering right now! In this one shelter, 20% of the animals are killed—that's six thousand every year *in one shelter*. Animals who have the right to a long and healthy life are being murdered. We're supposed to protect the weak! We're supposed to protect those who have no voice! What sort of people are we that mass murder goes on in our backyards and no one cares? Well, I care! I fookin' care! And I'm asking you to care, too.

"Last night, I tried to save 17 dogs. I broke into a shelter not far from here when I heard dogs crying. Heartbreaking, it were. Five of those dogs are on the kill list. I'd nearly made it out when the police nicked me. I don't blame the coppers, they was just doing their job.

"If you do one thing today for someone else, visit an animal shelter and see the conditions that these beasties live in, these sweet little bugs, tiny puppies, and you tell me that we care! You tell me that!"

His eyes were blazing as he marched down the steps with me and Rick trailing behind.

"Who is that guy?" asked one of the journalists.

"Vincent Alexander Azzo," said Vince proudly. "And that's Gracie Cooper, me lawyer."

CHAPTER FOUR

VINCE

We were sitting in the back of a taxi, and Gracie and Rick were staring at me.

"What? Is it me farts? They're like a weapon of mass destruction. It's the beans they gave me for breakfast—I was on the bog for hours."

"Mate," Rick said, leaning forward, "what was that speech all about?"

I grinned. "Yeah, well, I saw a camera crew and just went for it. Media whore, right? All about the opportunity, me."

"It was wonderful," Grace said faintly.

"Yeah? Cheers, Gracie!"

I was surprised and pleased that she'd actually paid me a compliment. Maybe my strategy was working.

"Dinner tonight, my treat?" I asked hopefully, deciding to strike while the woman was hot.

"Not if you paid me in gold bars," she said, her eyes returning to her phone.

She didn't even look up. Rick did, and the grin he gave me was well irritating.

"Crash and burn," he muttered.

"What did you say?" Grace snapped, turning her frown on Rick.

"Nothing," he lied.

He melted into the back seat as her eyes bore into him.

She turned and tapped on the taxi's dividing panel. "You can drop me here." Then she turned back and stared at both of us. "*You*," she said, stabbing her finger at Rick, "keep *him* out of trouble," and then pointed at me as if she wanted to poke me in the eye.

Throwing another scathing look, she swept out of the taxi like royalty. Fookin' hot!

"Are you sure you want to keep trying to date her?" asked Rick. "She's a bit scary."

"Nah, she's a softie really, I can tell."

I watched her march down the street and sighed when she disappeared into her office building.

"Right, you want to come and run me dogs?"

"Nah," Rick grimaced. "I've got some paperwork to do at the gym. We still on for the suit-fitting at three?"

"Yep, I'll see you there." I was about to wave him off when I realized I had no money. "Eh, you couldn't lend us fifty for the cab, could you?"

Rick groaned. "Sure. What's fifty on top of ten thousand? You're killing me, buddy."

"I'll pay you back, no worries."

I grinned and gave him a thumbs up as he climbed out of the taxi and headed for his gym.

Now I spend a lot of time in the gym. Physical perfection—that would be me—takes time and effort to get my body as amazing as it is, but I don't *live* at the gym like Rick does. The dude literally has an apartment over his fitness center. Until he met Cady, he didn't have anything else in his life. I did persuade him to try Tinder once, but that didn't go so well. *Cough, stalker!*

The kids were happy to see me when I opened my front door and walked into the hall. Zeus yipped loudly, telling me in no uncertain terms that he wasn't impressed by my absence. Tyson hung back, grinning at me goofily while his tail ricocheted off the wall. And sweet little Tap was trying to climb my leg and jump into my arms, but she couldn't quite make it. So I scooped her up and let her lick my face, giving her the reassurance she needed.

There's nothing like the welcome from your four-legged (and three-legged) family. Always happy to see you. Always sharing the love. Best feeling ever.

I let them all outside for a slash and a crap while I changed into my running clothes. But Tap followed me around the bedroom, nuzzling my calf from time to time, as if she was checking that I really was home.

"Poor little lass, aren't you?" I said, stroking her soft fur. "But don't worry—dad's home now. So, what did you think of Gracie? I know you ate the Milk-Bone she gave you so I think you must like her. You don't take treats from just anyone, do you?" And I pulled her ears as she stared up at me like I was her sun and moon.

That's the other thing about having dogs in your life—*you* are their whole life. It's not like they're going to write their novel while you're out and about. They're pack animals for a reason, and I was the pack leader, I was their everything. And in return their love was unconditional. Human beings are never that cool. Dogs don't stab you in the back.

It was an awesome responsibility and one I didn't take lightly. If I couldn't get a good sitter when I was on a shoot, I didn't take the job. Simple as.

And I was still worried about those dogs at the shelter. I needed to go over there and check on them, even though Gracie had told me to stay away.

I looked around my apartment and wondered how I'd fit in five more dogs, even temporarily. I sighed, wishing I had room for all 17, but now I was completely sober, it didn't seem like my best idea ever, but five more I could manage until they were re-homed. It would be a squeeze, and my kids would be jealous, but I couldn't let innocent lives be lost. I'd get over there after the suit-fitting.

Tyson and Zeus came barreling into the bedroom, letting me know that they were ready for their run.

I locked the back door, collected three leads and a pet sling for when Zeus and Tap got tired. I looked like a dick, but I didn't care.

It was half a mile to the dog play area at Pier 6. That was far enough for Zeus and Tap, but Tyson was just getting going and loved to find another dog his size to play with. Tap was too nervous to play with dogs she didn't know, so she curled up on my knee and Zeus snoozed in the pet carrier.

As soon as I sat down, a hot bird with a nice pair of knockers was on me like white on rice.

"Oh my God, that's so cute! Are these your dogs?"

She leaned down to stroke Tap, giving me an eyeful of her tits, but Tap curled away from her, peering up with worried eyes.

"She's a bit shy with strangers," I said. "Zeus is more of a slut— he'll let anyone stroke him."

She giggled and tossed her hair back. "I love your accent. Are you Scottish?"

I got that a lot. Americans heard my northern accent and assumed I was a kilt-wearing Jimmy.

"Nope, Derby born and bred, me."

She obviously had no clue where I meant, but I was used to that. She stroked Zeus who raised his head and yawned, causing Miss Tits to back off as she caught a whiff of his rank breath.

"Oh, yuk!" she huffed, waving her hand in front of her and screwing up her face.

At which point I lost interest in her. I knew Zeus had bad breath, but there was no need to hurt his feelings.

Love me, love my dogs.

After I'd grabbed Tyson from the dog play pen where he'd just shoulder-barged a Jack Russell he was playing with, sending the little fella rolling like a beach ball, I apologized to the owner who at least understood that it wasn't malicious. Tyson just got over-excited and forgot he was the size of a ten-ton truck, and he wasn't at all keen to leave his new playmate behind. The Russell was up and shaking himself, tail going like the clappers. No grudges held.

We jogged back slowly while Tap and Zeus curled up together in the pet carrier. Being with my dogs was my happy place. Although hot sex with a raging fox was up there, too. My thoughts turned to Grace. Was she softening towards me?

I checked my watch and sighed; time to get back, feed the hounds, then meet Rick for a suit-fitting with Uncle Sal.

Uncle Sal's real name was Signor Salvatore Finotello. He was a top bloke and top tailor with Armani. In his youth, sometime in the last century, he'd been the fitter at all the catwalk shows and was definitely the best at tailoring bespoke suits. Most people had to wait six months or more for an appointment with him, but he thought I was the dog's bollocks and made sure he had time to sort out a couple of wedding tuxes for Rick and me.

Some models can be such wankers, and think that only the couturiers count and that fitters or senior tailors like Uncle Sal don't matter. But it's like a Formula One car—a nice design is going to get the fans drooling, but it's the mechanics who make it fly. Same with designer clothes: you show some fookin' respect.

The kids were sleepy after I'd fed them so I didn't feel too bad going out again. Even so, Tap tried it on.

"Enough with the sad eyes," I said, kissing her on the top of her furry little head. "Your dad has responsibilities. I'll be back soon, promise."

She sighed heavily as if my promises meant nowt, which was a bit harsh, and limped off to her bed.

I was running late, as usual, so I didn't check my phone as I hurried out the door.

It was ringing when I found Rick waiting for me outside *Emporio*. I was already a few minutes late so I just let it go to voicemail again.

"You could have waited inside, you tosser," I grinned at him. "It's freezing out here."

He shrugged and looked uncomfortable, frowning at the enormous glass-walled entrance, several storeys high.

"Blimey, it's only a suit-fitting—you're not going to be stood against a wall and shot, you sad muppet! It's for your wedding. Cheer up a bit!"

He grimaced, although it might have been a smile. "Let's get it over with," he said, the grumpy bastard.

Uncle Sal looked about a hundred years old, maybe more. He'd been with Giorgio since the start and no one wanted to guess what would happen when he finally snuffed it. He'd come to New York to promote the opening of the Fifth Avenue store ten years ago and stayed because he said New York was his spiritual home.

"Ciao, Vincent! *Come sta il mio bellissimo ragazzo? Vieni a dare a papà un bacio!*"

He was gay as a coot and flamboyant as a flamingo, always wearing eye-watering waistcoats and matching cravats in orange, yellow or salmon pink. He belonged in a 1950s film with Doris Day. I fookin' adored him.

I bent down so he could kiss me on both cheeks, and then he pressed my hands to his chest.

"You are naughty boy, Vincent! You break my heart to stay away so long!"

I winked and didn't bother to remind him that I'd dropped by the previous week to arrange our fittings.

"And who is this beautiful brute?" he asked, eyeing Rick up and down.

The look on Rick's face was priceless.

"This is me mate Rick Roberts, the happy groom," I said

introducing them. "Rick, this is Signor Salvatore Finotello, top tailor in the biz."

"Bellissimo!" Uncle Sal sighed, pulling Rick down to kiss him. "But why you boys so big? You are like *un toro*."

Uncle Sal had known me a lot of years. We'd been based in Milan together when I was doing the catwalk shows. I was straight out of school and skinny as a rake. I had muscle tone because I was into kickboxing at the time, but I'd never really put on any weight. My teeth were crooked as fook, but even so, that's when I got talent-spotted to be a model. As long as I didn't smile.

Runway models are tall, skinny aliens—the women and the men. On the catwalk, we were kings, but see us in real life and we looked like we'd been made in Plasticine and stretched, all gangly arms and knobbly knees.

That's what Uncle Sal was used to and that's what he liked. He didn't approve of the muscles I'd gained since I stopped fashion modelling. Now *fitness* modelling—that was a different world, and one I was still exploring.

"I know, Uncle Sal," I grinned at him. "Built like a brick shithouse these days, but you'll fix us up."

"I don't know how I work with all this *mooscle*," he wailed, pulling out his tape measure. "Clothes off! *Adesso!*"

Rick looked horrified but I just shrugged. I was used to being down to my keks or less in front of twenty other dudes, girls, too. No glamor behind the scenes at a catwalk show.

My phone started ringing again but I ignored it, stripping off and getting ready to be sized up by a professional.

Rick took it more slowly, side-eyeing me as I let Uncle Sal wedge the end of the tape measure up by my meat and two veg, and measured to the ground (my leg, not the crown jewels, although my wanger is nearly to the ground). Uncle Sal muttered something and his assistant pencilled it into his notebook, then Sal measured the circumference of my thigh.

"No, it's impossible!" he said, throwing his hands in the air. "You are too much meat, Vincent! The pants will not hang well."

"Nah, it'll be fine, Uncle Sal," I grinned at him. "You're a wizard in the cutting room."

"Wizard, yes; miracles, no," he muttered unhappily.

Then he turned his tape measure on Rick. "Dresses to the right," he commented, and the assistant made a note in his book as a red flush started at Rick's neck.

"Don't worry if he tickles your tiny todger," I said cheerfully. "It's all part of the service."

"You are cheeky boy, Vincent," Uncle Sal said, wagging his finger at me. "Why do I stand for this?"

"Because I'm your favorite," I winked.

Uncle Sal muttered to himself but I could see that he was smiling.

Rick looked as miserable as a turkey in November while Uncle Sal fluttered around him, measuring and muttering and thoroughly enjoying himself.

Rick completely tuned out when me and Uncle Sal started discussing whether these tuxes should have peak lapels, shawl collars or notch lapels; nixed a slim fit, discussed traditional cut, but went for modern fit in the end.

Rick just nodded when I told him to, about a million miles out of his comfort zone. At the end he handed over his credit card and said he didn't want to know, unless it was more than my bail charge. It was close. Quality costs.

"Eh, trust me, mate. You don't want to know. But Uncle Sal will cut you a deal."

Rick winced and stuffed the receipt in his wallet without looking.

We fixed up a time for our next fitting, then I hugged Uncle Sal and gave him a big smackeroo. Rick tried to shake his hand but ended up getting kissed anyway.

While we took the stairs back to the ground floor, I was vaguely aware that my mobile phone had hardly stopped buzzing with texts and messages. But I was in a rush to get over to the animal shelter.

Rick was going back to the gym (what a surprise) and I headed through the busy streets, but as I neared the shelter, the road was partially blocked by news crews and crowds of people. Police were frantically trying to keep the traffic moving, and losing the battle.

As I neared the shelter, the crowd was thicker and then I heard someone yelling.

"There he is! The Canine Crusader!"

I glanced over my shoulder to see who they were talking about, but suddenly a reporter with a microphone the size of a koala was in my face.

"Vincent Azzo! You're back at the scene of the crime!"

"Uh, well..."

"How does it feel to know that every single dog at this shelter has been adopted because of you?"

A broad grin swept across my face. "Really? Every single one? Even the old fella with the torn ear? They've all been adopted?"

"Yes! You didn't know? Would you like to give us a quote, Mr. Azzo?"

"It's fookin' fab! I'm really happy that all the dogs have gone to good homes."

"Every dog shelter in the state of New York is reporting the same phenomenon, and dogs are being adopted all over the city. They're calling you the Canine Crusader!"

"Wow! I got a superhero name! That's cool! Do I get a cape?"

"Ha, I don't know. But you're certainly a hero to these dogs."

"I'm right happy about that."

"I believe that you've been charged with burglarizing this shelter, is that correct?"

"Yeah, I had to go to court this morning, but it weren't too bad. The judge let me out on bail."

"Would you break the law again to save a furry friend?"

I answered seriously. "If a dog is on a kill list, then yes I would.

No dog deserves to be on death row just because he hasn't got a home. What kind of people let that happen? It's wrong!"

The reporter turned back to the camera.

"And there you have it. The Canine Crusader would break the law again to save the life of another dog. And they say we don't have real heroes anymore."

I winked at the camera because I didn't know what else to say, then pushed my way towards the entrance to the shelter.

A harassed woman with a clipboard didn't want to let me through, but when she recognized me, I was allowed in. I found myself face-to-face with a stiff in a suit who was the shelter's director.

"Do you know what you've done here?" he hissed at me. "We've been under siege all day. I've personally been threatened with violence!"

I stare at him, puzzled. "But I thought all the dogs had been adopted. What's the problem?"

He turned purple and spittle flew from his mouth.

"The *problem* is that people are calling me a dog killer!"

My gaze hardened.

"Five dogs were on your kill list. Five dogs who now have a home. If you'd been doing your fookin' job right in the first place, this wouldn't have had to happen."

"How dare you!" he screeched, pointing a trembling finger at me. "You have no idea of the pressures we're under! Costs go up year on year but our budget doesn't. We've lost another part-time member of staff, and now we've got a broken door to pay for, no thanks to you!"

I felt a bit guilty about that. "I'll pay for your door."

"You most certainly will!" he snapped. "I'll make sure of it." He took a breath, his piggy little eyes narrowing. "You know, nothing about this is easy—we have shelters in five boroughs for the whole city and take in 30,000 animals every year. One in five have to be euthanized because *we have no space!* We know which animals we can help and the ones no one wants. Even if we had the room—which we don't—is it better for an animal to be in here for three, four, five years with no hope of being rehomed?"

He had me there. I had no idea that homeless dogs were such a huge problem in the city. And I had to consider the idea of a kill list against a beastie being kept in prison for years instead. Neither was something I wanted on my conscience.

"You need more money, mate," I said. "And better publicity. And seeing as I seem to be flavor of the month for the next 15 minutes, why don't I use it to try and get the donations flowing in?"

He gave me a skeptical look and answered stiffly. "All donations will be gratefully received."

"Right then! The Canine Crusader is on the case!" and I stepped back outside. "Right! Everyone here, give us five bucks for the shelter. Yeah, and you journalists! It's the price of a coffee and a muffin—you'll hardly miss it. Come on, hand it over!"

Twenty minutes later, I had a fistful of money, hundreds of dollars, which I gave it to the shelter's director who just stared at me.

"There'll be more where that came from," I assured him.

Then it was time for me to go home and take care of my own pack of hounds. Plus, I had some thinking to do. I knew I wasn't the sharpest tool in the toy box, but I needed to come up with a plan to raise more money.

My phone rang again but I ignored it. I might remember to check my messages when I got home, or I might not. I worked on the principle that if anything was important, they'd call back.

Which turned out to be a tactical error if I was trying to win Gracie over, but I didn't know that at the time.

CHAPTER FIVE

GRACE

I wanted to kill Vincent Azzo as slowly and painfully as possible, but right now I was too busy answering phone calls for him. Naturally, Vince wasn't answering *his* phone, messages or emails—the knob-head was driving me insane.

His little stunt outside the Supreme Court had gone viral and everyone wanted to know more. And since he'd named me as his lawyer, the press had hunted me down at work and had even gotten hold of my personal cell phone number.

All three of my assistants were answering one call after another, and I had to give them something to say other than 'my client has no further comment'.

I'd drafted a statement on Vince's behalf and emailed it to him but the asshole hadn't even looked at it or replied to the half-dozen texts I'd sent him. How was I supposed to represent him when he wouldn't answer his damn phone?

Although to be fair, I'd never have guessed that social media would jump on this so quickly. I'd been blindsided and I guessed Vince had, too. So I fobbed off everyone by saying that Mr. Azzo would be releasing a statement later in the day.

Everyone wanted to know if the dogs had been saved. I'd like to know the answer to that, too, and had tried calling the shelter but their line was constantly busy. I didn't know what to make of it.

I'd just finished up on yet another call, this time from a West Coast TV station wanting to know if my client would fly out for an interview, when senior partner Carl McCray knocked on my door and walked in before I could say anything.

I sat up straight. Visits from one of the upper echelons to one of the minions was unheard of. Usually, you were summoned to the fifteenth floor by the assistant to the senior partner's assistant.

"Ms. Cooper, I've heard you're much in demand today. An unusual client."

"Yes, sir. He's ... my *pro bono* work for the ABA. I like to keep up my hours."

"Good to hear but we're closing on the Rogers & Cranston deal this week. We need you up to speed."

Stung, I carefully straightened my legal pad in front of me. "I've already emailed the third draft to be disseminated to all parties. There was an error in the covenant regarding future income tax filings. I've now rectified that. The project is *up to speed* at my end."

He gave a cool smile and nodded. "I know we can count on you, Grace. Now ... your *pro bono* work is bringing our little company some publicity. I hope that will continue to be positive?"

It was easy to read between the lines: *your pro bono case is on TV, which means Kryll Group is on TV—don't do anything that will reflect badly on the company: don't fuck up.*

"It's an interesting case," I said, my answer deliberately noncommittal.

He rapped his knuckles on my desk. "Bring your client to the staff party on Friday—I'd like to meet him."

My mouth dropped open. "The staff party?" I said faintly and utterly horrified.

"Yes, the senior partners would like to meet the man who's making the news."

He gave me a chilly smile and sauntered from my office.

I rubbed my face twice before I remembered that I was wearing makeup. Today was turning out to be a complete nightmare. My phone rang again before I had time to think any further.

By 6pm, Vince's face was on every news channel, and the clip had garnered over 150,000 hits on YouTube. He was a ready-made celebrity, and everyone was contacting *me*, his lawyer.

> *Fascinating factoid: the man who played Robin in the Adam West series of Batman has re-homed more than 15,000 dogs through his charity, and as he specialises in dogs like Great Danes, most are bigger than him.*

I couldn't get a read on McCray but I guessed that the senior partners weren't happy with me ... unless I could turn this into a media coup for the company. I kind of hated them a little for that because it was supposed to be about homeless dogs, not how some very wealthy lawyers could spin this for their own benefit. But I was cynical enough to know how the corporate game was played.

Vince still hadn't replied to my messages and I needed a break. Luckily, I was meeting my BFF for an early supper before I headed back to the office to do my *real* job.

Cady looked fabulous as always as she sashayed into the restaurant, plopped down at my corner table and immediately slid one of the blintzes I'd ordered onto her plate.

"Grace, sweetie, you've got ugh-face. What's up?"

"My face is ugh?"

"Stop stalling. What's bothering you?"

"Nothing," I moaned.

She peered across the table and raised an eyebrow.

"I've been your best friend for 19 years and I know you. I call bullshit."

"I can't tell you."

"What? Of course you can!"

"I really can't!" I whimpered, feeling utterly pathetic.

"Hmm, well, mime it then."

"Mime it?"

"Yes, you know, charades."

"Are you serious?"

"As serious as my love of lemon-glazed donuts."

"Fine."

I leaned back in my seat and raised five fingers, then mimed the harbinger of my doom.

"Um ... five letters ... um ... it's got a horn? A rhino? No? Uh, unicorn? Not a unicorn. Dinosaur?"

"Ugh, no! You're teasing me!" I yelped.

"Well ... could it be ... *knob-head?*"

I nodded.

"So, is it Vince?"

"Of course it is! You were enjoying that, weren't you? You're evil!"

"Nah, I'm your BFF."

"Same thing."

"If you say so. So what's the knob-head done now? Apart from getting himself arrested and his face appearing on every news channel and gossip website."

I dropped my head into my hands. "Isn't that enough? Although it gets worse. He never answers his phone and I've promised a statement from him that reporters are waiting on. I thought four hours would be enough but so far he hasn't even read my email or returned my calls! And that's *still* not the worst of it!"

Cady pulled a face. "There's more? What's up, Grace? You're putting me off my blintzes, and that never happens."

"Nothing important," I laughed hysterically.

"It's bothering you; you're my bestie BFF..."

"What are we, twelve?" I said snarkily.

"...so if it matters to you, it matters to me."

"It sounds pathetic..."

"Please! You listened to me whine about Rick last year, all moody about whether he liked me or not."

"You were never moody."

"Thank you, but that's not the point. You're re-directing, Counselor."

"I know. Okay, fine. I have no one to go to the annual staff party with. Again."

Cady blinked. "You hate the annual staff party. You usually go for five minutes then make an excuse and run for it."

"I hate it because I'm the only person there who doesn't have a date. Everyone stares and looks sorry for me."

"Screw 'em! You're a strong, successful, beautiful..."

"Thank you. You're right, I know it. But I just feel..."

"I'll come with you," said Cady cheerfully. "I'll be your date."

I gave a reluctant laugh. "Thanks, but the senior partners already think I'm a closet lesbian."

"Seriously? Did I already say screw 'em? So spice it up. Let them think it! Anyway, I think you're hot. But really, does it matter what they think?"

"Unfortunately, yes, if I want to make partner any time in the next decade."

"That attitude is Stone Age!"

"Welcome to corporate law. But Carl McCray came into my office today and that *never* happens. Then he mentioned Vince and all the press coverage and now he wants to meet him—at the staff party! It wasn't a request!"

Cady leaned back in her chair, her expression aghast. "Are you telling me that *Vince* is going to be your date to the annual staff party?"

"YES!"

"Wow! That's ... unexpected."

"You bet your ass it is! What am I supposed to do? It'll be a disaster."

Cady finished her blintze. "At least it'll be memorable."

I let my head rest on my arms and moaned.

Then my phone rang.

"It's him! *Knob-head!*" I stared at the phone as if it was about to bite me.

Cady picked it up and answered for me. "Vince, this is Cady. I hope you're nowhere near Katz's Deli because Grace wants to tear you a new asshole. Yup. You said it. Yup. Well, put it like this: one, she's gotten no sleep last night because she was helping you; two, she's gotten no work done all day because she was helping you; three, she's emailed and messaged you a ton and you haven't replied until now. Yup. That's right. Yup. Hell, yeah! Your life hangs by a thread, buddy. Your excuses had better be outstanding."

She handed the phone to me with a smirk.

"Vincent," I said coldly.

"Hey, Gracie!" he said, his voice only slightly chastened. *"Sorry about that. Forgot to check me fookin' phone. Happens all the time. But no worries, I've got good news! All them dogs have got homes! Every single one of them! And the shelter bloke says that dogs all over the city are being adopted. They're calling me the Canine Crusader!"*

My mouth dropped open. "All the dogs? That's fantastic!"

"Yeah, right! But all the shelters are operating on tiny budgets, so I said I'd help them. I'm going to organise a Canine Crusader fashion show! I'll get all me mates to donate stuff."

"A canine fashion show?" I said faintly.

Cady's eyebrows shot up as she listened to my half of the conversation.

"Yeah! Fashion and dogs. I'm onto a winner, I fookin' know it! I'll do it during New York fashion week."

"That's the week before Rick and Cady's wedding," I muttered, unable to keep up with the conversation.

"Yeah, cool innit? So can you put that in the statement and send it to all

them journos you were talking to? Cheers, Gracie!" His excited voice slowed and became more intimate. *"So, if there's anything I can ever do for you, you just have to ask."*

I took a deep breath. At this moment in time, I really hated myself as much as I hated him.

"I need a date for my annual staff party on Friday. You're coming with me," I grimaced as Cady just about killed herself laughing.

"A date? On Friday? Sure thing, Gracie! That would be awesome. Tell Cady she and Rick are dog-sitting for us, yeah? That'll be fookin' fab! I knew you'd see sense in the end, babe."

I rested my head on my hands as despair rushed through me.

"Just kill me now," I whimpered.

Cady spat out half her blintze, she was laughing so hard.

"Some best friend you are," I grumbled.

CHAPTER SIX

VINCE

I was Grace's date to her office party—things were looking up.

The last few days had been crazy and I'd been doing interviews all over town as well as a bunch of online interviews. Sometimes I'd taken the kids with me, although Tap could be shy of strangers—it was either that or leave her home alone which I absolutely would not do. I'd even been on Cady's morning radio show and Tap had snuggled up on her knee the whole time, the little traitor.

And the news kept getting better—shelters in the city were almost empty, and even the harder to home dogs like older, large breeds were finding their forever families. They were even importing rescue dogs from other states. The idea of the fashion show was a goer and I was confident I'd get the people I needed. The Canine Crusader was on the case! I'd had a load of t-shirts made with my new Canine Crusader logo, and my IG and Facebook followers were buying them in bucket loads. I'd ordered a thousand and was about to run out. I'd paid a neighbor's kid to mail them all out and slung him a few bucks, so everyone was happy. Even better, the kid worked from my house and Tap, Zeus and Tyson had really taken to him.

I'd started to pull in a shit-ton of favors for the fashion show and promised a load more. But I knew it was going to be worth it. Uncle Sal had already spoken to Giorgio for me, and I had other people in the biz who I knew would help out. To be honest, it was fookin' fantastic the number of people who wanted in on it.

I grinned at Rick as I studied my reflection in the mirror.

"I am a god and women can't get enough of this fine specimen of manhood."

"You're an idiot, and no woman in her right mind will have anything to do with you," he said, playing some game on his phone.

"Oi! You're supposed to be me best mate!"

"I am. The world is doomed."

I stared at myself in the mirror, liking what I saw. I flexed my muscles, counted my abs, then turned sideways to check out the peachy globes of my amazing arse.

"Hot!" I grinned at my reflection. "Fookin' hot!" I raised one eyebrow and turned to stare at Rick. "And you were supposed to be persuading Faith to go out with me and that tonight will be fab, but I didn't notice you helping."

"Her name's Grace."

"That's what I said."

"Yeah, well, I can't help you."

"Why not?"

"Grace is my fiancée's best friend."

I arched an eyebrow at myself in the mirror as I answered him. "So?"

"I like her. I'm not telling her to go out with a tosser like you."

"Why are we best friends?" I laughed.

"Limited choices."

"Nah, you love me really, mate."

"I feel sorry for you."

At that moment Cady came in from the back garden with Zeus

and Tyson at her heels. Tap trailed behind looking sad. She knew that Rick and Cady were dog sitting for the evening and she hated it when I went out.

Rick pulled Cady onto his lap, which was a brave move since she wasn't a small weight.

"Cady, tell Vince that Grace isn't interested in him," he said.

"Course she is!" I defended.

"Sorry, big guy," said Cady with a smile. "She thinks that you're a jerk—ya know, a knob-head."

Rick nodded in agreement but I turned back to the mirror, ignoring them both.

"Nah, she's into me, I can tell. Otherwise why would she invite me to her office party?"

Cady sighed. "I didn't want to be the one to tell you … wait, I actually really did want to tell you … but she thinks you're a grade-A asshole, and the only reason she invited you is because her boss told her to."

"Prime stud, me."

Cady cringed. "I rest my case."

I glanced over and grinned at her. She was wearing a red sweater and it really suited her.

"Yer tits are looking nice today, Cady. Very firm and fruity."

"Oh my God! I can't believe you said that!" she bellowed.

"Don't talk about my fiancée's tits," Rick said, his voice a warning.

"What? I was paying her a compliment."

"No," Cady said patiently. "A compliment is saying my hair looks great or you like my dress. A compliment is not staring at the girls and leering."

"I can't help it," I admitted. "Your tits are so big it's like having another person in the conversation."

Cady slapped her forehead as Rick scowled. "You're a lost cause."

"Nah, I just need the love of a good woman to put me on the right track. Like Faith."

Cady and Rick yelled in unison:"It's *Grace!*"

"Yeah, her. Top totty," and I hid my smile.

Cady turned to Rick. "Why are you friends with him?"

"He's like a stray puppy. I can't throw him out now."

"He's 6'4"!" she yelped.

"He's still an idiot," Rick mumbled. "And a danger to himself."

"True," Cady sighed.

I winked at them both in the mirror. "I'm irresistible."

Cady tried once more to put me off.

"No, Vince. The reason Grace doesn't want to go out with you is because she has good taste."

"She wants a taste of my prime rib."

"I give up," she sighed.

I checked myself in the mirror once more then looked up as my door bell buzzed.

"My cab's here. Look after the kids for me and don't get too crazy—no shagging in my bed—unless I can join in."

"Get outta here!" Cady laughed. "And be good to my girl!"

"Always!" I grinned, then knelt to kiss the kids goodbye. "Group hug!"

Tap licked my face. It was her way of forgiving me and saying, *hurry home, Dad!*

The taxi ride to Grace's apartment seemed to take forever as it slid through the slushy streets that Friday evening. I'd been surprised when she'd asked me to be her date to her annual office party, and my enthusiasm was only slightly blunted when I learned that it was only because her boss wanted to meet the Canine Crusader, but I was all about the opportunity. Grace and me and an evening out—I wasn't going to waste it.

At her apartment, I rang her bell and she buzzed me in. I was curious to see her place. I imagined it to be very tidy but classy and a bit uptight, like her.

She met me at the door already wearing her coat over a knee-length black dress.

"I'm ready," she said, almost pushing me backwards.

"Nah, I've brought something for you to wear," I said, handing her the garment bag I'd been carrying and slipping past her. "Nice place you've got. I thought there'd be moose heads or something seeing as you're from Minnesota."

She stood in the doorway staring at me. "Moose heads?"

"You know, all huntin', shootin', fishin'. I'm glad you don't—I think animal heads look best on animals."

"Are you trying to insult me or does it just come naturally?"

My smile slipped as I experienced a brief and uncharacteristic loss of confidence.

"No. I've never been to Minnesota."

She continued to stare at me, her expression tightening with irritation.

"Uh, well, do you want to try it on?" I asked, pointing at the garment bag and hoping I could distract her from whatever had annoyed her.

"I'm already dressed," she snapped. "I'm a grown woman who can choose her own clothes and I'm ready to go. Now."

"Yeah and you're gorgeous, but please try it," I begged. "I borrowed it special like from Stella and I know you'll look amazing."

Her face twisted like she was sucking on a lemon.

"You brought me an outfit that you *borrowed* from a woman named *Stella?*"

I licked my lips, realizing that didn't sound quite right.

"Stella McCartney," I said quickly. "The designer. She's a mate of mine. It's from her new collection."

Grace blinked, then looked down. "Oh," she said faintly.

"Will you try it?" I asked hopefully.

"I usually wear a black cocktail dress."

"Nah. Boring. Try this—I promise you'll look amazing."

She nodded her head jerkily then headed to her bedroom. I really wanted to follow her but our date hadn't had the smoothest start so I just wandered around her living room looking at her photographs and generally checking out the lay of the land.

It didn't take long bearing in mind that this was Manhattan and a shoebox cost the price of a five-bedroom detached starter castle back home in Derby.

I sprawled on the mocha-colored sofa while I was waiting, leafing through a copy of *American Journal of Comparative Law*—a thrilling read it ain't.

I snapped a quick selfie that showed my Windsor knot tie and added it to my IG story, right after the undies shot I'd taken as I was getting ready. My followers loved it and I loved my hundred-thousand plus followers. Sponsorship was up which meant more dog biscuits for the kids and more pennies in the bank for me.

Then Gracie swayed into the living room looking fookin' fabulous but with an uncertain expression. Stella had loaned me a silver lamé halter-neck jumpsuit that turned Gracie from hot to knockout.

"A jumpsuit?" she said, her voice wavering. "I don't know ... I usually wear a dress at office functions..."

"Nah. They already know that you wear the pants in your office—may as well show them and look fook hot while you're doing it."

"I'm too skinny," she whispered. "All legs and arms. Like ... like a stick insect."

"Nah, more like a Whippet. I like Whippets."

"Gee, thanks," she snorted, sounding like Gracie again. "Can't I at least be a Greyhound?"

"Too short."

"Thank you, Vincent!" she snapped, her eyes flashing.

There was my girl!

"We'll look fook hot together," I grinned at her.

"You'll do, I suppose," she said haughtily, trying to hide a smile.

"Nah, you think I'm a scorcher, I can tell. You think I'm a solid ten, probably an eleven."

"No, you're more an equine nine."

"Eh? You think I'm a horse? Nah, luv, just hung like a horse—dick like a donkey, me."

"I don't care if you're a Shetland pony or a Shire horse," she hissed. "I'm not interested!"

She totally was.

CHAPTER SEVEN

GRACE

The jumpsuit was gorgeous and the material felt amazingly luxurious, almost decadent against my bare skin. There was no room for a bra, not that I had much to fill even an AA-cup. One (very ex) boyfriend had described my chest as two fried eggs on a plate. What a charmer.

But this jumpsuit made me feel incredibly sexy. The halter neck covered my front, but left my back bare then clung to my waist, the fabric draping softly against my legs and shimmering like molten silver.

I knew very little about fashion, but even I could tell that the cut and design was sensational.

I'd always played it safe when it came to clothes. In some ways that was part and parcel of being a corporate lawyer—a fitted gray, navy or black suit, and a token color in the shirt or shoes, with very little variation. But *this!* This was different.

I swung from confidence to concern as the taxi drew inexorably closer to the bar in the Village that Kryll Group had rented for the evening.

"Don't mention your IG account," I admonished Vince, "especially not your Fans Only page, and definitely don't show anyone photos of yourself in tighty whiteys."

He leaned in to me, his cologne clinging to his lightly tanned skin. "You've been peeking."

"You're *my client*," I said coldly. "I need to know the drivel you put on your social media."

That was probably a little ruder than necessary, but Vince just winked at me and sat back with a satisfied smile. He was irritatingly difficult to annoy.

"Can I show the photo of me in nothing but my Canine Crusader t-shirt and a smile?"

"No."

"What about the new S&M leisure wear that I've been modelling?"

"No!"

"How about those studded diamanté thongs I was gifted by that designer?"

"No, no, no!"

"Spoilsport."

"And don't swear," I said seriously. "The F-bomb is off limits. So is 'shite', 'tits', 'knockers', 'boobs', 'dick/dickhead' and 'cock'. Do you think you can manage that for an entire evening?"

"Taken under advisement, Counselor," he said, grabbing my hand and kissing it.

I pulled away quickly. "This isn't a date," I said severely.

He just smiled.

Every time I tried to keep my professional distance, he seemed to slip a little closer. It was annoying. And worrying. But mostly annoying.

As the taxi pulled up outside the bar, Vince surprised me by paying the fare.

"Can you afford it?" I asked. "I wasn't expecting you to..."

"I can be a gentleman," he said, then held the door open for me.

Stumped, I stumbled out into the icy street, and Vince held my arm to steady me.

"I'm sure you can," I lied, "but you told me you haven't got any money."

"I got a new sponsorship deal," he said with a faint smile. "S&M weekend wear. The photos are on my Fans Only site, but I'll show *you*. Just say the word. I have free samples, too."

"Oh," I said faintly. "Right. Thank you, but no."

An amused smile brightened his expression and I wasn't sure if he was teasing me or not. Probably not.

I took a deep breath as we entered the dimly-lit bar, arm in arm.

I hated events like this. At work, I had a role and a purpose and was too busy to worry what anyone thought of me. I was very good at my job, fair to my assistants and polite to everyone. At functions like this, I felt like I was freefalling. I never knew what to say or do. I hated just latching onto a group, but equally I hated circling the room hoping to find a conversation to join. I felt awkward, ill at ease, judged. I was liked, but I wasn't popular. And I was one of only a handful of other women who were also trying to make partner. Competition was fierce. I competed by being the best at my job. But I was savvy enough to know that was rarely enough. Partners were expected to be expert networkers. I sucked at that.

I glanced at Vince who was pulling faces at himself in one of the highly polished entrance pillars and checking his teeth.

"Oh, God, I'll never make partner," I mumbled, feeling my heart begin to race.

"You alright, Gracie?" Vince asked, turning towards me. "You look as though you're about to be invited to a colonic irrigation party."

"Do they have those in LA?" I asked distractedly.

He laughed as we checked our coats and snagged two glasses of champagne from a passing waiter, handing one to me. "I'm glad I moved to the east coast—Lala land is full of nutters."

"We have enough crazies of our own."

"Yeah? No wonder I fit right in."

I was vaguely aware that he was teasing me, but my mouth had gone dry as people started to turn and stare at us.

"How do you want me to introduce you?" I whispered. "As my client or..."

He dropped his voice half an octave and did a passable Sean Connery impersonation, complete with raised eyebrow. "My name is Azzo, Vince Azzo and I'm fookin' irresistible to women and dogs. Cheers!"

I choked on my champagne as Vince gave his trademark megawatt smile.

Then he bent towards me.

"Relax, Gracie. It's going to be fine."

I didn't like using alcohol as a social prop, but I downed that glass of champagne faster than a pie-eating champion at an all-you-can-eat buffet.

Then I saw Melissa, one of my assistants, with her long-term boyfriend, Neil, propping up the bar, as usual. She smiled and waved me over, which instantly made me feel better.

"Hi, Mel, Neil! How are you? This is my ... friend and client Vincent Azzo."

"Oh Em Gee! I know who you are! You're the Canine Crusader!" she said, giving him a sloppy grin, and I wondered how long she'd been here.

"And you're the wonderful Mel," he smiled, taking her hand and kissing the back of it like some latter day prince.

He shook hands with Neil who was eyeing him warily, then turned the full blast of his variable charms on Mel.

"Thank you for all your help," he said sincerely. "Gracie told me that you worked all the hours helping me out. I really appreciate it." He smiled down at her. "And the dogs appreciate it, too. You must be an animal-lover. All the best people are."

She blushed to the roots of her hennaed hair, and then she

spent the next five minutes telling him all about the pet rabbits she'd kept as a child.

Vince gave her his complete attention, fixing his dark blue eyes on her intently, listening to every word with utter sincerity, and absolutely charming her.

There wasn't a single inappropriate remark or F-bomb to be heard. I started to relax. Maybe this evening wouldn't be so bad after all.

We were joined by Gary and Penny, my other two assistants, both with their husbands, and Vince worked his magic on them, as well; thanking them, showing his appreciation, telling them more about the fashion show he was organizing, explaining about the funding the shelters needed. I could see adoration shining in their eyes. They were already #TeamVince.

Mel sidled up to me. "He is *so* nice! I always assume good looking guys are assholes, but you can't say that about him."

Oh, yes you can.

But I didn't say that to her. She looked completely smitten and a little dazed. Then she seemed to notice me properly.

"Grace, your outfit is wow!" she said, her eyes widening. "You look ... great!"

I smiled, but did she have to sound so surprised?

"Thank you, Mel. I ..."

We were interrupted by Carl McCray calling and waving at me imperiously from the other side of the room.

"You'd better go," Mel said knowingly.

"Thanks," I sighed.

I took Vince's arm and eased him out of the circle of his new fan club.

"We're going to meet my boss and several of the senior partners, so *behave*. I mean it! This is my job."

"Chill, Faith," he said with a wink.

"It's *Grace!*" I hissed at him.

"That's what I said."

By then, we'd reached the partners, and it was too late. My life flashed before my eyes and I mentally ran through a re-write of my CV when I had to start looking for a new job.

"Ms. Cooper. Or perhaps we can dispense with formalities tonight, Grace. Good to see you. You've met my wife Simone."

"Yes, of course, hello again. And let me introduce you to my client, Vincent Azzo."

At the sound of his name, Vince turned on his smile, and I had the impression that he was summing up Carl and Simone McCray in that one quick glance. Then he shook hands with all the partners. It was like watching a giraffe with a herd of buffalo—he was so different from our world.

"Of course!" said Carl with a broad smile. "The Canine Crusader. Welcome to our little soirée."

I wanted to cringe; Carl sounded so pretentious. Maybe he'd described the office party as a 'soirée' to impress Vince, or because Vince was British, and British accents always sound classy.

"Thank you for the invitation," said Vince. "I really appreciate that Kryll Group are right behind my campaign. It's good to know that influential corporations are helping to spotlight the misery of homeless dogs and pets."

For half a second, Carl looked completely taken aback then puffed out his chest, trying to stand as tall as Vince, and failing.

"Yes, indeed. We at Kryll Group pride ourselves on our community service."

That was the first I'd heard of it.

Vince nodded and looked at Carl seriously. "And I'm opening up sponsorship opportunities for the Canine Crusader fashion show..."

"Is that Stella McCartney?" Simone interrupted suddenly, eyeing my jumpsuit.

I was a little surprised as she'd never spoken to me in seven years of working here and seven years of meeting her at office events.

"Yes, it is. From her new collection."

She sniffed and turned away. Then one of the other senior partners congratulated me on the Rogers & Cranston merger. It was a perfect opportunity for me to network, but I was only half listening, afraid of what Vince might say when left to his own devices.

Simone asked him about living in Milan and working for Armani, and he regaled her with gossipy stories of mishaps behind the scenes and what the *maestro* was really like. He'd also spent time in Rome and Florence, and had even walked up every one of the 295 steps of the Leaning Tower of Pisa at night.

66 *Fascinating factoid: the tower has 296 steps, or 294, because the seventh floor has two fewer steps on the north-facing staircase.*

When he spoke in what sounded like fluent Italian, Simone lapped it up and ten minutes later, Carl and the senior partners had pledged $25,000 to Vince's event. I could only stare at him in awe. How did he get to be so smooth? Where was the goofy, accident-prone guy that I knew and sort of hated?

Eventually, our group broke up and headed to the buffet table.

Carl walked away looking very pleased with himself, and Simone cast several backward glances at Vince. He passed me another glass of champagne and winked at me.

"Why aren't you like that all of the time?" I blurted out.

Vince didn't even pretend that he didn't know what I was talking about.

"Because it's fookin' fake," he said seriously. "I can brown nose and kiss arse for a good cause. Just because I'm good at it, doesn't mean I like it."

"And you can speak Italian!"

"Not really."

"But I heard you speaking to Simone!"

Vince eyed me with amusement.

"I learned a few phrases for pulling birds, that's all. I just told Simone that her backside was as beautiful as a pig in muck. It sounds better in Italian."

I shut my eyes. "You didn't! Oh my God, what if she'd understood you?"

Vince laughed, "It was a compliment."

I huffed angrily then sighed.

"You were amazing," I admitted. "Honestly, I've never known Carl to pledge that sort of money before."

Vince shrugged. "Maybe he's a dog-lover."

He took my arm as we wandered through the bar and inspected the buffet—the usual fare plus mini vegan shroom-burgers as a nod to Vince.

He stuffed a whole one in his mouth then reached for another.

"Tastes like crap," he said cheerfully, coming close to spraying me with crumbs.

I took a step back, faintly disgusted with his eating habits. I wondered if he did it on purpose.

We sat at an empty table as Vince wolfed down several of the bite-sized *amuse-bouche*, as Carl McCray insisted on describing them. Vince pulled a face with every enormous mouthful and I got the impression that they weren't amusing his big bouche very much.

"Oh, gee, sorry to bother you but can I have your autograph, pl—?"

I glanced at up at one of the junior members of staff, then watched in complete horror as Vince stood up so quickly, his head clocked her under the jaw, and the poor girl staggered around looking dazed.

"Oh, gosh! Are you alright?!"

I rushed toward her and we grabbed an arm each as she tottered about, then Vince brought a chair for her and a class of water.

"Sorry about that, luv," he said. "When I come up, I come up fast."

Then he winked at me.

"Noted," I deadpanned.

He didn't get much chance to eat after that because it seemed like everyone wanted to meet him, and the girl he'd nearly knocked out sat next to him, her eyes glassy with champagne and a mild concussion.

Vince lit up the room and behaved like everyone was his new best friend; he made them laugh, he made them want to spend time with him. They barely said 'good morning' to me and I'd worked with them for seven years. How did he do it? Well, no one could accuse Vince of being shy. Not like me. I hid behind my suits and smarts. I wasn't a networker and I envied his ease in his own skin.

I was good at my job; Vince was great at being Vince.

After we'd made a complete circuit of the room, I'd had three glasses of champagne on an empty stomach and I was feeling ashamed of feeling sorry for myself. Vince had done a good thing here; it wasn't his fault that people liked him more than me. Did that make it *my* fault?

Vince was concentrating hard and staring at his phone. Huh, probably updating his IG feed *again*.

"What are you doing?" I asked crossly.

"Just deleting me Tinder account," he said without looking up.

I was surprised. "Oh, right. Why?"

He pressed one more button and winked at me. "I'm upgrading."

"Is that a new app?" I asked, a little confused.

"Yeah, no. Not exactly."

Yes, no, not exactly! What did that mean? Vince always said what he meant. Why had he chosen this evening to go all existential on me?

"What's up, Gracie?" he asked quietly. "You look as happy as a fart in a Jacuzzi."

That made me smile, it was so Vince. But then I sighed.

"Everyone likes you."

"Only 'cause they don't know me," he grinned.

"And the women were all over you."

"They know hot stuff when they see it," he nodded in agreement, smoothing his tie and giving me his patented James-Bond-raised eyebrow.

"I mean it," I snapped.

"You looked fook hot tonight," he said, squeezing my hand. "Them blokes would have been all over you if I hadn't been on guard duty."

I shook my head. "Men just see me as a skinny, uptight fun-sucker ... and don't make me say that again quickly!"

I thought he'd laugh it off. I was really being pathetic and obviously drunker than I'd realized.

"Okay," he said quietly. "But, Grace ... is that really how you see yourself?"

"Sometimes, yes."

The silence hung between us.

"Come on," he said. "Let's get out of here. I know a great vegan restaurant just around the corner. You'll love it."

"Thank you," I said. "I mean it."

Vince gave me a dazzling smile. "You like me, admit it."

"I tolerate you."

"Same thing."

"Not even slightly," I said haughtily. "And I preferred you when you were 3,000 miles away in LA."

He leaned down, his breath tickling my ear. "That's a long way to go for snuggles."

And I couldn't help laughing. Vincent Azzo was winning me over, too.

God help me.

CHAPTER EIGHT

Vince

The mistake people make when they're not used to cooking vegan food is that they try to replace the meat to copy a meat-based meal and it just doesn't work. Sticking veg and potatoes on a plate with a Quorn-burger and calling it a roast dinner don't cut it in my book.

The restaurant I took Gracie to was streets beyond that—it was a fart-friendly environment: more beans, pulses and lentils than you could shake a bog roll at, and an array of delicious dishes.

It was also a Buddhist place so had this cool, laidback, hippy dippy vibe. It was my go-to happy place, second after the dog park, or maybe third after a good shag—but that was debatable.

My mouth started watering like a leaky hydrant even before they brought the menus which I knew off by heart. Do you think vampires drool when they scent a tasty human? I've often wondered about that: it's one of the questions that keeps me awake at night.

Nah, I'm kidding. Nothing keeps me awake at night—I sleep like the dead.

Like the dead! Hahaha! The Vin-meister is a pun-master.

Back to the drool.

Triple mushroom noodles with black turtle beans (no turtles involved); bean curd with basil, cashew nuts, cranberry beans, split peas and lentils; pan fried turnip cake with lemon (a must); and their incredible sweet and sticky rice balls with sesame.

Grace wanted to go with something safe but I ordered lots of other things for her to try, as well. I never want to be one of those shit-necks who tell their women what to eat, but I was confident that when she saw what I'd be shoving in my gob, she'd wet her knickers, guaranteed.

When the array of food arrived, her eyes widened and she looked physically sick. I wasn't quite sure where I'd miscalculated, but I tried to reassure her it was all for me. She seemed incredulous, but I took to a trough like the world was ending.

As I chewed, half delirious with pleasure, I stared at her, watching her color rise as the warmth of the restaurant and the food took away the winter chill.

After a minute, she laid down her chopsticks.

"Please don't watch me eat, it's really off-putting."

And the penny dropped with a loud and familiar clang, so I concentrated on staring at my own plate.

"No worries, Grace. I'm too busy stuffing me own fookin' face."

"You're gross."

"But in a sexy way, yeah?"

"No, in a gross way. You're staring, again."

"You've got mustard on your lip," and I wiped a paper serviette over her face, trying to be helpful, but she reeled back, flushed with embarrassment.

I carried on eating, then asked in a conversational tone, "How long were you anorexic?"

Her whole body stiffened.

"Did Cady tell you that?" she asked angrily. "I can't believe she'd..."

"Nah, nothing like that. Cady barely tolerates me," I said

cheerfully. "You know I was a catwalk model for five years. I've seen it all. Most of the models were fookin' anorexic— chewing on tissue paper to fill 'em up, arses like elephants—all loose skin over butt bones. You need squats to get a juicy, peachy arse like mine," and I stood up pointing at the pert peaks of perfection in question.

"Sit down!" she hissed, uncertain whether to give me an ear-bashing or laugh.

"It's nothing to be ashamed about," I said. "You look perfect to me."

She blinked several times. "I'm not ashamed," she said quietly, "but it's not something I share with many people."

"But Cady knows?"

Gracie gave a brief smile. "She was the one who helped me through it. We were roomies at college." Her smile fell. "Mean girls used to call us 'Laurel and Hardy'. One day, Cady grabbed the bathroom scales and tossed them in the trash. She said no one was going to judge us for what we did or didn't eat."

I nodded, understanding how hard it was to re-set your body's eating demands once you'd gone a bit wonky.

"Cady persuaded me to see a counselor and, well, it's a work in progress, but I'm a healthy weight now." Her voice was defensive as she glared at me, then her shoulders slumped just a little. "I find it hard to eat around other people unless I know them really well."

"Fair enough," I grinned at her. "I'm counting on you getting to know me *very* well," and I gave her my patented panty-melting grin.

"Not gonna happen in this lifetime or the next," she snorted, but her eyes were smiling.

"Well, we *are* in a Buddhist restaurant and they believe in reincarnation, so I'll take that challenge."

"It wasn't a challenge," she huffed.

"It is now," I insisted, raising an eyebrow.

We sat in silence for several seconds which was way too long. I'm a talker by nature; can't be doing with uncomfortable silences.

"Tell me about growing up in Minnesota. That's up by Canada, eh?"

"Please don't do your *Fargo* accent. We don't all talk like that."

"But it's really good!"

"No, it isn't. You sound like Dudley Do-right."

"Who?"

"Never mind. Where are you from? And don't just say 'England'."

"Derby, in the middle of England: north of Birmingham, south of Manchester."

"Any brothers or sisters? Parents?"

I shook my head. "I'm an orphan, me. Dad died when I was 15 and Mum died last year."

"Oh!" Gracie was momentarily speechless. "I'm sorry—that must have been difficult," and she gave a sympathetic smile. "Although the legal definition of an orphan is someone who is a minor and has lost both of his or her parents. You're 35, even though you act like a great big kid."

"I feel like an orphan," I said. "I'm no one's child anymore. Haven't got anyone to call Mum."

She touched the back of my hand briefly, and I cleared my throat.

"So, what about you? You got family in Minnesota?"

"Yes, my mom and dad. Dad worked in the lumber industry before he retired, and mom is a homemaker." She shrugged. "Pretty typical, small town upbringing: lots of sports, especially football and ice hockey."

"Eh, can't see you as a wide receiver."

She laughed. I fookin' loved her laugh.

"Not so much, but I was a demon on the ice."

"Are you shitting me?"

"Nope. I was quite a tomboy when I was a kid. I was a great winger, got a lot of assists."

I stared at Gracie with new respect. I knew that ice hockey was fookin' lethal; pretty much a blood sport at times. Imagining someone as graceful as her slamming a puck into the net or taking her hockey stick to another player was turning me on.

"What about you? You said you did kick boxing—that's pretty brutal, isn't it?"

I had to dismiss the image of Gracie in my bedroom wearing a hockey uniform and carrying a big stick. Can I just say, *Phwoar!*

"Yeah, did it for a few years and got pretty high up the rankings for my weight."

"Why did you give it up?"

"Modeling came along and in one of my last fights, I got these teeth knocked out," and I pointed at the right side of my mouth. "Then I had a car accident a few days later and cracked the other side of my face on the steering wheel and lost the teeth on the left. I just had gums. I looked like an old grandpa. Cost me a fortune to get this lot fitted," and I tapped my teeth.

"They're all false?" Gracie asked in shock.

"Yep, the dentist screwed 'em into my jaw. Fookin' hurt! But it was worth it. Mind you, he was a sadistic bastard. I think he enjoyed it. This one was the worst," and I tapped my front tooth, but the fooker dropped out right onto the pile of white napkins on the white tablecloth.

Grace looked shocked then started to giggle as we scrabbled around trying to find it.

"It's ice-white! It's the same color as the sodding serviettes! That fooker cost me a grand! Can you see it?"

"That's an adorable gap-toothed smile you've got, stud," she laughed. "Like an eight year-old ... a 6'4", 190 pound, eight year-old."

Still giggling, she helped me search through the wreck of the table until I found my tooth glinting at me next to one of the candle lanterns.

"Phew! Found it! I need to glue that bugger back in. Can't have the Canine Crusader without his fangs."

I screwed it back into my mouth, making a mental note to glue it later. Gracie watched me with soft eyes and an amused smile. She was cute when she was drunk and I think she liked me a bit more. Unfortunately, once I'd fed her and she started to sober up, I could see her slipping back behind the hard shell of her professionalism.

So I let her talk about the next press release, the fashion show and my upcoming court case—those were her safe places.

"And we've got a wedding to go to," I reminded her. "I'm looking forward to stepping out with the maid of honor."

"A life-defining moment, I'm sure," she said coolly.

"Counting on it," I grinned, watching as she rolled her eyes.

She muttered something I didn't hear then glanced at her wristwatch.

"I need to get home. I've got to get an early start in the morning," and she raised an accusing eyebrow at me.

"On a Saturday?"

"Press releases to send, fashion contracts to review, and someone's court case to prepare."

"Me and the dogs thank you," I said with a wink.

Back at her apartment, she raced into her bedroom and stripped off the jump-suit. I wish I could say we had wild monkey sex in her bed, but she came out wearing a floor-length silky robe thing, and handed me back Stella's outfit.

"Please tell her I said thank you," she said primly, tugging the edges of the robe closer to her throat. "I felt very special wearing that."

"You're always special to me," I said.

"Very smooth, Vince," she laughed. "Thank you for dinner, it was delicious. Now *goodnight!*"

I left with a smile on my face and hope in my heart. A couple more evenings like that, and I was sure I could persuade Gracie to lower her standards. That woman was mine—she just wouldn't admit it yet.

I took the subway home, getting off at Borough Hall. The

slushy pavements had frozen into slippery mounds, and I relived my youth by taking a run at them and sliding along. I'd come a long way from a Council house in Derby, but that scrawny little kid was still inside me.

The lights were on in my apartment when I got back. I slid my phone out of my pocket, hoping I'd be able to catch a picture of Rick and Cady getting it on.

Instead, I got a photo of her snoring on Rick's chest while he watched an American football game on my TV.

"Blimey! You're not even married yet and you're falling asleep in front of the telly!" I yelped.

Cady grunted and sat up. "I was awake at 4.30am this morning for work, turd face," she said grumpily.

Rick grinned. "What she said."

The kids heard my voice and came rushing in from the bedroom. From the loud thumps as they jumped off my bed, they'd obviously decided that was more comfortable than their own dog beds.

Tyson stuck his nose in my crotch, the little sod, and Zeus yipped and barked, complaining that I'd been out again. Tap whined and tried to climb my leg, so I scooped her up with Zeus and plopped down on the sofa between Rick and Cady, dodging an elbow to my ribs as I separated the lovebirds.

"Home by yourself?" Rick asked slyly.

Cady threw a cushion at him. "Is Grace still talking to you?"

"Yep! I've made some progress there. She still thinks I'm a knob-head, but a loveable one."

"Yay for you," Cady yawned. "We're going home. I'm glad it went well, big guy, but I still say you're punching above your weight."

CHAPTER NINE

GRACE

"So, how did your date with Vince go?"

Monday lunch with Cady was a new tradition. We used to spend Sundays together when we could, but what with her being all loved up, it had become a short and sweet catch up on Monday lunchtime instead, plus dinner once every couple of weeks if I wasn't canceling on her due to working late *again*.

"It wasn't a *date*," I grumbled. "It was ... a business exchange."

"Okay, so did you *exchange* anything interesting?"

I gave her a jaded look and she shrugged. "A woman has needs."

"He dropped his false tooth on the table in the restaurant."

Cady choked on a croissant. "What? Seriously?"

"Yep. It was bright white, perfectly matching the table linens. Playing hunt the tooth was one of the evening's highlights."

Cady laughed. "That's ... that's so Vince!"

I smiled with her. "It wasn't all bad. And we found the tooth. He was kind of amazing with the partners," I said thoughtfully. "He even persuaded them to donate $25,000 to the Canine Crusader fashion show. He was so smooth with them. It was ... weird."

Cady cocked her head on one side. "You like him."

"I don't hate him. He's still annoying, but he's got a good side."

She raised her eyebrows but didn't speak.

I shook my head. "No, absolutely not. Don't even go there."

"Fine, I won't. How was your dress fitting?"

That brought a genuine smile to my face. "Fantastic! The fitter even made it look like I have a cleavage!"

"There's nothing wrong with your girls."

"Well, I like them, but you have to admit they're small. Mammograms are hell for someone with small breasts."

"They're hell for everyone," Cady said mildly, as I gazed enviously at her extremely well-endowed chest.

"I'm serious! When I take off my padded bra, the nurses..."

"You wear a padded bra?"

"Only because the air conditioning in my building is so cold," I said defensively. "But the nurses look at each other as if to say, 'what are we going to do with those peanuts?' So they tug hard to try and get some boob to squish, and all they end up with is a mammogram of my nipples! It's not funny!"

"I'm grimacing in empathy; it's different from laughing."

"Not very different, apparently. I have no boobs, no waist and no hips. Half the time, I have to shop in the boys' department in stores."

"You have great legs—your legs would give the Pope second thoughts."

"Ha, well, thanks. I got so fed up of sales assistants asking if I'm clothes shopping for my son that last time I said yes."

"Really? What happened?"

"I ended up in a very bizarre conversation about which school my non-existent son wants to go to, and which softball team he plays for."

Cady bust a gut laughing. "That's hilarious! I hope you said he was a Yankees fan?"

"Ugh! You're such a wench!"

Just as we were settling the bill, Cady said innocently, "Has Vince said anything to you about the maid of honor / best man dance?"

I froze, then my eyes narrowed as she tossed some bills on the table and ran for the door.

"Cady Callahan, get your ass back here and explain that!" I yelled as she waved from outside, striding down the sidewalk with a huge grin on her face.

I swear my colon clenched in horror at the thought of a maid of honor / best man dance with Vince, the hapless harbinger of doom. It would be a disaster, a very public disaster. Cady was in so much trouble.

And so was I.

I hurried back to my office thinking of a thousand ways to get Cady back for her disloyalty—she was really pushing the best friend code. Could Vince even dance? Because I knew I couldn't. I barely had a rhythmic bone in my body and found swaying in time to the music a challenge.

My eyes opened wide. No! This was way worse than Vince embarrassing me in public—it was me! I was going to be the one embarrassing him!

Flames of humiliation for the ignominy that hadn't yet happened shot through my body. I slid on the ice, half wishing for a sprained ankle; a small injury that would prevent dancing and indignity. Or I'd just fake it. I'd have to remember to buy a support bandage later.

Back at the office, Gary shot to his feet the moment I returned, but I was surprised when he followed me into my office, Melissa and Penny crowding in behind him.

"What's up, guys?"

Gary held out a cream envelope, made from expensive linen paper, and embossed. Melissa had my silver letter opener laid across her palms like an offering.

"It's from *Vogue*," Penny whispered. "Hand delivered."

I didn't even pretend not to be excited but still prepared myself for a polite 'no', so I had to read the short note twice.

"It's from the editor's personal assistant: Anna Wintour is coming to the Canine Crusader Fashion Show!"

Penny looked like she was going to faint, and Gary and Melissa jumped up and down, screeching with excitement.

She'd said yes! The doyenne of fashion had said yes!

> *Fascinating factoid: nicknamed 'Nuclear Winter', Anna Wintour is thought to be the inspiration for Miranda Priestly in 'The Devil Wears Prada'.*

"Right, everyone!" I shouted, clapping my hands above the noise. "I need you to hit the phones. Gary, prep a news release that tells the press that Ms. Wintour will be at the Canine Crusader Fashion Show, and remind everyone that no animal products will be used in the clothes, shoes or accessories; Penny, call everyone who hasn't RSVPed and let them know; Melissa, contact all the reporters, bloggers, vloggers, YouTubers and Instagrammers you can think of and kindly inform them that *Vogue's* Editor-in-Chief will be attending. Go!"

They ran back to their desks while I took a deep breath.

And that was the moment that I knew I'd do everything in my power to make Vince's dream come true.

Unfortunately, that feeling didn't last long. By 11am the next morning, I wanted to stab him with my silver letter opener.

Gary knocked on my door while I was just finishing a phone call with the fashion show's insurers. I'd managed to shave $1100 off the initial quote, but they maintained that by having dogs at the event, the risk was much higher, therefore the premium—including a premium for anyone catching rabies—was higher. I'd put the cost on my credit card. Personally, I thought having Vince at the event was the riskiest part of all.

"Ms. Cooper, I have Mr. Azzo for you."

"Put him through," I said tiredly, replacing the phone in its cradle and tucking my credit card in my purse.

"No, he's here!" Gary said excitedly.

I stared at him queasily. Here? That couldn't be good.

"Okay, send him in."

A pair of legs entered carrying an enormous bouquet of colorful flowers, and something that looked like a broomstick with pink and yellow birthday balloons tied to it. It was loud and lurid and hard to miss—just like Vince.

"Fook me! Them balloons are heavier than they look," he said, plonking the huge bouquet on my desk and sending the contracts I'd been reading sliding to the floor.

Then he presented me with the long, thin gift-wrapped broom handle, plus balloons.

"What's this?" I asked faintly.

"Birthday present," Vince grinned at me.

"But my birthday was two weeks ago."

"I know! Fook me! Missed that one! Cady only just told me so I thought I'd make it up to you." He nodded his head at the broom handle/gift/unknown item. "You'll love it."

Gary, Penny and Melissa peered through the doorway while I unwrapped my gift. The hastily Scotch taped paper revealed a thin, shiny pole about nine feet long.

Vince was watching me, his expression excited. I stared at the pole then I stared at Vince; he stared at me, willing me to say something.

"Um, it's a pole."

"Yeah!" he grinned.

"Thank you," I said faintly.

Gary, Mel and Penny looked just as perplexed as me.

"It's great, isn't it?" said Vince, happily taking the pole from my hands and walking to the middle of the room. "I thought it could go here."

I blinked. I understood the individual words, but I was still trying to make sense of his sentence.

"You want to put a pole in the middle of my office?"

His radiant smile faded a few degrees. "It's not just a pole—it's a pole for pole dancing."

Gary and Mel exchanged looks as I cleared my throat.

"You bought me a pole for pole dancing?"

"Yeah! Innit brilliant!"

"Isn't pole dancing for strippers?" I asked in a flat voice. "Do I look like the sort of person who would do that?"

Vince looked horrified then hopeful then horrified again as I almost snarled the final words at him.

"No! No, I don't ... I mean it's not ... I thought it would make a change from yoga. It's ... it's a great workout routine. You can learn some moves at Rick's gym—they do classes—then every time you take a break at the office, you can get some exercise: do a few spins, stretch out your muscles, clamp your thighs around it..."

Penny giggled.

"Thank you, Vince," I said carefully biting my tongue and speaking with dented dignity. "It was very thoughtful of you. But you see, I use this office for meetings—I don't think it would be appropriate to have ... that ... in my office."

"But ... you haven't got room at home," he said sadly, causing my assistants to throw me questioning looks.

"Don't you have work to do?" I asked crisply, nodding at the door.

Once they'd shuffled out and closed the door behind them, I turned to Vince, indignation warring with softer emotions.

"Can you return it and get your money back?" I asked.

"Dunno," he said moodily. "Are you sure you haven't got room? Maybe in the boardroom—spice up meetings," and he looked so hopeful, my anger drained away; he was just being Vince.

I rubbed my forehead.

"Have you got a headache?" he asked.

"Yes," I sighed.

"Exercise will help that," he said with a half-smile, pointing at the pole. "And you'd look fook hot."

"Vincent! A stripper pole is not going to help with my headache!"

"It's an exercise pole," he said defensively, then sighed. "Hey! We could use it for the best man and maid of honor dance!"

"Absolutely not. No way. Never."

"So you don't want it?"

"No." *Not in this lifetime.* "Thank you."

"Okay," he said defeated. "I'll have to think of something else for your birthday. What about a ThighMaster? You could keep that under your desk."

"No."

"Kettlebells?"

"Still no."

"A mini trampoline?"

I rubbed my forehead again. "No, Vince. You don't have to get me anything for my birthday—the flowers and balloons are more than enough. They're beautiful, thank you."

He rubbed the stubble on his chin. "Maybe I could donate the pole to the kids' playground."

I had a vision of six year olds spinning like they were about to join a revue bar.

"Yes, great idea," I said as I escorted him to the door.

"I'm good with kids," he said happily. "I used to be one."

"You still are," I muttered.

"Thanks!"

"That isn't a compliment."

"Yes, it is."

"No, it isn't!"

"Is."

"Isn't!"

"Are we arguing?"

"YES!"

"Can we get to the part where we kiss and make up now?"

"Aaaaagh!"

"Is that a yes?"

"NO! Good*bye*, Vincent."

He brushed a kiss onto my cheek as he departed with the nine-foot pole under his arm and a swagger in his step.

CHAPTER TEN

VINCE

I was gutted that Gracie had turned down the exercise pole. I'd had a lot of fantasies about watching her use it, which was probably the primary reason I'd bought it. But exercise poles could be a great workout and sexy as fook.

I stared at it sadly while I navigated the Manhattan sidewalk traffic. It's funny, you can be invisible in a crowd, but add in a nine foot pole, and you get a lot of looks. I'd have to mention that on my IG page. Maybe I could learn some moves for *Fans Only*. I'd have to plant the pole in the back garden and remember to clear up the dog shit first.

As I headed back to the subway, I ran through the problem that was giving my gray matter its own workout.

I needed some more models for the fashion show. Well, I needed *different* sorts of models. Most of the ones I knew from the biz were skinny giraffes; I wanted a bit of variety, and being somewhat distracted with my pole, so to speak (the Vin-meister is on form!), I made the cosmic mistake of sending a mass text to everyone on my phone's contacts list. I hadn't meant to, and it was only when my plumber said he was well in there that I realized what I'd done.

Erik the plumber was a top bloke: five foot nothing and five foot around, with a bald head and enormous mustache. But as he was a huge dog-lover, I just shrugged it off and sent a text message to Uncle Sal's assistant (because the old codger didn't do text messages) to give him the happy news that one of his suits for the show might need a bit of alteration.

The reply was a lot of exclamation marks and emojis of ducks shagging (if I had to guess, I'd think he was telling me to fook off, but I could be wrong).

Unfortunately, there was way worse to come and I really was earning my knob-head credentials.

I got tagged on Instagram by someone I'd hoped never to hear from again for the rest of my life.

> **Shout out to the darl @CanineCrusader @VinceAzzo an old squeeze of mine begging me to be part of the #CanineCrusaderFashionShow and im IN! Beautiful people only. No fuglies!**
> **@fabulousMollyMckinney**
> **#fuglies (Fansonly pix in my profile)**

I took a deep breath. Molly was the last person I wanted to see/speak to/spend time with *ever*—but she had a fuckton of followers, so maybe it would work out. She couldn't be as bad as she used to be, right? Squinting slightly to hide from bad news, I read her previous post.

> **Being hated is hard work. You think Piers Morgan wakes up in the morning and suddenly has an idea about who he's going to skewer today? No way. Ive worked hard to be the girl**

whos most hated. Why am I hated? Because Im hot, rich and awesome. And I tell it like it is.

If your an ugly ho its not like its gonna be a surprise to you if I mention it. In public. Or on my social media. You already know your a troll —do something about it. Thats what plastic surgeons are for.

@fabulousMollyMckinney

#fuglies (Fansonly pix in my profile) #fataintfunny #fixyourteeth #nosejob #facelift #boobjob #lipfiller #drmarkdimpler

Nope, she was still a mean bitch. I sent her a text uninviting her and didn't think any more about it.

It was a lot harder work producing a fashion show than just being the skinny tosser who shows up unwashed and unshaven to be transformed into a catwalk model. I'm talking about myself, of course, but I'd seen some female models arriving for a show looking hairier than a wookie with the temper to match.

If it hadn't been for Grace, Rick and Cady, I would have fallen arse over tit a hundred times a day getting the show off the ground.

Grace did the boring-as-shit work like contracts, insurance, timings and sorting out the catwalk space. We'd started off with 1500 ft^2 at the Spring Studios, the venue that most of the designers were using for New York Fashion Week. By the end of the first day, they'd upgraded us three times, and we'd already sold all the tickets to the largest space they had—4,800 ft^2 in Studio 4 on the sixth floor. (Should have been called Studio 6—just sayin'.)

And as the week went on, we could have sold that again many times over. If I'd thought it wouldn't be pissing with rain in February or arse-freezing cold, I'd have tried to get Central Park or Yankee Stadium. Go big or go home, right? I wanted to call Aaron Boone just in case, but Grace wouldn't let me.

"Do this event well, and you could put it on every year. Screw up, and you'll look like an amateur—and a knob-head—but you'll also lose the chance to raise more money. Walk before you can run, Vincent."

I opened my mouth to argue but she closed me off faster than Usain Bolt ordering a pizza.

"Nod if you understand me."

Message received and understood. I nodded.

I'd tried to get Grace to be one of the models but she'd shot me down so many times, I had more holes than a cheese grater.

Cady had agreed cheerfully to be one of my models, and Rick was just told that he was in the show. He grunted, I shrugged, Cady smiled. Nuff said.

I wished everything was that easy because the models were giving me a headache—some of them, that is. Rafe and Elias hated each other (this week) and refused to share the same dressing room. I told them they could share with the dogs, but didn't mention that there was only one dressing room anyway.

I had ten guys (including me and Rick), and ten girls (including Cady) and ten dogs (including Tap, Zeus and Tyson). Cady and Grace had tried to argue against having the mutts, but to me, that was the point of the show. And they all had to be rescue dogs, like mine. Zeus and Tyson would walk with Rick and Cady, and Tap would come with me. I'd carry her because I was a bit worried that she'd be overwhelmed by the crowd.

So as well as the models, I had seven rescue dogs ranging from a ten year-old Wolfhound called Wolfie (yeah), a Malamute called Nanuk (yup) with one blue eye and one green eye (I'd have called him 'Bowie'), and four sweet mutts ranging in size from teacup to giant— Alfie, Mitch, Delilah and Sparky. Their 'clothes' were Canine Crusader neckerchiefs designed by my mate Stella. I was well chuffed with them.

But there were a thousand details that were doing me head in: the lights, the music, the seating plan, the invitations, where to put the press peeps, food and drink for the models and volunteers, getting the outfits to the studio, having enough fitters for last minute alterations, getting hair and make-up artists to work for free.

Grace had come over to my place to help me iron out the fine print.

Most things had been donated, but there were still some upfront costs that had to be paid, and if I ever meet the sod who fleeced us for the one day's insurance, I'll let Tyson crap in his shoes. Maybe *I'll* crap in his shoes.

Gracie interrupted my evil plan.

"You told me that you've asked two professionals to do hair and makeup, right? Well, my spreadsheet shows that even if they only spend 20 minutes per model—which is half what's usually allowed—you'll either have to get everyone in two hours earlier or you need two more hair and makeup artists."

She hovered with her phone in her hand, waiting for me to make a decision while I sat like a muppet staring at her.

Then she waved her hand in front of my face. "The lights are on but there's nobody home. Vincent! Decision, please. Do you have two more makeup artists you can call?"

"You're so fookin' hot when you're all serious."

She rolled her eyes. "Do you have low blood sugar? Focus!"

"That's a great idea," I said, leaping to my feet and waking up the kids. "We all need a break and I'm hungry as fook. Let's all go and get something to eat."

She immediately shook her head. "I don't have time. You go. I need to work on the timings."

I grabbed her hand and she looked up at me, puzzled and irritated.

"Gracie, take a fookin' break. We've been at this for nearly three hours. I need a walk, the dogs need a walk, and you need..." *a shag* "something other than coffee."

She huffed and pulled her hand free. "Three hours planning is nothing! I've been in meetings that have gone on for nine hours."

"Where? In Hell?"

Her eyebrows snapped together in a familiar scowl. "Look, I'm giving up my Saturday to make sure that *your event* is perfect!"

"Yeah, you are and I'm right grateful, but you need to take a break, woman! Come on, Tap will be worried about you if you don't come with us."

Gracie glanced down at Tap whose anxious eyes were flitting between us.

"That's blackmail."

"Yeah, did it work?"

"Fine," she huffed. "Just don't blame me when mistakes happen because we weren't ready in time."

"I wouldn't do that, Gracie," I said seriously. "You've sweated your balls off for me and I won't forget it."

Finally, she smiled.

"You say the sweetest things."

"Yeah, fookin' smooth, me."

Outside, the sky was slate gray and heavy with the prospect of more snow. Grace pulled on a coat that looked like a duvet and had me thinking an array of dirty bedtime thoughts. Meh, watching her brush her teeth was a fookin' turn on. Spending time with her left my balls bluer than a blueberry cobbler, without the cobblers—whatever they were.

I put coats on Tap and Zeus but didn't bother for Tyson because he never felt the cold. Then we all traipsed outside and walked briskly toward the dog park.

Tyson immediately found his Jack Russell friend and knocked him over in a friendly greeting. The little fella shook himself then raced Tyson, lapping him a few times, beating him on the curves as they chased each other happily.

I couldn't help smiling—there wasn't much wrong with the world when two happy dogs playing together put a smile on your face.

"Have you always had a dog?" Grace asked as I handed her a steaming hot chocolate and plate-sized chocolate chip cookie.

"Not always. But I nagged me mum and dad for a puppy pretty much from the time I could talk."

"Good Heavens, you mean there was a time you couldn't talk? What bliss!" Grace teased.

"I know. I'm eloquent as fook," I grinned at her. "Anyway, they said I was too young to understand the responsibility and I'd get tired of looking after a dog. Finally, when I was ten, they gave in and that's when Gnasher came to live with us. He was a Bull Terrier crossed with a Staffie and ugly as fook, but I thought he was better than margarine on white sliced bread. He came with me on my paper round before school. When he was little, he sat in the saddlebags, and when he was older, he ran next to me. Never needed a lead or nothing. I gave up playing football after school so I could come home and play with him. He was the best thing in my life."

I swallowed and looked down.

"I loved that mutt."

Gracie was watching me, her brown eyes soft as she fed pieces of her cookie to Tap and Zeus.

"What happened to him?"

"Me dad got sick. Lung cancer. Took him three years to die. Gnasher was what stopped me from losing it. All those trips to hospital, all the times we thought he'd got it beat, all the times we knew it had come back, and at the end, Gnasher was the only one I could talk to." I shrugged. "A fifteen year old kid can't talk to his parents about *feelings*, so I talked to Gnasher."

"He sounds like a great dog," she said quietly.

"The best," and I gave her a weak smile. "He was there for me at the worst time of my life but I had to give him away."

"No! Why?"

"The Council were redeveloping the street I lived in and we had to go into temporary accommodation while our new flat was being finished. Trouble was, this B&B didn't allow dogs, so Gnasher had to go. Mum came with me to the dog shelter when I handed him over. He just stood there with his tail between his legs like he knew what was happening but he didn't understand why I was abandoning him, why I was leaving him with strangers. He started barking as I walked away, then howling, and I knew he was crying, begging for me to come back for him. Fook me, worst day of me life." I took a deep breath as tears came to my eyes at the painful memory. "Six months later, we were in our new place and I went back to the shelter to find him, but he'd been rehomed and they wouldn't tell me where. All they'd say is that the people were nice—had a couple of young kids. I didn't care, I wanted Gnasher back. But it was too late."

Gracie reached out and held my hand. "And you've been rescuing dogs ever since."

I looked down at the table. "Every dog should know it's loved."

We were quiet then for several minutes but Gracie didn't let go of my hand.

"I'm so sorry about Gnasher," she said at last.

I nodded because I couldn't speak. Twenty years later and I still felt like I'd failed him, still felt the grief of loss. I'd watched my dad get ill and watched how frail he became, how much pain he was in. By the time he died, we were all willing him to let go. But Gnasher ... I hadn't been ready to let him go. And anyone who told me he was *just a dog* was going to get knee-capped.

"Vincent," she said quietly, "you're going to do so much good with this fashion show."

"Yeah," I said, nodding slowly. "We are."

CHAPTER ELEVEN

GRACE

The chaos and noise was unbelievable and I was tempted to put my hands over my ears to be able to think.

The studio was packed to the rafters and despite the security I'd organized, there had been a ton of gate-crashers. I was worried that the Fire Officer would shut us down; so far our luck was holding. And it was a star-studded crowd: Anna Wintour was wearing her trademark dark glasses, seated in the front row between Stella McCartney on one side and whispering to Victoria Beckham on the other; Blake Lively was laughing with Katie Holmes; Alicia Silverstone was looking for a seat with Ellen DeGeneres; journalists were snapping away at them but the celebrities ignored the flashes like the pros they were. Even so, heads turned when the enormous figure of Jason Momoa strode into the room and squished his giant frame into one of the plastic seats.

The heat was starting to build so I grabbed a member of staff and instructed them to turn down the air-conditioning before greenhouse temperatures were reached and tempers were lost.

I desperately wanted this to go well for Vince. Yes, he was a jerk and an asshat and a total *knob-head* who thought stripper poles were appropriate office furniture, but he was a good man with a good heart. I wasn't sure his brain was always engaged, but I'd come to realize that even when he annoyed the hell out of me, he didn't mean to—even though it was pretty much every time he opened his mouth.

But if the entrance was bordering on looney tunes, backstage was way worse—because that part was organized by Vince. I could hear dogs barking, one howling, people yelling, and when I saw a red-faced Cady desperately trying to attract my attention, I abandoned my job at the front, telling security that we were full and no one else was getting in, not even Jason Momoa's better-looking twin brother.

Models of all shapes, sizes and ages were crammed into the backstage area with their harried dressers, racks full of couture clothing that combined cost more than my mortgage, plus seven dog owners and assorted canines, Vince with one leg in a pair of electric pink pants, the other trailing behind him, trying to calm Tap who was cowering at the back of the room.

"Here's Mummy Gracie," he said with relief to the quaking dog, and bless her if she didn't give a tiny wag of her tail even though her eyes were large and fearful.

"Give me your pet sling," I ordered, trying not to notice how ripped he was or the way the V-for-vegan tattoo on his thigh flexed as he moved. "If she can't see and can't hear so much, it might calm her down."

Sweating through my blouse, I stuffed poor little Tap inside the sling, relieved to see her relax slightly.

Two of the other dogs were growling at Elias and Rafe, the models they were supposed to be walking with, and Elias looked terrified then blamed Rafe for the animosity, which turned into a shouting match.

Before I could intervene, a high-pitched screech made me jump and the hairs on the back of my neck stood up.

Cady was standing with her hands clenched into fists, glaring at her arch nemesis, the totally ghastly reality 'star' Molly McKinney.

The horror. The horror.

"Where's my dressing room?" she yelled. "Where's my hair and makeup? This place is shit!"

"What are you doing here, Mol?" Vince asked, pushing his other leg in the pink pants and zipping up his fly.

"You invited me, you fucking arsehole," she bellowed in a sweet, understated way.

"And then I uninvited you, you rampant bitch," he shouted back.

"If I don't get an outfit and a dog, I will fucking crucify you!" she shrieked. "I have *five million* followers. I'll bury you!"

"Just give her a damn dress, someone," said Cady, her lips white with anger. "We don't have time for deviant divas."

Vince nodded, his handsome face pulled into a sneer. "Get her on and off the fookin' catwalk as fast as possible."

"And I don't want an ugly dog like that mutt," Molly yelled, glancing at Cady then pointing at Tap who was trying to hide her head under my arm. "I'll have *that* one!" and she pointed to the Malamute who sat serenely watching the chaos.

"Uh, that's not a good idea," the owner said nervously. "Nanuk is better with men."

Molly barely glanced at him as she snarled out a response. "No one asked you, you duh-brain ameba."

The owner's mouth fell open in shock.

"Everyone shut up," yelled Vince. "You're upsetting the dogs!"

Immediately, the volume dropped and even the dogs stopped barking.

Vince grinned happily. "I am the Canine Crusader, dog whisper extraordinaire."

"Admire yourself later," I growled, still annoyed that the vile Molly McKinney had gotten her own way again.

I'd have been very happy to kick her heinous butt all the way back to Britain. But this was Vince's show, and he said she could walk the runway.

The sisters Bella and Gigi Hadid exchanged glances but sat quietly having their makeup applied, and I said a short prayer of thanks because they'd been so amazing: they'd arrived early and prepared, hadn't made a fuss about the outfits and had taken time to greet all the dogs and volunteers.

Vince's plumber was clearly in love with both of them but happily admired from afar in his Armani suit and Paul Smith leather-free shoes which altogether made him look pretty good, bless him.

He'd been another one who was a godsend, helping everywhere, sweet to everyone, great with the dogs, stepped in between Elias and Rafe's bickering, even though he was a foot shorter than both of them. He even fixed a leak in the women's bathroom.

I gave a nervous giggle when I saw Wolfie relieve himself on Molly's enormous coach purse. Still, what the mind doesn't know, the heart won't grieve over, and by the time she found out ... who cares? I wondered if Wolfie could be persuaded to do it again.

"We're live in five, people!" I bellowed above the hubbub, looking at my watch.

I was sweating freely now, especially with Tap's little body pressed against me. Only half the models were ready, the dogs were getting angsty, Vince had disappeared somewhere and Cady was wedged half in, half out of her dress. Rick was getting it in the neck because the zipper was stuck and he was desperately trying to pull it up to cover Cady's boobs.

> *Fascinating factoid: the average breast size in the US is 34DD (not me, of course), but the most popular bra size is 34B, which either means women are stuffing their boobs into bras that are too small, or bra sizes are B.S.*

Suddenly, the music started and *You Ain't Nothin' But A Hound*

Dog pounded out, leaving me a nervous wreck until a flash of pink made my eyes long for sunglasses as Vince strode onto the catwalk with five other male models all in neon-colored suits.

A huge cheer went up which sent the six rescue dogs that the models were walking into a lather, barking, howling, snarling and snapping in fear. The models were equally panicked, not knowing whether to go forwards or retreat, let the dogs go or drag them. Vince stopped in the middle of the catwalk and held up his hand to the five other models. It was complete chaos as dogs pulled at their leads, growled and barked at the audience.

I slapped my hand against my forehead: *it was a disaster!* I'd *told* Vince not to include dogs!

But then he raised his right hand with his thumb, second finger and pinkie finger sticking out like horns, the other two curled under, and he started humming loudly, staring at the dogs mesmerizingly as he gradually lowered his hand.

I grabbed Rick's arm. "What's he doing?"

"Uh, it looks like ... I think he's doing Crocodile Dundee."

"What the...?"

And sure enough, all six dogs turned to listen, then trotted up to Vince and sat down in a line in front of him. The five other models finished their walks looking relieved, and Vince strode down the runway with all six dogs trotting behind him, as the music changed to *I'm Too Sexy* just before Vince ripped his off, sending buttons flying, then flexing his muscles at the audience before heading off stage.

"I bet you've never seen that before," said Cady.

"The striptease or the impersonation of Crocodile Dundee?" I shook my head. "No and no, and I'm still not sure I believe it even though I've seen it. Oh crap, Cady! You and Rick are up next and you're not dressed!"

Cady's zipper was still stuck and Rick was desperately tugging at it.

"Aagh! That pinches!" she squealed. "You'll have to walk in front of me so no one can see and..."

"Let me," I said, shouldering Rick out of the way, releasing the caught fabric and pulling up the zipper. I slapped Cady on her ass. "Go! Walk that catwalk!"

"Yes, boss!" she yelled as the music for *Lady and the Tramp* started.

Rick seemed slightly miffed but Cady slapped *his* ass, and they were off down the runway with Tyson tugging Cady, and Zeus trotting along in front of Rick.

A huge cheer went up and Cady waved to the audience. She'd become even more popular since her incredible efforts to run the New York Marathon last year had gone viral, and she'd raised a ton of money for veterans, too.

Tyson towed her down the catwalk, his tongue hanging out of his mouth as usual, and Cady went with the flow, teetering slightly on her high-heeled sandals, but catching her balance at the end. Rick followed with tiny little Zeus looking like he'd been born on the catwalk, the dog, not Rick, who looked self-conscious and uncomfortable as well as unconscionably hot.

They got to the end of the runway, posed, turned, and then the leads got tangled. Cady was laughing her ass off and Rick's beautiful grin was seen at last as he scooped Zeus into his arms, while the audience sighed at the sweetness of it all, then burst out laughing again as Cady let go of Tyson who went charging up and down the catwalk, assuming everyone was there to see him.

Suddenly another dog appeared, an escapee from backstage, and Tyson completely disgraced himself by trying to mount the Collie-Alsatian mix named, appropriately, Delilah.

Vince sprinted onto the stage dressed only in a pair of tighty whities, waved at the audience and dragged a grinning Tyson from the catwalk.

Delilah wagged her tail and followed them. I wondered if our insurance covered puppy maintenance payments.

Sisters Bella and Gigi were up next in their Cri de Coeur outfits, showing everyone how it should be done, leading their beautifully behaved mixed-breed dogs, Mitch and Sparky, with smiles on their faces. And I realized how unusual it was for models to grin like that, but the sisters looked happy, and I wasn't sure if it was the dogs, Vince's enthusiasm, or they were just having such a darn good time.

It was the perfect example of what a runway walk was supposed to look like. I sighed with pleasure at seeing two professionals at the top of their game, and sighed even more when they returned backstage and fussed and cuddled the two dogs while their owners beamed.

Erik the plumber took to the catwalk like a natural with two male models towering over him but all three working the stage and moving in sync, which couldn't have been easy what with the height differential.

Erik got a huge cheer when he did his pose, then bent down to kiss his borrowed dog on the top of her furry little head.

And I think he must have enjoyed his five minutes of fame because he wiggled his hips all the way back up the catwalk with the strangest walk I'd ever seen, stopped again and waved to the audience.

"Vincenzo! I will remember this always!" he cried, tears of joy running down his face, then hugging Vince tightly and patting him on the shoulder.

"Wow! Everyone loves Vince!" Cady said to me, then pulled a face. "Not you, of course."

I didn't even bother to answer because Molly was the next to walk.

As she hadn't been planned (and because after five minutes of getting to know her, none of the other models would walk with her), Vince arranged for Molly to strut down the catwalk by herself, which she was very pleased about.

She was wearing *my* Stella McCartney silver lamé halter-neck jumpsuit, with her enormous breasts pouring out of the flowing material, and I wished she'd been wearing anything but that.

She dragged Nanuk in one hand, not seeing his lip lifting in warning, and then the music for Black Sabbath's *Evil Woman* blasted out. I turned to Vince and he winked at me.

Nanuk was *not* taking well to being dragged, and when he stopped dead in the middle of the catwalk and started to produce a large and steaming pile of poo, Molly yelled at him then let go of the lead. The audience were in stitches as Molly scowled all the way to the end of the catwalk, did her turn and pose, then stepped over Nanuk's deposit but skidded in urine that she hadn't noticed. The shriek as her ass landed in the poo was louder than a police siren, but the audience loved it and I knew what was going to be front page on the gossip sites tonight.

Vince shoved two fingers in his mouth and whistled. Nanuk looked up, very happy with himself and trotted off the catwalk winking his one green eye.

I did hope Molly's outfit was washable.

The apologetic owner rushed on stage wearing a plastic bag on each hand, with a bunch of toilet tissue as he tried to scrape dog poo off of Molly's backside, but ended up making it worse. She slapped him around the head, slipped again, her arms and legs cartwheeling as she slithered to the end of the stage, then stomped off screeching.

From the corner of my eye, I saw Cady cheering.

The embarrassed owner finished mopping and scooping, then bowed sheepishly as he received a rousing bout of applause, and I even spotted Anna Wintour sharing a smile with Victoria Beckham.

Four boys were up next. Well, I say 'boys' because that's what Vince called them but they were all in their early- to mid-twenties with prominent cheekbones and ever so slightly vacant eyes as they focussed on the back of the room. Rafe and Elias were the outside of the group of four since they were still not talking to each other, but Caleb and Kwame were professional, thank goodness. They shared two rescue dogs between them and ended up cracking smiles when one of the dogs tried to leap off the catwalk when he saw his 'mommy' in the audience. Kwame scooped him into his arms and strode into the crowd to give the little fella a chance to lick his owner.

It was like no fashion show that had ever gone before. It was wonderful, joyful chaos, and I realized then that this was Vince's secret weapon—find joy in everything you do, even when it goes completely ass-in-the-air wrong. So simple to say, so hard to do, and I had to wonder if working 14+ hours a day for Kryll Group was what I wanted to do with my life.

It was a very inconvenient realization to have in the middle of this fashion show.

And then there was just Vince left, making his final appearance to the theme from *Superman*. I gasped when I saw him, and he winked at me as I placed Tap carefully into his arms.

He'd shed the pink pants and the Armani jacket and was wearing a gold Lycra body suit that showed every muscle, ripple and bulge, with his Canine Crusader logo on his chest, a long green and red cape that flowed behind him with a sort of hood that had—oh God—floppy dog ears.

Behind him, with Tyson in the lead, the other dogs were walking in the shape of a perfect V-formation, beautifully behaved.

He paused at the end of the catwalk, raised his fists in the air and shouted out, "I am the Canine Crusader! Throw your fookin' money in the bucket on your way out! Yeah!" and all the dogs started barking in agreement.

A laugh followed by a soft sigh rose from the audience, and then everyone was on their feet, clapping and cheering. Tap looked up briefly, licked Vince's face, and the assembled photographers went crazy as the other nine dogs galloped around the stage for a final moment of mayhem.

When Tap followed Vince back up the runway, the audience

realized she had just three legs, and the sound of cheering and applause was enough to raise the roof.

I was *so* proud of Vince.

Words I never thought I'd say.

"That was incredi—" I began as he strode from the stage, but Vince picked me up in his arms, swung me around, then carried me the length of the catwalk as my cheeks turned fire-engine red.

"This is Gracie Cooper!" Vince bellowed over the laughter and shouted encouragement. "She's me lawyer!" and then he kissed me soundly, deliberately, lovingly.

And me? I couldn't help melting.

Just a little.

CHAPTER TWELVE

VINCE

I woke up with a tongue in my ear and hot breath on my neck.

If my dreams were coming true then I'd open my eyes and see Gracie lying naked next to me, but when I rolled over, Tyson was grinning at me and Zeus had jumped onto the bed, then stood on my chest and peered down into my face. Little Tap's nose appeared at the side of the bed and she whined, unable to join in the fun.

"Alright, alright," I yawned, "it can't be that late."

But when I looked at my phone it was two hours beyond the team's usual breakfast time. They must have been busting for a piss by now.

"Aw, thanks for letting me have a lie-in, guys," I yawned, then flailed about to find a pair of sweats before I took them to the backdoor, shivering when the cold air hit me.

They lolloped happily around the backyard as I stared up at the overcast New York sky, wondering if it was going to snow again.

The fashion show had been a massive success and donations were still rolling in more than two weeks later. Press coverage had been fookin' fab and the photo of Molly covered in dog shit had gone viral. Couldn't have happened to a nicer person.

I'd already been asked about doing the show again next year. I wanted to, but fook me, it had been hard work. And I was smart enough to know that I wouldn't have been able to do any of it without Gracie's mad organizational skills, Cady's media contacts and good humor, and Rick's quiet support. I had some bloody good mates.

Mates. I brooded over the word. I wanted to be more than mates with Gracie, and despite the fact that we'd worked closely together on the fashion show, I hadn't completely cracked that hard shell of hers.

The catwalk kiss had been completely on impulse but felt fantastic. She'd grabbed me by my ears (my costume ears, thankfully) and gave as good as she got, but then she hadn't returned my calls since. Was I back to just being Rick's knob-head friend?

I shivered again and headed inside, then caught a glimpse of myself in the mirror, flexed my biceps and grinned. Nah, she wanted me. She just didn't know it yet, poor luv. The Vin-meister never gave in!

I wondered how I could impress her. Maybe if I organized Rick's stag night without us getting arrested?

My first thought for the big event had been to rent a Caribbean island, import the strippers from Thailand and have a mud-wrestling competition, but it turned out that my budget of $2,000 wasn't going to cut it, even with the deals I could get from some air stewardesses I knew. For the flights, not the mud-wrestling, although some of those girls could get pretty wild.

To be honest, Rick was being boring as fook and kept saying he didn't want a big party or anything crazy, so naturally my job as best man was to ignore him. He'd definitely want to remember his stag night when we're a couple of wrinkled old gits.

Thankfully, two of his old rugby friends were flying out from

England today and I knew they wouldn't let him get away with doing nothing. I'd booked their flights and hotel, but Rick refused to invite anyone else, even from his own gym, and Cady's soldier brother was on deployment and wouldn't get back until the rehearsal dinner. That was a shame—Army blokes knew how to party hard. Luckily, two guys from the fashion show were up for a laugh, so there'd be six of us commiserating on Rick's decision to chain himself to Cady for the rest of his life.

I liked Cady, I did, but she had bigger balls than most blokes and she was *loud*.

Still, I had plans and I was getting through my list:

- Friends from UK, sorted √
- Clothes for the night, sorted √
- Transport, sorted √
- Entertainment, stage one sorted √

I just had to figure out the best place for a stripper competition. This was Manhattan, baby, and there were a ton of places to choose from. I was like a pig in muck planning it all.

But the first note that I might have bitten off more than I could chew was when Rick called me an hour after breakfast.

"This is the Vin-meister at your service." I could hear him breathing but he wasn't saying much. "Alright, Rick?"

"I just got a call from Leon. He said you booked his and Ben's flights from the UK."

"Yep, all booked up, and the hotels."

"You got the date wrong."

"Eh, no I didn't. Arriving at lunchtime today, stag night tomorrow, hangover Friday, wedding on Saturday."

"Their flights arrive on Friday lunchtime."

My stomach clenched. "Nah, not possible, mate. I checked."

"So did Leon when he went to check-in for the flight that should have been an hour ago."

Rick definitely sounded a tad testy.

"I'm sure it's just a mistake," I said weakly. "Let me look into it and I'll call you back," cutting off his comment that he *knew it was a mistake.*

But when I studied the booking, I saw that I'd definitely made a balls up. My head dropped into my hands. It was Rick's fault for leaving a dickhead like me to organize his stag night.

I phoned the airline and felt a jolt of hope when they told me that they could exchange the tickets—but only for flights on Thursday, but not till the evening, and the penalty fee would be $950 for two.

That was pretty rubbish since it meant they'd miss Rick's big event tomorrow night anyway. I looked up other airlines but the prices were nuts, and when I found my balls and called Rick back, I admitted defeat.

"I'm sorry, buddy, I fooked up."

"Don't worry about it," he sighed. *"I didn't want to have a stag party anyway."*

"Are you kidding me? We're still going!" I yelped. "Rafe and Elias are up for it."

"I hardly know them," Rick said in a grumpy voice

"Which is good, 'cause they won't know what a miserable bastard you are," I answered cheerfully.

"And I thought they hated each other."

"Not this week. I'll be at your place tomorrow at six."

"Why so early?"

"Got a lot to pack in, mate," and I hung up before he could argue anymore.

Not only that, I wanted to prove to Gracie that she wasn't the only one who could organize a night to remember.

She'd planned and executed Cady's bachelorette party last weekend like a military exercise with a printed itinerary and comments in the margins—something I'd spotted when I'd visited Rick's apartment—

and nobody had been naked, lost, or arrested. It sounded tame to me. Cocktails at the Aviary on the Upper West Side with views across the city from the 35th floor and a new cocktail invented by some famous mixologist named for the woman of the hour, 'Cady's Easy Street'—*meh*; dinner at Boqueira on Second Avenue where they made Cady's favorite Churros con Chocolate and individualized party candies—*too girly*; champagne at Be Cute in Brooklyn, a famous drag bar where they'd danced till dawn—*whatever*: Gracie, Cady and twenty-five of Cady's nutso friends. Gracie had even organized a London bus to drive them around with a singing conductor—*puh-leeze*.

I was pretty certain I could top that. Whatever happened, it was going to be an epic stag night.

Gracie and Cady were already unsteady when I opened my front door at five o'clock the following day and found them leaning against the wall. I wondered if they were in a fit state to look after the kids, but Tap headed straight for Gracie and Zeus jumped into Cady's arms.

I was relieved Tyson didn't try that trick or he'd have flattened her.

"You girls been hitting the booze already?"

"Yes, Dad," snorted Cady, and thrust a plastic bag at me that rattled with the sound of bottles.

Gracie tottered inside with a massive pizza box under one arm and a bag full of donuts, chocolate, candies and Milk-Bones in the other. Tap followed her faithfully and they settled on the sofa together.

"So what's the plan, ladies?" I asked with a grin. "Porn Hub and eating chocolate dicks?"

"Yes," said Gracie, and my smile fell.

Cady sniggered. "Well, it's a sort of porn: nostalgia porn."

"What's that?" I asked, wondering if this could be a niche market I hadn't covered in my *Fans Only* IG.

"Well, let's see: there's *Dirty Dancing*, of course; followed by either *Footloose*—the original because, yeah, Kevin Bacon, why wouldn't you?—or *Step Up*, although Grace put in a vote for *Strictly Ballroom* because she thinks Paul Mercurio is hot in it, but I'm still holding out for *Magic Mike*; and then *Ghost* when we get to the weepy part of the evening."

I scratched my head. "Whatever grooves your truffles, ladies. Look after the kids. I'll be back, um, some time."

I kissed the kids goodbye, and even Tap seemed happy enough curled up between Grace and Cady, and Zeus was already snoring on Cady's lap. Tyson was stretched out under the coffee table which made me wince. He always forgot where he'd fallen asleep, then tried to stand when he woke up and headbutted the table. Every time. I had no idea why it was his favorite place.

"Right, I'm off! Stay out of trouble," I grinned at them.

"Enjoy the bachelor party, but not too much, Vincent," Cady said. "I'm warning you!"

Gracie met my eyes for the first time even though hers were slightly crossed. "Don't get arrested because I'm not coming. Or going. But definitely not coming."

A squiffy Grace was very, very cute and I wanted to kiss the scowl off her face.

Sighing, I left them to it and jumped in the taxi they'd arrived by, then headed over to Rick's.

CHAPTER THIRTEEN

GRACE

"Ooh freeze and burn!" Cady snickered.

"What?"

"You were so cool with Vince, I could see icicles dripping from every word."

I shifted on the large sectional, making myself more comfortable without moving Tap.

"No, I wasn't. I just don't want him getting any ideas, especially crazy ones," I said defensively.

Cady shrugged. "Vince already has ideas: I see them flashing across his face every time he looks at you." She paused. "At least tell me you don't hate him, because I saw that steamy lip lock you had with him at the end of the fashion show. Everyone did. Woah, call the Fire Department and bring a bucket of water!"

I shook my head. "I don't hate him. And it was a very nice kiss."

"Nice? Damned by faint praise!"

"Okay, it was a *great* kiss," I admitted sheepishly, "but that was just because of adrenaline from the show."

"What if it wasn't?"

"Excuse me?"

"What if it wasn't just the adrenaline rush? What if you two have genuine chemistry?"

"I doubt it."

"Well, Counselor, to test that theory, you'd need to stage a re-enactment."

"I've had too many glasses of wine to have a sensible conversation," I replied, dodging her suggestion.

Cady grinned at me. "Then don't have a *sensible* conversation—tell me how you *feel*."

"I don't want to go to work anymore."

The words leapt out of me before I had a chance to analyse them or call them back.

Cady blinked at me. "You don't want to work at Kryll's? What's that got to do with Vince?"

"Nothing, everything! It's hard to explain."

"Grace, I'm your oldest friend. Have another glass of wine and try. I won't judge you. Much."

We each poured another glass of wine as in the background Baby announced, 'That was the summer of 1963'.

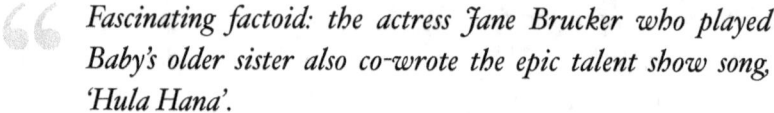

Fascinating factoid: the actress Jane Brucker who played Baby's older sister also co-wrote the epic talent show song, 'Hula Hana'.

"Vince is really disorganized," I began.

"True. And?"

"I'm super organized. I hate mess, I hate being late for things, I hate my to-do list not being finished at the end of the day. I work *hard* to be the best on details; I find mistakes in other lawyers' work all of the time and I fix them. That's why the partners pay me well. Their wages and bonuses have been enough to keep me from looking around elsewhere. They've hinted that next year I'll make partner myself—in one of the most powerful and prestigious law firms in New York. And I'll have done it before I'm 40."

Cady nodded. "Go on."

"I work 14 hours six days a week, sometimes more. I take work home with me most nights. And I don't mind that, I really don't. I take a hot yoga class once a week and I get to have lunch with my bestie most Mondays..."

"When you don't cancel on me."

"I know, I hate that."

"It's okay. Ooh look! She's carrying a watermelon. Sorry, go on. What's this got to do with Vince? Although I think I can guess."

"Vince's life is chaos and..."

"Woah, woah! Objection, Counselor! Look around you. Do you see any chaos in his home? Does he ever forget to feed or walk his dogs? Has he ever left beer bottles or pizza boxes lying around when we've visited? Are there dirty skivvies under his bed? Is there a scurf line around his tub? I bet you've looked! Vince's home is neat and tidy, and he doesn't even have a cleaner, he does it all himself." She gave me a hard look. "You're over-ruled."

"Okay, fine, his apartment is tidy but his life isn't. He models in his underwear for his online fans. He teases them with his you-know-what! His latest sponsor makes S&M leisure wear! And before you ask, I know because he told me and because I read the contract for him. His life is just..."

Cady grabbed my hand as I started to get agitated. "Okay, just breathe for a minute before your OCD kicks in for real."

I took a shuddering breath, annoyed to find that I had tears in my eyes as my chest felt constricted. Then Tap licked my arm, giving me a worried look.

"I'm okay, precious," I said. "Mommy Gracie is just having a midlife crisis meltdown."

She wagged her tail cautiously, and Cady chuckled.

"I think she understands you and she says that it's okay for life to be messy because we can't control everything around us. If we try, we'll always be disappointed. People *are* messy and contrary and a pain in the ass, but if you dismiss all those things, you'll dismiss everything that's quirky and different, too."

I sniffed and gave her a watery smile. "Tap says all that?"

"She is a very wise dog. She's very fond of you and she worries when you're upset."

I stroked Tap's soft fur as she nestled against my hip, slowly relaxing again. "She's very special to me, too. Did you know that Vince rescued her from Dubai and spent months getting her well enough to travel home?"

"Yeah, I heard that story. Pretty incredible."

"He *is* incredible," I said softly. "Everything he's done as the Canine Crusader is amazing..." I shook my head. "I never thought he'd do any of it, but he's proved me wrong." I looked up at Cady. "He's not just a knob-head, is he? Not just a big joke."

Cady shook her head. "No, he's not."

I sighed. "You know he bought me a stripper pole for my office as a late birthday present?"

Cady sniggered. "Yeah, that was an epic fail!"

"Well, I decided to try it out."

"Excuse me?"

"I took a class at Rick's gym."

"You took a pole-dancing class?"

"Yes, I was terrible, but I really enjoyed it."

Cady eyed me with interest. "Would you do it again?"

"Maybe. It was fun. It made a change from yoga."

Cady lifted her eyebrows. "And what wisdom have you concluded from this interesting departure from your nice, tidy life?"

"Ugh, you make me sound so boring!"

"No, but you're careful. You plan things, and there's nothing wrong with that. But then you get upset when your perfect plans are torpedoed by life, and that stresses you out. I'm happy that you decided to shake things up a little."

I gave a quiet laugh. "I think being Vince's lawyer has taken care of that! But at the fashion show, there was a moment—well, several —when I thought it was going to be a complete disaster, but even though it was totally chaotic, it was *fun*."

"I certainly laughed my ass off when a certain someone's shit hit the fanny," and Cady high-fived me as we both enjoyed that particular memory.

After we'd stopped laughing, Cady looked at me seriously. "And how does this make you feel about our favorite knob-head?"

I looked down at Tap as her eyes closed with pleasure while I continued to stroke her.

"It made me think that maybe he's the one who's gotten it right and I'm the one who's gotten it wrong all of these years."

"Or maybe there's a place somewhere in the middle?" Cady suggested gently.

"Maybe," I admitted. "Probably."

"You like him?"

"I do. That doesn't mean I could date him, I'm sure he'd drive me crazy..."

"Yep, I'm sure of that, too. But you're warming to the idea? Because he's a nice guy? And kind of hot?"

"Again, maybe."

"And he hasn't called you 'Faith' for ages."

"Ha, true!"

"And you've been avoiding him since the fashion show."

I sighed. "Also true. It's just ... I can only deal with one unpredictable thing at a time. And I did make a decision about something else, something important..."

"Well, don't leave me in suspenders!" Cady quipped.

I laughed then took a deep breath. "I decided that I'm going to leave Kryll. I don't care about making partner anymore. If I'm going to work 14-hour days, I want it to be for myself. I want to look into setting up on my own. I could still freelance as a Mergers & Acquisitions consultant, but I could also explore doing more project work..."

"Like producing a fashion show?"

I grinned at her. "Exactly!"

"Because it was fun?"

"Because I could see the whole thing through from beginning to end. Because I negotiated the hell out of those contracts to make sure that the event made more money for Vince's charity. Because I wasn't just making money for the sake of it. And because I had the *best* time doing it!"

"Good for you, girl!" Cady smiled. "Those asses at Kryll take advantage. They'll feel a cold wind when you're gone."

"Well, I'm not making any announcements yet; I need to look into a few more things first; but mostly, I need to get Vince's trial out of the way."

I slapped my hand over my mouth as Cady stared at me wide-eyed.

"His case is going to trial?" she gasped. "But I thought you'd agreed a plea bargain with the prosecuting attorney?"

"I had," I sighed. "I wasn't going to say anything yet, but with all the publicity Vince has gotten, the DA's office is making noises, and Randolph Barclay really wants to make his name and get re-elected. I'm guessing that by being the man who took down the Canine Crusader, or something, he'll prove that no one is above the law. I read an interview that he did just a couple of days ago where he says they can't have vigilantes getting away with burglary. I guess he's not a dog-lover."

"Holy crap! Have you told Vince this?"

I winced.

"I'm still hoping that I can persuade Barclay that it's not in anyone's best interests to take this case to trial, but apparently there have already been some copycat vigilantes breaking into animal shelters, and not just here, but in other states, too."

"Oh, that's not good. Do you think you can still get a plea bargain?"

"Maybe. But it's looking less likely every day."

"And if not?"

"We'll have to go to trial."

"So, when are you telling Vince?"

"I'm still hoping I won't have to..."

"But?" Cady prompted as my shoulders slumped.

"I thought I'd wait until after your wedding. It's one of the reasons I've been avoiding his calls. Ugh, I probably shouldn't have told you either. Are you mad at me?"

Cady groaned. "No, but is there any chance that Rick and I will need to cancel our honeymoon to pay for our best man's fine?"

"Nope, because Vince has a great lawyer," and I winked at her, raising my glass.

"Oh, baby, it sounds like Vince might get lucky!"

"Maybe," I grinned, clinking my glass against hers.

CHAPTER FOURTEEN

VINCE

Gracie, she was one of a kind. I couldn't stop thinking about her. So how could I prove to her that we'd be fookin' amazing together? Dinner? Nah, done that, lost me tooth. A picnic in the park? Nah, it was still February and cold enough to freeze the balls off a brass monkey. Maybe another playdate with the kids, then coffee and cake at my favorite café? Yes, that sounded like something she might agree to. I'd have to work on it. She'd also mentioned wanting to get together to talk about me getting community service or whatever from that old court case. But I didn't want it to be about work all the time. I wanted to show her that *we* could be good, too.

Fook me, women were complicated.

And so was me best mate. I'd also been thinking a lot about how to get Rick to loosen up for his epic stag night, because I knew that just diving into my plan would have him heading for the hills. He needed the wheels of his sense of fun oiling first, which meant heading to a really sleazy sports bar where we could have triple shots during happy hour and a few beers to get Rick revved up. It wouldn't take long—he couldn't handle his drink, the lightweight plonker.

Rafe and Elias were waiting for us at the bar when I dragged a grumbling Rick through the door.

Rafe was frowning and Elias was scowling—they looked a lot alike.

"The barman ... who does *not* deserve that title ... doesn't know how to mix a Cosmopolitan or a Kir Royale or in fact *any* cocktail because *they don't serve them!*" Rafe huffed, his tone full of disgust.

"Yup, we're starting with beer and shots," I said, slapping him on the back. He was another bugger who needed to loosen up. "Don't worry, lads, the Canine Crusader knows how to get the party started."

Rick shook hands with the guys and thanked them for coming, then I ordered triple tequila shots and beer chasers as we stood at the bar.

Elias necked his three shots and frowned at the food menu. "What's the GI of this?" he asked, pointing to a picture of a burger wrapped in a bun with cheese and relish dripping out of it.

"Fifty-five or less, mate," I lied. "The Canine Crusader says enjoy! But we've got dinner plans later."

Rafe sniffed and turned to Elias, "If I hear Vincent mention the Canine Crusader once more, I'm going to vomit. I don't even like dogs. This is a totally lame bachelor party."

He was such a kidder, always up for a laugh.

After another set of shots and beer, Rick seemed a bit unsteady on his feet.

"I'm just going to the bog," he announced in a slurred voice, then weaved his way through the crowd.

"Me, too," said Rafe, and Elias nodded in agreement.

Rick reappeared a couple of minutes later.

We waited, but Rafe and Elias were still missing in action, so we sat there sipping our beers, eating crisps (what the natives called 'chips'), and watching highlights from last Friday's Kansas City Chiefs versus the Forty-Niners.

"Didn't you see Rafe and Elias in the bog?" I asked after a while.

"No, I didn't. What, they both went to the toilet at the same time as me? I think they've ditched us."

"Nah, they wouldn't do that, they're good lads," I assured Rick.

"They've been gone half an hour."

"No one ditches the Canine Crusader!"

"Mate, stop talking about yourself in the third person. It's not cool."

"My personality is so big, it's like there's three of me. Anyway they're probably going to meet us as the strip club."

Rick stood up, leaning slightly to the left as he grabbed the bar top. "Bloody hell! I told you, no strippers—Cady would kill me. And then she'd kill you. Then she'd dig me up and make sure she'd done it properly."

I patted him on the shoulder and he lurched forwards. "You can trust the Vin-meister."

"No, I can't," he mumbled. "He's got a death wish."

"Of course you trust me!" I said, throwing an arm around my lightweight mate. "This way to our limo."

Outside, a Pedicab was waiting.

"You wanna pedal first or me?"

Rick scowled. "I'm not getting in that."

"But it's environmentally friendly! I'm the Canine Crusader—I have to think about my Instagram feed. Here, get a shot of me on the bike!"

Rick gave in with good grace, and since he was only the groom and I was the best man, I made him do the pedaling for the five blocks to the strip club.

Rick's first clue that this was no ordinary strip club were the crowds of screaming women lining up outside.

"Don't worry, I know the doorman," I yelled over the noise as we parked in a side alley. "I've pulled a few strings to get us in."

"What is he talking about? What are *you* talking about?"

"Trust me! Have I ever led you astray?"

"Yes, every time you open your mouth."

I pushed a reluctant Rick inside, wondering if all stag nights were such hard work. I couldn't remember much about the ones I'd been to before because after the first hour, everything was a bit hazy, so I was working from ideas I'd found on the internet.

"Your costumes are over there, guys," said one of the theater staff. "Enjoy your bachelor party. Don't forget to sign your personal injury waiver before you go on."

"What costumes?" Rick asked warily. "What are you talking about?"

"Oh, man, this is going to be epic! You'll love it!" I said gleefully, proud of my plan.

I'd brought the costumes to the theater yesterday, having thought really hard about our party personas. I shoved a bag toward Rick as I shed my keks and slid into my neon green mankini, tucking in my knob which kept trying to escape out of the thong part of my outfit as if it was some sort of executive toy. I'd originally planned for us to wear matching mankinis but somehow I didn't think Rick would go for it.

Rick looked horrified. "What the bloody hell are you wearing, Vin?"

"Cool, innit?" I grinned at him, tugging at the skimpy material. "Borat has nothing on me. Those women are going to love it. I didn't get you one because you're a bit of a stiff, but your costume is cool, too. It's got a 90s Mr. Motivator theme."

Rick frowned as he pulled out a rainbow-colored, knee-length Lycra workout suit, circa 1993, with matching neon fanny pack and a British policeman's helmet.

Rick shook his head. "No. No way."

"Just go with the flow, it'll be fun!" I wasn't taking no for an answer. "Come on! Let's get out there! They're waiting for you!"

"Who's waiting for me and why do I need a helmet?"

"Uh, health and safety. Do it for me, Rick?" I begged, eyeing the enormous MC who was looking pissed that we weren't ready yet. "Do it for the Canine Crusader!"

"Alright! Alright! I'll do it if you stop talking about yourself in the third person like that."

Oozing reluctance, my fun-sucking friend changed into his epic costume and I pushed him on stage.

Bright white spotlights hit Rick between the eyes and he stood there like a rabbit about to be hit by a Mack truck, completely frozen except for a twitch in his left eye.

"Dance, you muppet!" I yelled, and women started screaming as Tom Jones' voice bellowed out *You Can Leave Your Hat On*. "Follow my lead!"

And I started grinding my hips and doing that thing ladies love where my pecs dance, hoping against hope that Rick had unfrozen. Those women out there looked vicious—maybe this hadn't been my best idea—but at least Rick had a helmet if things went south.

"Get your kit off!" I yelled as he stood there like a lemon, then ducked as a water bottle flew out of the audience at him.

"Dance! Dance! Dance!" they chanted.

An enthusiastic woman climbed onto the stage and ripped Rick's Lycra to his navel. This seemed to wake him up and he legged it for the exit with her tugging on his shorts.

"Come back!" she yelled. "We ain't seen the full monty yet and I want to know if there's meat with them potatoes!"

At this point I decided that a strategic retreat might be a good idea, and ran after Rick and his new fan.

The MC grabbed my arm. "You said he was a professional!" the seven-foot man-mountain yelled in my ear.

"He is! But not at stripping—he's just a bit shy."

We were thrown out of there so fast, the door literally hit us on the arse on the way out.

"What the hell was that, Vin?" Rick growled, sounding a bit stressed.

"I don't know, mate, you really let me down," I said looking at him seriously. "What about my street cred?"

Rick's face turned an angry purple as if he was about to hit me —maybe he was just sobering up.

Then Alf the doorman tossed our clothes out, unfortunately my trousers were missing and I didn't think asking for them would be a good idea, but at least Rick seemed happier and at least I had a coat to wear over my mankini since it was a bit nippy around the nethers in February. Thankfully my socks matched.

"I can't believe they did that to the Canine Crusader! Oi, Rick! Where are you going?"

"Home!"

"Nah, you can't do that, we're the star guests at a Broadway show—totally legit, trust me."

He stood with his hands on his hips. "You've got us tickets for a show? As in singing?"

"Yeah, but they're not expecting you to sing—no one needs that kind of ear-pain. And we're VIP guests—we can't disappoint them. I've got it all organized."

Rick pointed his finger at me. "Okay, but only if you *promise* me on Tap's remaining three legs that I won't have to a) sing, or b) take my clothes off on stage."

"Sure, sure! Of course! Although I can't believe you made me swear on Tap's legs! That's not cool, buddy."

"And you have to wear some trousers."

Before he changed his mind, I shot into the nearest consignment store, scored a pair of worn Levis and tugged them on over the mankini. I'd thought about ditching it but I should at least wear it to the beach once, although I wasn't sure about the tan lines.

I took my turn pedaling to Broadway, hoping that it would give Rick a chance to calm down.

The Lion King was one of my favorite shows. Who doesn't love it when they sing *Hakuna Matata*? That song could have been written for me.

"What's it about?" Rick asked suspiciously as I flashed our VIP tickets.

I gaped at him. "That's fookin' crazy, man! You've never seen *The Lion King*? Did your parents hate you?"

Rick ignored me and stared at the posters. "Is it about a lion?"

I shook my head in despair as I lead him to our seats. "It's a good thing you've got me as your cultural ambassador," I said. "When you finally hit puberty, you'll need to know the facts of life."

I couldn't hear what he replied because the house lights dipped and the music started. I was completely swept away, sometimes feeling like Pumbaa the slow-witted warthog, and sometimes feeling like Simba who made one bad choice and fooked up everything.

I didn't look at Rick until the interval, then confiscated his phone and shoved a pre-mixed vodka and tonic at him, handily disguised in a water bottle.

"Mate, this is a quality show—it's won awards and shit."

"I know. I googled it to see how it ends."

I clapped my hand to my forehead. Rick really was a lost cause.

The second half was even better and I had to wipe a couple of tears from my eyes.

"Thank God that's over," Rick muttered, yawning.

I ignored him but sat up straighter when then lights came on and a man in a tuxedo appeared on the stage.

"We have a real treat for you tonight, folks!" he said. "To celebrate 10,000 shows here on Broadway, we thought you'd like to meet Simba for real, although his name is Jabari and he's really from Central Park Zoo."

"Bloody hell! That's real!" Rick gasped as an elderly-looking lion prowled onto the stage with a keeper next to him.

"I told you tonight would be special!"

The audience oohed and aahed, and the lion yawned, showing a set of long, yellow teeth.

"And now, ladies and gentleman, we have another treat for you: a very special animal-lover is in the audience tonight. Let's give a big round of applause for Vince Azzo, better known as the Canine Crusader!"

Rick turned pale and slid lower in his seat as the spotlight swung towards us.

"I'm not getting on stage with a lion."

"I thought you liked cats, or are you just a pussy?"

"Vince, it's a freakin' lion!"

"But ... this is the best part!" I protested, trying to drag him with me.

Rick was gripping the arms of his chair as if it was a lifeboat, so I had to leave him there and headed to the stage by myself.

The lion didn't seem very interested in me, but then the keeper handed me a large Hula hoop.

"Eh?"

"Hold it up, he'll jump through it. For some reason, he likes doing it. We put a hoop in his compound at the zoo and he's been doing this trick for years."

Feeling a bit nervous, I held up the hoop and the lion swung his slanting golden eyes towards me and then started to run. I squeezed my eyes shut, waiting to feel his jaws around my favorite head, but instead of taking me down and turning me into kibble, he jumped through the hoop and the audience cheered.

"Mate," I whispered to the lion when the keeper told me I could stroke the rough hair of his mane, "you took years off me life, but it was fookin' well worth it."

It took ages to get back to Rick because of all the people who wanted to get a selfie with me and even autographs, which was really old-school. I grinned at him when he held up his phone and showed that he'd filmed the whole thing. That was going to get at least 20,000 likes on my IG page, probably more.

"I thought I was going to have to find a new best man," Rick said as he sent the video to my phone.

"Nah, I've got the eye of the tiger, mate."

"It was a lion."

"Yeah."

Rick looked at his wristwatch. "What do you think the girls are doing?"

"Wrestling naked in a vat of chocolate and filming themselves," I sighed and Rick slapped the back of my head. "What? That's one of my favorite fantasies!"

"You're talking about my fiancée, *mate*."

"Oh, yeah. I keep forgetting that."

Rick shook his head. "Shall we call it a night?"

"No way! It's been brilliant so far, but we've only just started. Ah, come on, buddy! At least let's have dinner," I pleaded, a bit deflated that Rick was ready to throw in the towel despite all my super cool efforts to force him to have a little fun.

"Fine," he grimaced, giving me a friendly punch in the shoulder that nearly knocked me over. "Let's eat."

Relieved that he wasn't bailing on me just yet, I even offered to do the pedaling and we rode to Central Park in style, heading for the Tavern on the Green. I usually just went there for coffee as their menu consisted of meat and fish, but I knew that it was one of Rick's favorite places to eat. We'd been friends a long time but when I finally persuaded him to try a plant-based diet, he only lasted six months. I think it was all the gas.

When I'd made our reservation at the Tavern, I asked them if they could make something vegan for me. It got boring have grilled vegetables with salad everywhere if I didn't plan ahead.

Rick looked genuinely pleased when we arrived. "No strippers? No dancing telegrams? No ritual humiliation? Just food?"

"Just food," I promised.

Of course, at the time, I didn't know that I wasn't going to be able to keep that promise.

We sat down at our table for six, ignoring the irritated look the hostess threw at the empty seats, but Rick scanned the menu happily. I already knew what I was having, so now was the time for me to do the most important part of my best man's duties.

I leaned forward. "Mate, it's not too late for you. I can get you to the airport in 40 minutes."

Rick looked up and frowned. "Too late for what? What are you talking about?"

"To get a flight back to Britain. I'll tell Cady you've had second thoughts and the wedding's off. It's okay, it happens to lots of blokes. There's no shame in it—well, not much."

Rick slapped the menu onto the table and started strangling his napkin. "When have I ever said that I don't want to marry Cady?"

"Um, not sure, let me think about that, um..."

"How about never," Rick offered crossly. "I've never said that because I *do* want to marry Cady. I love her. And I'm not sitting here talking to you about my feelings!"

I pretended to wipe sweat off my forehead. "Just checking, mate. Part of the best man duties."

Rick smirked. "You reckon you could have pedaled me to JFK in 40 minutes?"

"Don't be a muppet—I'd have called an Uber."

The server came out with two loaded plates and we'd just started our meal when a woman behind me screamed. I wondered if she'd found an earwig in her soup, but it turned out to be a bit more serious than that.

Several other people joined in with the screaming, and suddenly there were people yelling and a mass exodus of diners trying to lock themselves in the kitchen or the restrooms.

We both stood up, uncertain what was going on.

"Run!" yelled the man next to me. "There's an escaped lion out there!"

"What?"

"A lion!" he shouted and pointed behind him.

The lights outside the restaurant glowed brightly and suddenly I saw him. "That's not a lion," I said.

"It bloody well looks like one to me," Rick muttered. "What with the mane and teeth and everything."

"No, I mean obviously it's a lion, but it's Simba from the show—you know, Jabari!"

Someone started yelling about calling the police and shooting it. I couldn't let that happen: I knew what I had to do.

I headed for the door but Rick grabbed my arm.

"Don't be an idiot, Vin! You can't go out there. You don't know if it's the same lion!"

"Course it is! Look, he's got that little scar by the side of his nose—it's definitely him. I don't know how he escaped from the theater, but he's probably heading home to the zoo. It's not far from here. But if the police get here first, they might try and shoot him. We can't let that happen!"

I shook off Rick's arm and went outside.

"Jabari," I said quietly.

The lion followed me with those hypnotic sloping eyes, then opened his mouth in a roar that had me crapping my pants. It occurred to me several seconds too late that coming out here might not have been the smartest thing I'd ever done. Perhaps this was the sort of shit that was always getting me into trouble with people —people like Gracie.

"Jabari, buddy," I said, my voice a little more high-pitched than usual as my balls shrank to the size of grape seeds. "What are you doing here? Did you follow me from the theater? Been a long night, eh?"

He padded towards me and I wondered if it was too late to hide behind a table. But instead, he butted me in the stomach with his heavy head like a big ole cat asking to be stroked.

Once I could breathe again, I ran my hands through the wiry tufts of his mane and stroked the softer fur of his ears, feeling relieved as his eyes closed in pleasure.

"You had me a bit worried there for a moment, Jabari," I said. "I'll have to change me underwear."

The restaurant door opened and Rick appeared holding a chair in front of him with one hand and a large, heavy candlestick in the other.

"Vin! You still alive?" he whispered. "The police are on their way and someone from the zoo with a tranquilizer gun."

"Ah, mate! That's just overkill. Jabari's an old fella—he doesn't want to get shot!"

"Yeah, and I don't want to get mauled to death," Rick muttered.

"He won't hurt you," I scoffed. "They wouldn't have brought him to the theater if they were worried he was dangerous."

"Then why are they sending someone from the zoo to shoot him?"

"Look, I'll talk to him."

"What? Who?"

"Jabari! You know, like Dr. Doolittle. Animals listen to me."

"Vin, get back in the restaurant now!"

"Seriously, it's cool. I think he came here to find me. It's like I'm the chosen one or something."

And then I had a brilliant idea. If I got in the Pedicab, I could lead Jabari back to the zoo and there'd be no need to tranquilize him!

Persuading Rick wasn't easy, and he refused to go anywhere unless he could take the chair and candlestick with him.

"I don't think you're supposed to take souvenirs from this restaurant, Rick. Did you pay the check, because I forgot?"

"Shut up and pedal," he snarled, side-eyeing Jabari who was padding along beside us.

It was different pedaling through Central Park at night without any people around and I was rather enjoying myself, but Rick didn't seem to be feeling very chatty. He was probably tired: great coming out of the gate, but not too much for stamina. I think I heard that in a film once.

But when we arrived at the zoo, there was another problem: it was locked.

Jabari sat down and yawned.

Still looking wary, and still holding his chair and candlestick, Rick climbed out of the back of the Pedicab and stared at the locked entrance.

"I can't find a doorbell," I said.

Rick threw me a look that was supposed to mean something. I shrugged.

"How do we get in?"

"We wait for the police and the man with the tranquilizer gun," said Rick, one eye still on Jabari who seemed to have fallen asleep.

"Ah, come on! We can't let him get shot! He's snoring!"

Rick sighed. "Okay, can you climb the gate and find some way of opening it from the inside?"

I eyed the wall. "Maybe. If you stand on the chair and I get on your shoulders, I should be able to reach the top of the wall."

Glancing again at Jabari who was now drooling in his sleep, Rick stood on the chair. It wobbled slightly as I climbed onto Rick's back then slowly fumbled my way up until I was swaying on his shoulders like amateur hour at Cirque Du Soleil.

"Stand still!" I grumbled.

"I am standing still!" he hissed. "You're bloody heavy so hurry up!"

Taking a deep breath, I launched myself at the wall and managed to get one leg over it, wincing when I found some sharp bits sticking into me knob. Then with an embarrassingly girly yelp, I tumbled over the other side, landing on my hands and knees.

"Did you fall on your face?" Rick's muffled voice came from the other side. "Because Cady will have to hide you at the back of the wedding photos."

"My face would win awards," I grinned, coming around to peer at him through the gates.

Rick looked relieved that his best man was still alive. "Can you find a way to open the doors?" he asked.

"I dunno. Is Jabari still sleeping?"

Rick's face seemed paler in the lamplight as he realized that he was on the same side as Simba, and Dr. Doolittle, *moi*, was on the other side of the gate.

He grabbed the chair and candlestick again. "Yes, he's still asleep," he whispered. "Hurry up!"

I looked for something I could use to force the padlock. "Oi, Rick! Throw that candlestick over the wall."

"But ... but it's my weapon," he said feebly.

"Shut up and chuck it over, you loser!"

Reluctantly, he threw me the candlestick, and I had to use all my strength to lever open the heavy, iron padlock. Just when I thought I'd have to give up, it finally snapped, and the gates swung apart.

I walked back out, then Rick and I both stared at Jabari.

"You'd better wake him up," I said.

Rick shook his head. "He's your lion. You wake him up."

We both looked at Jabari. He seemed very peaceful but ya know, no one likes being woken up from a deep sleep. I swallowed and glanced at Rick.

"Can I borrow your chair?"

He handed me the wooden chair then watched as I gently prodded Jabari with a chair leg. He grunted but didn't wake up.

"Harder," said Rick.

"Mate, I've been waiting my whole life to hear you say those words," I quipped.

Never let it be said that the Vin-meister missed a chance for a joke.

"Shut up and wake him up!" Rick whisper-shouted. "I can hear police sirens!"

I prodded Jabari a bit harder and he opened one eye, then sat up yawning. He had a lot of teeth.

"Come on, buddy," I said, pointing toward the zoo with the chair. "Time to go home before someone shoots you in the arse."

Sighing, he rose to his enormous feet and padded quietly towards me.

"Um, I think he wants you to go with him," said Rick. "He probably wants a midnight snack."

Ignoring Rick, I led Jabari back into the zoo just as the police arrived along with a harried looking zoo keeper.

"It's okay!" I yelled. "I've taken Jabari home! You don't have to shoot him."

"Who's that clown with the lion?" asked one of the police officers from behind a gun.

"That's the Canine Crusader," said Rick, grinning at me.

"Dude, seriously! You rescued a lion?" the police officer gaped. "I thought you just did dogs?"

"Any animal in trouble can come to me," I replied. "I am the chosen one."

"What a guy!" said the police officer, shaking his head.

"Oh, bloody hell," Rick sighed.

I helped the zoo keeper put Jabari back in his compound. The poor old fella looked knackered after his unplanned evening out. "I'll come and visit you, buddy," I said, stroking his ears.

He blinked at me, yawned again, then ambled off into the darkness as the zoo keeper wiped his forehead and locked the door to Jabari's compound.

By the time I was back at the main entrance, a TV news crew had arrived.

"Is it true that you rescued a lion?" the reporter asked in amazement.

"Yes, it's true," I grinned at her. "Animals understand me. It's like I can talk to them. I think it's because I was hit by lightning when I was a kid. Ever since then, I've been able to know what animals think."

"Wow, that's amazing!"

"Yes, it's a gift," I agreed.

"Sorry to interrupt, folks," said the police officer. "But I'm going to have to arrest Mr. Azzo for breaking into the zoo."

"But ... but I was putting the lion back!" I protested.

"It's still burglary," said the police officer as he snapped on a pair of handcuffs. "You have the right to remain silent..."

"Rick!" I yelled. "Call me lawyer! Get Gracie!"

CHAPTER FIFTEEN

GRACE

Tears were pouring down my face as Patrick Swayze ran his invisible hands over Demi Moore.

"Why is life never that good?" I sobbed.

"Yeah," Cady sighed. "Except for the fact he's dead."

"Men suck," I nodded in agreement.

Cady's phone rang and she got that dopey look on her face which told me Rick was calling her. I hugged my cushion tighter and sighed. I couldn't imagine having that look on my face when some guy phoned me. Especially not Vince. When he called, if I happened to see my reflection, I'd probably look like I was sucking on a lemon.

And then I remembered *that kiss* from the fashion show and sighed again. My own for real *An Officer and a Gentleman* moment, except Vince had been wearing Lycra and floppy dog ears rather than crisp Navy Whites. Okay, not quite as romantic, but still...

 Fascinating factoid: John Travolta turned down the role of Zack Mayo; he'd also turned down 'American Gigolo', which

was a huge hit for none other than Richard Gere. Way to make lousy movie choices, John.

Cady sat up straighter, spilling her glass of wine as she slammed it onto Vince's coffee table.

"He did *what?* You're *where? How* long? *Who* else? *When?* For God's sake, Rick! *Why?*"

The thought crossed my mind that you could tell Cady had a background in journalism. Personally, I'd always thought that she missed her calling as a kick-ass FBI agent. But then her words sunk in as she turned her *uh-oh* face to me.

"Right, I'll tell her. You are in *so much trouble*, Rick Roberts!"

Cady tossed her phone onto the coffee table next to the spilled wine, then swore and grabbed her sweater to mop it up.

The dogs were all awake now, looking at us expectantly as if it was time for a game or a walk or another round of Milk-Bones.

A cold rush of sobriety had me sitting upright and I rubbed my eyes, blotting drying tears with a tissue.

"What did Vince do?" I asked with ominous foreboding.

Cady gritted her teeth. "He's been arrested."

I nodded.

"For burglarizing Central Park Zoo."

I nodded again.

"For rescuing a lion and trying to take it home."

I blinked. "A lion?"

Cady exploded. "Yes, a goddamn lion! A lion! With teeth and claws and an untameable desire for raw meat! Your *client* is a maniac! Rick could have been eaten! I could have been standing under the *chuppah* on my wedding day next to a can of Chum! I cannot *believe* Vince has done this! I'm going to kill him! Slowly! Or maybe quickly! I am *so* mad at him!"

"I'll help. Um, did Rick get arrested, too?"

She calmed down a little, the murderous rage fading from her eyes.

131

"No, thank God. He's down at the 20th precinct where they took Vince."

I glanced up as I worked my phone, the liquor receding rapidly from my veins. "They didn't take him to Central Booking?"

"No. Is that good?"

"Yes, it means they're still deciding whether or not to charge him."

"We have to get over there!"

"I'll go. You have to stay with the kids. Tap gets anxious if she's left alone."

For a moment, Cady looked mutinous but then sighed and nodded. "Fine, you're right. And I'd probably be arrested for assault or intent with a deadly weapon."

"You're holding your phone," I pointed out.

"You haven't seen what I can do with my phone when I'm mad!" she said darkly.

"True."

I stood up and found my coat.

"You're taking this very calmly," said Cady, looking me up and down.

I gave her a thin smile. "It's not my first rodeo. And let's face it: Vince + bachelor party + New York City = disaster." I shrugged into my coat. "I'll call you."

The Uber I'd summoned honked outside the door and I bent down to kiss the kids, with a special squeaky one for Tap, then hurried out into the night.

To rescue Vince.

From himself.

Again.

CHAPTER SIXTEEN

VINCE

If I was honest with myself, Rick's stag night hadn't gone entirely as planned.

The sports bar had been good, except for those tossers Rafe and Elias ditching us; and the striptease show had been fantastic, except for Rick having his family jewels felt up by a strange woman with purple eyeshadow; and the Pedicab had been brilliant, except it was a bit chilly if you weren't the one pedalling; and *The Lion King* had been epic, except for Rick checking his phone every five minutes; and the meal would have been good, except we didn't get to taste it (although on the plus side, we hadn't paid for it either). But then I'd been arrested, and if anyone was arrested on a stag night out, it was supposed to be the groom.

So mostly a successful evening.

I hoped Gracie wouldn't be too mad about the last part.

But after what seemed like hours of listening to the drunk in the next cell to me singing *Freedom* off-key, I wasn't quite as optimistic.

Finally, my door rattled and a police officer told me that my attorney was waiting for me in an interview room.

I had a huge smile on my face when I saw Gracie sitting at the table, her lawyer briefcase next to her chair and a notebook lined up in front of her with two pencils.

"Gracie!" I grinned.

She looked up, her face unmoving. "Vincent, we must stop meeting like this."

Her tone was a tad cool but fair enough—I'd left her getting happily plastered with Cady for a girls night in, and now she was at another police station after midnight saving my sorry arse.

She pointed to a chair that was bolted to the floor opposite her and then introduced me to a dude sitting next to her. Somehow I hadn't seen him when I'd walked into the room.

Pow! This is what love is like! I only have eyes for Gracie! Fook me!

My smile grew wider.

"Vincent, allow me to introduce you to Mr. Greg Pinter, Central Park Zoo Director."

The dude stood up and offered his hand to me. "Mr. Azzo, it's a pleasure, sir! A great pleasure! We at Central Park Zoo can't thank you enough for bringing Jabari back to us safe and sound." His voice dropped as he finished pumping my hand and slumped back into his chair, rubbing his forehead. "To be honest, this would have been a total PR disaster if it hadn't been for your timely assistance. Jabari is completely harmless, as you know, but if he'd wandered into traffic ... and he is quite scary if you don't know him." He rubbed his forehead again. "The welfare of all our animals and the safety of the general public is our primary concern, always. Tonight ... well, there are questions to be answered ... but I wanted to give you my personal assurance that the small matter of burglary..." he waved his hand in the air. "Forgotten! Never happened. And, ah, I know it's hardly the appropriate time, but I couldn't let this fortuitous meeting go by without asking if you'd consider being a Patron of the Zoo?"

I glanced at Gracie, feeling like I'd just been slapped around the face with a wet kipper, and still a little confused.

"So ... I'm not being arrested?"

Gracie shook her head. "Not tonight, Vincent," she said with something approaching a smile. "Although I'm sure there will be other opportunities."

"Mr. Azzo," the suit-dude began again, "you've become an icon for animal welfare in this city—your voice has shouted louder than we've ever been able to. If you were our Patron—an advocate for the animals, you might say—you could continue that with a framework of..."

"Eh, cheers and all that," I interrupted him, "but I'm not good with frameworks," and I shook my head.

"He's really not," Grace added with a smirk. "Rules, frameworks, *laws*—he breaks out in hives."

I blinked. Had she just made a joke? Things were definitely looking up.

I grinned at her.

"The thing is," I said, turning back to suit-dude, "I don't like seeing animals in cages. Safari parks, yeah, I get that, for breeding programs, but zoos ... it's not really me."

Suit-dude deflated but nodded understandingly. "Well, perhaps I can entice you and Ms. Cooper to visit—in daylight..." and he laughed carefully. "So you can see the extent of our conservation efforts and work to preserve wild habitats. I assure you, our resources reach beyond Central Park," he said seriously, then gave a kind smile. "And you can visit Jabari. I believe he's become rather attached to you."

"Alright, you're on!" I said, brightening up at that prospect. "It'll be good to visit my buddy."

Then we all shook hands and the suit-dude left the room.

"That was unexpected," I said cheerfully.

"Very," Gracie agreed, packing up her briefcase. Then she looked up. "A lion, Vincent? Really?"

"It just sort of happened," I said lamely and shrugged.

"Only to you," she muttered, snapping closed her briefcase.

"It's great to see you," I said more softly and she looked up, her expression unreadable. I cleared my throat. "On a scale of one to ten, how mad at me are you?"

She waved her hand dismissively. "It's not me you have to worry about."

"It's not?"

She gave an amused smile. "No, but I can't speak for Cady."

My smile fell. "But ... but Rick's fine! He had a good time. It was a fantastic night and…"

"I'm sure it was memorable," Gracie said shortly, putting on her coat. "But I think she's just the tiniest bit ticked off that her fiancé was nearly eaten by a lion."

"Oh," I conceded, my shoulders slumping.

"Yes, oh." And she linked her arm through mine. "Come on, Vincent, time to go home."

I really liked the sound of that.

"What, you and me?"

Her gaze frosted over. "I just saved you from being arrested *again*. Don't push your luck."

I gave her my winning smile: *Message received and understood.*

For now.

CHAPTER SEVENTEEN

GRACE

The aftermath of Rick's bachelor party was not pleasant. Cady, usually so even-tempered and with a God-given gift of laughing things off was furious and tearful, spending half-an-hour reaming them both out until the guys looked completely whipped.

I had a theory about why that might be, but now was not the time.

Finally, to draw a line under the evening and bring an end to the emotional beatdown, I ordered an Uber for Rick and Cady, pushed them inside and promised my best girl that we'd talk soon.

It was certainly a lot more peaceful after she'd gone. Vince seemed slightly stunned by the tirade that had lashed down on him from the moment he and Rick had walked through the front door and been met by Hurricane Cady.

"Fook me," he said quietly, as the dogs crept warily into the living room now that the shouting had stopped. "I think I've upset her." He looked up at me sadly. "I always fook things up, don't I?"

I lifted my eyes to the ceiling. "You do have a talent for getting into the craziest situations," I agreed, "but no, you don't always mess up."

He dropped his head into his hands. "Just most of the time."

He looked so sad, and it probably would have been a huge mistake if I'd tried to comfort him, but Tap got there first, nuzzling against him and laying her head on his knee.

"You still love me, don't you?" he said with a soft smile, stroking her gently.

I watched him, sitting there quietly with his dogs around him, so different from the walking, talking, *shagging* disaster that was the Vincent Azzo I'd first met more than a year ago. I knew that version was still there, but now I also knew that there was a kind heart behind all the mouth and muscle.

"Vince," I said, waiting until he looked up. "Sometimes you do real good."

He blinked, as if he was waiting for a qualifying statement, but when he realized that it was a real compliment, he gave me the most beautiful smile.

"Thank you, Gracie. I don't know what I'd do without you."

"Well, so long as I don't get eaten by a lion, I can keep Cady from beating you to death with her phone and you won't have to find out."

He gave a light laugh. "Promise?"

"Promise."

He cleared his throat. "I don't want to come over as a knob or say anything naff, but do you want to stay here tonight? I don't mean with me—I'll take the sofa—but it's really late and ... and me and the kids want to take you out to our favorite place for coffee and cake in the morning. No funny business, Scout's Honor."

I thought about another long cab ride across the city to an empty apartment and I had to admit that his offer did sound pretty good. I'd taken several vacation days from work for wedding week, so I had nowhere particular to be until the rehearsal dinner tomorrow evening.

"I don't have a toothbrush."

"You can use mine."

I wrinkled my nose. "Um, no!"

He laughed. "I've got a new one you can have."

"Thank you. Much better. And, uh, do you have a t-shirt or shirt I could sleep in?"

Something hot flashed in his eyes, but then he just nodded.

"Follow me," he said, heading for his bedroom.

He handed me a t-shirt with a Canine Crusader logo, and a pair of his briefs with purple paw prints on the fabric.

"For the morning," he grinned. "They're fairly clean. Only wore them for a week."

"Don't be gross," I said, slapping his arm as he laughed.

His smile faded. "Don't take this the wrong way, Gracie, but could you leave the bedroom door open tonight?"

"Excuse me!" I yelped, wondering if I'd made a huge mistake and glad I had my Uber app primed and ready to go.

"No, no, not like I'm a creepy pervert, but you've got the dog beds in there and they'll know I'm next door so it would probably be easier if they could come and check on me—just to reassure them."

I relaxed.

"You can come and check on me, too, if you like," he said suggestively, raising one eyebrow.

"Don't push it, buddy! Three cold, wet noses is enough—yours just doesn't make the cut."

"Harsh," he said sadly, shaking his head. "Okay, well I'll just take them out for a slash then I'll tuck them in."

"Do you read them bedtime stories, too?" I couldn't help asking.

"Yep, their favorite is *101 Dalmatians*; Tap likes *Old Yeller*, but it always makes me cry."

"Get outta here," I laughed, tossing a pillow at his head that he caught easily.

> *Fascinating factoid: Lassie is still the most famous fictional dog in history.*

I changed into Vince's t-shirt in the bathroom and brushed my teeth with the new brush he'd left out for me. I didn't have to worry about cleanser, toner, moisturizer, body lotion or anything else like that because Vince had more products than I did—probably a habit he'd acquired in his modeling days—and all top brands for men. Nothing icky left by an ex.

I scooted into bed, feeling the cool sheets against my skin as I caught Vince's cologne faintly on the pillows.

When he came back into the bedroom, the dogs were following him like the Pied Piper.

He gave a huge smile when he saw me. "You look great in my bed," he said. "Sure you can't be persuaded to let me join you?"

"Quite sure," I said primly. "We're not married."

His face was a picture as a shocked range of emotions charged across, and then he relaxed when I laughed.

"Blimey! You had me going there for a minute, Gracie. I saw me life flash before me eyes!" and he pretended to check his heartrate.

"Hmm, dodged a bullet there," I teased. "But it's a good thing my dad doesn't know I'm here in your bed or he'd hunt you down, him being from Minnesota and all."

"I hope you're pulling my leg," he said, "because if your dad is anything like you, he'd be well scary."

"If you hear someone banging down your door at dawn, and he's wearing camos and carrying a deer rifle, better run for the back door," I said with a yawn.

Still smiling, Vince shook his head then tucked the dogs into bed, with a kiss and a quiet word for each of them as he pulled their little dog blankets over them, carefully tucking in the corners.

"All done," he said. "Now be good for Mummy Gracie—Daddy Vin is right next door." Then he stood up and stretched his back, looking at me longingly. "Night, Gracie. Sleep well."

"Night, Vince."

Sighing, he left the room, leaving the door ajar in case the dogs wanted to go walkabout.

I could hear him in the living room making up a bed on the sofa, the creaks of the furniture as he got himself comfortable, and then silence.

I listened for a few minutes but all I could hear were the dogs snuffling, Tyson already letting out rumbling snores. Not long after that, I drifted asleep with a smile on my face.

I woke with a warm, wet tongue in my ear.

"Gerroff, Vincent!" I mumbled, but when I cracked an eye, it was Tyson looking up at me with a sloppy smile. "Oh, my mistake," I yawned. "What time is it?"

"Time for coffee!" a voice yelled from the kitchen.

Ooh, what a good idea. I shuffled to the bathroom, splashed some water on my face then groaned when I glanced in the mirror, grumbled a bit, ran Vince's brush through my hair, then borrowed his enormous fluffy robe that reached to my ankles.

I trudged into the kitchen, still only half awake but with the happy knowledge that I didn't have to work today. And then I saw Vince. His feet were bare, his chest was bare, and only his long legs were covered in a pair of ill-fitting jeans, at least four inches too short.

As my eyes traveled greedily across the colorful tattoo on his upper right arm, the line of black ink peeking out of his waistband, the ridges and valleys of his abdominal muscles, and his firm pecs, my face grew hot. At 6'4" that was a lot of half-naked man making me coffee, and now I was wide awake.

"Hot?" he asked.

"Excuse me!" I squeaked.

He turned and grinned. "Do you like your coffee hot or with a drop of cold water?"

"Oh. Ah, hot, please."

He winked. "Some like it hot—coming right up."

I climbed onto the high stool at his breakfast bar and swung my feet, feeling light and carefree while Vince puttered around the kitchen.

"Nice jeans," I commented sarcastically, sipping my piping hot brew.

Vince pulled a face. "Best I could buy after I lost my trousers last night."

I spluttered, dribbling coffee down my chin. "You lost your pants last night? Seriously? How on earth did that happen? Or maybe I shouldn't ask."

"Well, me and Rick were on stage doing our strip show and..."

I choked again. "What?! You did what? Oh, God, you had Rick stripping on stage?"

Vince leaned forward confidentially. "Don't tell Cady, but he wasn't very good."

I laughed suddenly, snorting coffee, and coughed so hard I nearly lost a lung. The dogs were barking and Vince thumped me on the back with too much strength, making me face-plant on the breakfast bar. Tears were streaming down my face and I rubbed my sore nose.

"Oh, fookin' hell! I'm really sorry!" Vince yelped, trying to dry my face with a dish towel as if I was a five-year-old.

"Stop! Stop! Don't help me anymore!" I wheezed, then sat hiccupping, wiping my eyes, blowing my nose and still half-giggling.

When my bodily functions were finally under control again, I glanced up at Vince who still looked worried.

"Tell me you got photos," I gasped.

He relaxed slightly and perched on the stool opposite me, the perfect height for him, unlike us more normal-sized humans.

"No, but one of the women in the audience put a video on

YouTube," he grinned. "But it's too grainy to tell who we are, otherwise I'd put it on me *Fans Only* page."

I shook my head, still smiling. "As your lawyer, let me give you this piece of valuable advice: never tell Rick that there's a video."

He laughed out loud but I could tell by the gleam in his eye that he wasn't taking my advice seriously.

I pointed my finger at him. "Let me add an addendum to that free piece of advice—never tell Rick, never tell anyone, or Cady will have your balls for breakfast."

His smile fell so quickly I heard it hit the floor.

"Yeah, good point," he admitted. "Do you think she'll forgive me for fookin' up?"

I patted his arm. "Cady doesn't hold grudges—she's just a little emotional right now. It'll be fine."

He nodded absentmindedly, looking down at my hand on his arm.

"Can I have a hug?"

Surprised, it took me a moment to respond, then I stood up and walked around the breakfast bar, reaching up to put my hands around his neck, feeling the heat of his bare chest through my robe. He immediately wrapped his arms around my waist, hugging me tightly and leaning his head against my shoulder, his breath warm on my cheek.

"This is nice," he mumbled.

And it was. It was friendship and caring and something more.

Then the dogs decided that they wanted to be hugged, too, and trotted over to join in, Zeus at our ankles, Tap at our knees, and Tyson shoving his nose into our crotches.

Laughing, we pulled apart and Vince grinned at me.

"Can I have a shag now?"

I rolled my eyes. "No."

CHAPTER EIGHTEEN

VINCE

"Can't blame a bloke for asking," I said with a wink. "It worked for the hug."

"You're incorrigible!" Gracie huffed, pushing me away, but she was still smiling.

Being a gentleman, I let her use the shower first; and being a red-blooded male, I imagined the hot, soapy water sliding over her sweet little tits and naked body, and ended up with a stiffy the size of the Empire State Building.

It was hard work doing the friend thing while she warmed up to the fact that we'd be awesome together. Getting her to trust me enough to spend the night had been a massive step, and it had given me hope when generally as a commodity it was in short supply. I should have won a medal for forcing myself to stay on the sofa all night when the woman of my dreams was a few feet away all soft and warm and tucked up in my bed.

I was beginning to understand why Rick had been such a grumpy bastard last year while he was trying to persuade Cady that the course of true love never ran straight but sometimes ran marathons. They still seemed an unlikely couple to me, and after last night's tongue-lashing, I hoped that Rick really knew what he was letting himself in for.

The strange thing was, last night I'd been waiting for the other shoe to drop and for Gracie to take a turn at the verbal battering, but she hadn't. She hadn't reamed me out at the police station either. In fact, she'd been the one to stuff a sock in Cady's gob and shove her in a taxi. Even then, I thought my turn would be coming and she'd start yelling at me, telling me that I was an irresponsible twat, but again she hadn't. And then I thought she might give me that look of disappointment that I was so familiar with, but she'd just smiled and shook her head saying, "Only you, Vincent. Only you." Which I took as a compliment.

All these things were positive signs. I just wish I knew what she was so worried about. Was it men in general or me in particular? Cady had been very close-mouthed about Gracie and only told me that she didn't date much. Which told me sod all.

I was hoping that a relaxed day with the dogs would get her to lower her standards a bit more and maybe consider dating me. After all, I was a catch. I was the Canine Crusader!

I heard the shower turn off and she finished dressing in the bedroom. Me and my pet trouser-snake had a painful ten minute wait until she returned to the kitchen.

"Clean in body and mind," she smiled.

"I can do one out of two," I said hopefully.

She glanced down at the truncheon in my pants and her eyes widened. For a second, I saw a flicker of interest. I swear I wasn't imagining it, but then she looked away and reminded me that the shower was free.

I walked away like John Wayne after a long ride through Death Valley. And if this sex drought kept up, that's exactly where I'd be.

Before the shower was even hot, I grabbed my knob and gave him some healing hands, reminding the poor sod that I really did still love him and promising that he wouldn't drop off from lack of use.

Three strokes and a quick tug and I was creating a shower of my own.

I looked down breathlessly, feeling sorry for my dick who was hanging exhausted and limp.

"Listen, mate. I wish I could promise you some action in the near future, but I'd be lying. I'm working on Gracie and believe me, she's worth waiting for. You've just got to hang on in there and try not to get too eager. You're not a heat-seeking missile—try and have a bit of fookin' class. I'll take care of you, buddy. And no more shit second-hand jeans that cut off your blood supply."

I finished washing lazily, had another quick wank to cheer up my depressed dick, and then dressed for the day ahead. By now it was time for morning coffee and cake, and my stomach was almost as hungry as my cock.

I tried to be a bit careful with food around Gracie. Left to my own devices, I ate huge portions, but I knew that large plates filled with food were off-putting to someone who was still dealing with anorexia, so my tried and tested method was small amounts but lots of them.

Gracie was smart, so she probably knew what I was doing, but it seemed to help. She'd scoffed more at breakfast than I'd ever seen her eat before. I figured that meant she was getting more relaxed around me. *A score for the Canine Crusader! Sensitive to the needs of dogs and women.*

Yeah, probably not an award-winning marketing motto.

By the time all five of us were dressed and ready to go, the sun had come out, reminding us what it looked like, a pale watery disc in the sky. I grabbed Gracie's gloved hand and she threw me a surprised smile. When she didn't let go, I felt happier than I had in decades.

But ya know, if some soppy fooker had told me last year that holding hands with a girl was enough to make me this happy, I'd have told him to piss off and get a life. Funny how your values change when you meet a woman who stops you in your tracks and rewires your brain, and I had no doubt that Grace Cooper was the one for me.

"Wotcha thinking about, Counselor?" I asked.

"Happy non-thoughts," she smiled. "I'm just glad not to be at work and..."

"...the company is great," I added for her in case she forgot.

"Yes, I'm really enjoying being with the dogs," she teased. "Oh, and you. You're not so bad."

"Bloody hell, Gracie! You make me sound like the consolation prize at the lucky dip!"

She laughed but didn't disagree. Instead, I got a hand squeeze, and that launched my happiness like an Apollo space mission.

"Why do you call me 'Gracie'?" she asked, out of the blue.

"Dunno, really. It suits you though. And no one else calls you that, do they?"

She shook her head, her cheeks pink, then changed the subject.

"So, now you've reached $500,000, what plans does the Canine Crusader have?" she asked.

I grinned, very pleased with the awesome amount I'd raised.

"Everything!" I said. "All that dosh going to shelters around the city. It'll keep them in Milk-Bones for a while. They'll even be able to refurbish the dog runs."

Tyson looked up in approval when I mentioned Milk-Bones—he was a complete slut for them—he'd do anything.

"What about long term? Are you still thinking about setting up your own charity? You know I could draw up the papers for you if that's the direction you want to go. Or maybe you'd prefer to be a fundraiser for other charities? That could work for you, too. And you've got the offer from Central Park Zoo to be their Patron."

I still hadn't made any decisions—except one. "I definitely want to do another fashion show next year—that was brilliant fun!"

"It really was," she nodded enthusiastically. "I'll help you."

Suddenly, I was so fookin' happy, I had the very unfamiliar desire to cry.

I sniffed loudly. "Yeah, cheers. That would be great."

Gracie smiled. "I think you prefer dogs to people."

"I've never been treated badly by dogs."

Clever Gracie didn't miss anything. She didn't call me on it, she didn't tease me: instead, she stood on tip toe and planted a quick kiss on my cheek.

We carried on walking and didn't talk about anything important —it was the best day of my life.

At the dog park, I dropped off Tyson at the play run, then found a table in the café where we could watch him racing laps and playing with the other dogs. Tap snuggled on Grace's knee and Zeus snoozed in the pet sling, worn out by the walk. I'd noticed that the little fella was slowing down and wanting to walk less. A twinge of sorrow settled in my chest. He was already about seven or eight when I found him; all I knew was that he'd needed a new home and a second chance. He was nearing 14 now and I hated to think that his days were numbered.

Shaking away the sadness, I smiled at the two beauties sitting across the table from me. Gracie was already studying the menu, a small frown on her face.

"I always have the blueberry vegan muffin," I said encouragingly.

"Um, just a cappuccino for me, I think. After all, we've only just had breakfast and we've got the rehearsal dinner later."

"Oh yeah. What time do we have to be there?"

"Four o'clock. Haven't you looked at the schedule?"

"Meh, loads of time."

She shook her head. "How can you go through life being so oblivious of deadlines? I know I can be a little OCD, but you, you're just..."

"A manly hunk of loving?"

"I was going to say always last minute. I envy you in some ways."

I blinked at the unexpected comment and gave her a half smile. "I don't like being stressed."

"But not being organized *is* stressful!" she argued.

"I am organized," I disagreed. "I just organize myself at the last minute."

She smiled uncertainly but was silent for several seconds. I took the opportunity to stuff half a muffin in my mouth.

"I'm thinking of leaving my job," she said quietly, side-eyeing me as if I'd tell her she should chain herself to her desk until she retired.

"Great! When are you leaving? We'll have a party."

"I haven't decided definitely," she said hesitantly.

I leaned forward without squashing a snoozing Zeus, and took her hand.

"You know your problem, don't you?"

"Yes," she said snarkily. "You."

"Nah, I'm the best thing since sliced bread. Your problem is you: you never know when to piss or get off the pot."

She sucked in a shocked breath. "*Excuse me?*"

"You know ... make a decision."

She tugged her hand free and used it to stir her coffee. I don't know why, she hadn't put any sugar in it.

"You're right," she said simply without looking up. "It's just, when I was a kid, I always felt like I was a day late and a dollar short. When I went to high school, I didn't cope very well—so many kids who all seemed to know what they were doing and where they were supposed to be. Obviously most of them were faking it, I know that now, but I didn't at the time. I forced myself to be more organized and that's when my OCD kicked in and everything had to be done just so." She gave a strained laugh. "I drove my parents crazy because everything had to be my way or I'd completely freak out." She gave me a faint smile. "It might surprise you, but I'm not nearly so bad now. It did get bad when I left home for college and then I had to deal with my eating disorder, too. Therapy taught me that both conditions are all about needing to be in control, but that trying to be in control of life is not possible most of the time—all those curve balls, right? If it hadn't been for Cady, I'm not sure I'd have made it. I want to leave Kryll Group, I know that, but I need to have my plan ready—it's how I function, being in control as much as possible."

She'd opened up to me at last, and it explained a lot. I wanted to hold her and protect her and tell her she was fookin' perfect as she was. So I did.

I took her hand across the table and looked into her warm brown eyes. "I think you're fookin' perfect."

She gave a quiet laugh and tried to pull her hand free.

"I mean it," I said, still holding tight. "You're kind and clever and hotter than two camels shagging in the desert."

She snorted into her cappuccino and even that seemed cute to me. She tugged her hand free and blew her nose, her cheeks a rosy pink. Gorgeous. Making her laugh was the best part of being the clown prince.

"Anyway," I said, "I get that you want to plan ahead 'cause being out of work isn't fun. What do you want to do?"

"Well," she said, almost shyly, "I thought I'd like to be an events planner ... because I really loved working on the fashion show and I love being involved in that level of detail."

I beamed at her. "And you were fookin' awesome at that. I know you'll be amazing. I'll write you a great reference."

She laughed. "Perfect! And can you sign with a paw print?"

"Yeah, that can be arranged."

She smiled, leaning back in her chair and stroking Tap who gazed up at her adoringly.

"So, what's your story, Vince? Why did you give up the catwalk life? I know it's not as glamorous as it seems after recent experience, but still ... I looked you up. You were the face of some huge campaigns, I had no idea!"

I shrugged lightly. "I burned out. I was traveling all the time, never in my apartment, a different city every week. It stopped being fun." I looked at her seriously. "Life's too short not to enjoy what you do for the day job, doncha think?"

She sipped her coffee slowly before she replied.

"In theory, yes. But we can't all be superstar models and just decide to quit. Most people have college loans, credit cards, rent or mortgages to pay, families counting on us, responsibilities. Quitting isn't that easy."

"Sometimes you've just got to walk away when things aren't working if your health and sanity are paying the price."

Gracie eyed me carefully. "Are we still talking about jobs?"

"Yes. Mostly."

"Relationships?"

"Toxic ones, definitely."

I could have kicked myself for walking down this stinking back alley of memory lane.

"Do you want to talk about it?" she asked quietly.

No, I fookin' didn't. Not. Ever. But...

I pulled a face. "Woman I was dating was a nutter, a complete psycho. She was a model, too, but wasn't getting a lot of work. Basically, she was jealous and accused me of cheating on her. Which I didn't, but I couldn't take it anymore and moved out."

"You were living together?"

"Sort of. She couldn't make the rent on her apartment so she moved in with me. It was supposed to be short term but ended up being for over a year. I was a way a lot. Thank fook."

"Sounds pretty bad."

"Yeah, she could get violent, too."

Gracie's eyes widened and then her eyebrows pinched together in a frown. "She hit you?"

"Yeah," I said quietly, the shame and humiliation as cutting today as it had been five years ago. "I know it sounds ridiculous, a big bloke like me, but she was vicious. I'd walk in the door and she'd throw a bottle at my head or a vase or a drawer of cutlery, then start slapping and kicking me. I never hit her back, not ever. I'm a trained kickboxer—if I'd hit back, well, I just wouldn't. I couldn't."

Grace looked shocked. Not a lot of people knew about Olivia. Rick was one of the few.

"Did you report her?"

"No, who would have believed me. She was half my size—weighed less than a hundred pounds. And I thought it was my fault because I was away so much and she hated being alone. But in the end I realized that was just an excuse to take out her anger on me. So I walked. But I promise you, I never laid a finger on her. Never."

Grace touched the back of my hand. "That's because you're a good person. I'm glad you managed to get away from a bad situation."

I nodded, half wishing I hadn't brought it up, but found that I really wanted Gracie to know all about me.

"Anyway, after Liv, I promised myself I'd never do serious again." Gracie gave me the hairy eyeball. "Until I met you, obviously." I cleared my throat. "What about you? Cady says you don't date much but I don't know why, 'cause you're a fookin' knockout."

"Thank you, I think." She looked out of the window, watching Tyson playing tag with another dog.

"I dated a little in college but I was very self-conscious about my weight—or lack of it—so I never let anyone get close. When I went to law school, there just wasn't any time. We had classes all day and studied all night—it was intense. I saw one guy for a while, but he became really competitive and not very nice when I beat him in tests, so that didn't work out. And when I started working, first as an intern, then as a junior, it was expected that you put in 12 hour days or 14 hour days, and I'm still doing that. I have dated, but the men I've met didn't like coming second to my job, and frankly, none of them were worth the compromise."

"Until now," I suggested hopefully.

She smiled without answering directly. "Cady says I'm a

hopeless romantic because I'm picky, but I'd say that I'm a hope*ful* romantic."

"I'm a romantic, too. I'm dead sensitive, I know poetry."

"Really?" Gracie asked, her tone curious with a note of skepticism.

"Yeah! Here's one me gran taught me.

My dearest, darling ducky,
I loves thee clean and mucky.
I loves to hold thee in my arms
And squeeze thee just like putty."

Gracie laughed out loud. "Romantic poetry now has a whole new meaning for me!"

I grinned proudly. I loved making her laugh.

CHAPTER NINETEEN

GRACE

The wedding rehearsal went smoothly, and Cady was wreathed in smiles and glowing with happiness. Rick was quieter but a pure joy curved his lips every time he looked at my best friend.

I was introduced to his parents, who were quiet and reserved like him, and completely overwhelmed by Cady's exuberant Jewish family. They were hugged and kissed and hugged again until they looked dazed.

I took pity on them and found a quiet alcove where they could sit down and drink a glass of champagne in peace before the dinner started.

Rick's two friends from his rugby playing days had bonded immediately with Cady's soldier brother, and the three of them were drinking shots before dinner, getting louder and louder. I thought that Vince would probably join them, but instead he was being unusually mature, and charming Cady's two grandmothers.

Then he turned and nodded at me, said something to the grandmas who eyed me carefully, then he strode forwards carrying two more glasses of champagne.

"Alright, Gracie?" he asked, his voice carrying over the hubbub.

"Fine," I smiled.

"I saw you rescue Rick's mum and dad. They look gob-smacked."

"Just a little. I think they're like Rick—they prefer the quiet life. I'll go chat with them in a minute."

He passed me the champagne and kissed my cheek. "You're top totty, Gracie."

I shook my head at his choice of endearment, smiling despite myself. Vince was an acquired taste, and God help me, I'd definitely acquired it.

We were interrupted by Cady's mother, Rachel.

"Hello, Grace honey, how are you?"

"Good, thank you, Rachel. I think you've met Vincent Azzo, Rick's best man."

"Only briefly," she smiled. "It's nice to meet you again, Vincent."

"And you, Rachel," Vince said. "I can see where Cady gets her luscious looks from."

Rachel laughed. "Thank you very much! Cady has told me all about you, Vincent, or should I call you the Canine Crusader?"

Vince leaned in and whispered to her. "Only when I'm wearing me superhero cape."

Rachel fluttered her eyelashes and glanced at me. "Oh, he's got some slick lines, Grace honey. How long have you two been dating?"

"It feels like our whole lives," Vince said before I could spit out a denial.

"We're not dating!" I said, shocked, stepping away from him, stupid, annoying man.

"She'll fall for my charms eventually," Vince grinned unrepentantly, winking at Rachel.

"Only when the Earth stops spinning," I muttered.

"You two make such a cute couple," laughed Rachel. "I'll be

expecting an invitation to your wedding next." And she strolled off to visit with Rick's parents.

"Why did you tell her that?" I griped. "She'll be gossiping about us now!"

Vince shrugged. "It felt true."

"Well, it's not!" I said, pointing a finger at him.

He grabbed my finger and pulled it gently to his lips, kissing it before sucking it into his mouth. I inhaled sharply, feeling an unexpected tingle of lust as my skin heated with a full-body blush.

Then he gave me a cheeky grin and leaned closer.

"You'll change your mind, Gracie. I can wait."

And he sauntered off, smiling to himself. Which is when Cady found me with my mouth still hanging open.

"Oh my friggin' God, that was so hot!" she gulped, fanning herself. "What's going on with you and Mr. Knob-head?"

It had been so long since I'd thought of him that way, it took me a second to realize who she was talking about.

"Just Vince being Vince," I said, still flustered.

"Hmm, methinks you protest too much, Counselor. I mean, phew! I could feel the heat from 20 feet away."

"He's being annoying," I countered. "I'm irritated not turned on. He told your mom we were dating. She asked for an invitation to our wedding!"

Cady laughed so hard, there were tears in her eyes. "Oh, hell, that's awesome! I can't wait to be your maid of honor."

"Stop it!" I said crossly. "People will hear you."

She sniggered, then gave me a big hug. "Whatever you say, hon. But that guy has it bad for you. Don't break his fluffy little heart."

She reeled away in a zig-zag pattern across the floor, groping Rick's ass along the way as he gave her a tolerant smile.

Was it true? Did Vince really like me that much? I knew he was attracted to me and we'd become friends, sort of, but surely I didn't have the power to break his heart? It was an unnerving thought. I'd felt his vulnerability when he'd told me about his ex-girlfriend, and I understood much better now why he'd kept all other relationships as shallow as possible. But was he asking me for something else, something deeper...?

He'd already invited me into his life and entrusted me with his dogs, and they were his family—far more precious to him than anything. I tried to examine how I felt about Vince: what would it be like to date him? Chaotic and confusing, definitely; he could still be arrogant, and he was very vain, spending more time looking in the mirror than I ever did; but he was also fun and exciting, completely impulsive, living life by the seat of his pants. He was kind, he could be sweet. And I had to admit that he was hot.

So the question was, *why wouldn't I date him?*

Not while he was my client, of course. But after?

With so many thoughts whirling through my brain, it was lucky that I remembered I had a job to do and went to check with the hotel staff who were ready for Cady and Rick's guests to be seated.

There were 16 of us, including the rabbi who was going to conduct the ceremony and her husband.

The seating placements had been planned with precision, trying to ensure that everyone would be happy with their places. Cady assured me that at least one member of her family would undoubtedly be pissed but she could live with that.

She was at the head of the table with Rick, of course, then going around it was Mr. and Mrs. Roberts, me, Vince, Ben and Leon the ex-rugby players, Cady's Uncle Gerald and Grandma Callaghan at the foot of the table, then Cady's brother Davy, with Nana Dubicki next to Rabbi Lisa Buchdahl and her husband, and finally Cady's parents, Rachel and Sandy.

Cady had tried hard to meet everyone's conversational requirements, but failing that, she'd ordered enough champagne to drown a herd of hippos.

> *Fascinating factoid: the collective noun for hippos is pod,
> school or bloat, which seems a bit unkind to hippos.*

"Well," said Nana Dubicki loudly as she allowed Davy to help her to her seat, "I never thought this day would come."

Cady laughed. "You and me both, Nana."

"Girls your age would have been considered on the shelf in my day," added Grandma Callaghan. "Spinsters. But times have changed."

"Mom!" Cady's dad yelped from the other end of the table, but his mother was on a roll, enjoying being the center of attention.

"A woman over 29 was an old maid if she wasn't married and you're, what, 45?"

Cady choked on her water. "Still a mere stripling of 38, Grandma."

"Yes, that's what I said, pushing 40. You were lucky to have someone take you off your father's hands."

"Huh," Cady said accompanied by a roll of her eyes, "I thought I was off Dad's hands once I landed my first job after college and paid back my loans five years later, but I could be wrong."

"And I'm the lucky one," Rick said quietly, but Grandma Callaghan was too deaf to hear him.

"Thank you, honey," Cady said, kissing her fiancé sweetly.

"You'd better not get lucky with my sister before the wedding tomorrow," Davy said with a threatening leer before bursting into loud laughter.

Cady picked up a bread roll to toss at him but her mom grabbed her hand and made her put it back.

Rick's parents were watching it all like a tennis match, wondering if there was an umpire.

"Doug and I married when we were in our late thirties," said Rabbi Buchdahl with a calming smile, putting an end to that conversation.

Vince leaned toward me and whispered, "Fook me! I should have brought me tin hat! Those two grans are lethal!"

I nodded. "I think they're just warming up."

"Are you two young men married?" asked Nana Dubicki as she looked over at Leon and Ben. "Or are you homosexuals?"

"Mom!" yelped Cady's mother.

"What? I can't say 'homosexual'?" Nana Dubicki frowned.

"Er, no, we're just mates," Leon said, tugging at his collar. "Um, friends. Former teammates. We were in a rugby team with Rick."

"Rugby? That's like football without helmets, isn't it? No wonder all you boys get concussions. Does it affect your memory?"

"I'm not sure," Leon said with a straight face. "I've forgotten."

Ben coughed into his napkin, and Davy laughed out loud.

"I can't eat this spicy food," Grandma Callaghan complained, poking at her starter course.

"It's only got a little black pepper on it, Mom," Cady's dad sighed.

"Like I said, far too spicy, it gives me terrible gas."

"I'll ask the chef to make you a plain salad, Gran," Cady said with a gentle smile. "No pepper."

"Thank you, dear. I hope you'll learn to cook now that you're about to be married. The way to a man's heart is through his stomach."

"Or his dick," Vince whispered. "Best to start with a bit of dick and order take-out."

"This pear and blue cheese salad is delicious," I said loudly, elbowing Vince in the ribs as he grinned at me.

"It's nice to see you looking so well, Grace dear," said Grandma Callaghan. "You were always such a skinny Minnie but you've got a little more meat on your bones these days. Men like a little meat."

Cady's Uncle Gerald went red in the face as he tried not to laugh, and everyone else suddenly found their plates fascinating as Davy added, "I prefer fish."

I know that Cady's grandma didn't mean to upset me, and I was well aware that both grans had no filter, but I *hated* my size being discussed like that. My throat closed up so I couldn't eat another bite.

"Ignore the old bat," said Vince, throwing his arm around the back of my chair. "You're fookin' gorgeous."

Cady threw me a commiserating look, then took charge. "How are your piles now, Grandma? Are they still giving you trouble?"

"Oh, yes, I'm a martyr to my bowels, dear. When I went to see Dr. Smithson, he said that I should sit in a warm salt bath for 20 minutes every morning. But who has time to do that? Besides, those cashiers at the market are nosy—they'd ask what I wanted with all that salt. And I'm hardly going to talk about my piles in public."

She sounded so indignant, I couldn't help smiling.

"Can we *not* talk about bodily functions or illnesses while we're eating," said Cady's mom firmly, then turned to Vincent. "Tell us about your plans for the Canine Crusader, *please!*"

"Oh, yes," said Rabbi Buchdahl excitedly. "We donated to your campaign. It was wonderful. We have two rescue pugs at home: Sid and Ollie."

Vince threw her his patented grin. "Cheers, Rabbi! That was fookin' fab of you. Well, I've got a few ideas and I'm definitely going to do another fashion show next year. Maybe an underwear special. I've started a new clothing line for dog-lovers—boxers and briefs with paw prints on them. Gracie's tried them—they're alright, in't they?"

I blushed as everyone turned to stare at me. "Very comfortable," I muttered.

"Ooh, awesome!" said Cady. "Can I have some of those for Rick —he'd look so cute! Do they come in gold?"

Now Rick was blushing and his parents looked utterly bemused.

"And I'm working with a designer for S&M underwear with a dog theme—we're looking at what we can do with studded collars and vegan leather," Vince announced cheerfully.

"Leather underwear?" Nana Dubicki questioned. "Won't that chafe?"

The table exploded in laughter as the old lady kept repeating, "What? What did I say?"

But I did notice Cady's Uncle Gerald asking Vince for details of his IG page.

Soon after we'd reached the dessert stage, Cady rattled a spoon against her champagne glass and stood up.

"Unaccustomed as I am to speaking in public..." she grinned as everyone chuckled, "and being the shy, retiring type..." more laughter, "I do have a few words to say tonight before the big tamale tomorrow. First of all, Rabbi Lisa, thank you so much for being our officiant and for joining us here this evening—and thank you, Doug, for jumping on the crazy train with us—it means a lot to both of us," and she smiled down at Rick before turning to me.

I felt Vince's arm across the back of my chair, his thumb rubbing soothing circles on my bare shoulder.

"Grace, I'd like to thank you for organizing an amazing bachelorette party—I've paid the blackmailer and we can get our panties back soon—but seriously! It was awesome and everyone had a great time. I know how much like herding cats it is to transport twenty-seven over-excited women around Manhattan without anyone breaking so much as a nail or losing more than a false eyelash. And thank you for organizing our dinner tonight and so much of our wedding day with your usual flare and patience. These are from me and Rick to say thank you."

And then she presented me with an enormous bunch of flowers and a tiny jewel box containing a pair of stunning diamond earrings.

I looked up to see that the tears in my eyes matched hers.

"But mostly," she said, her voice becoming hoarse, "I'd like to thank you for being the best friend a woman could want. Since we met at college twenty years ago, you've seen me at my best and at my worst, and you've always had my back. The woman I've become today thanks you with all her heart. So, everyone, please raise your glasses to the most awesome woman, the most fantastic friend, whose kindness and loyalty I've always been able to count on: to Grace!"

I dabbed at my eyes as everyone toasted me, and Cady walked around the table.

"Love you, Grace Cooper," she mumbled into my neck as we hugged tightly, wobbling on our high heels.

"More than lemon-glazed donuts?" I half-sobbed.

"More than every Dunkin Donut store in the whole damn world! Thank you. For everything." Then she let me go and turned her weepy gaze on Vince. "You look after my best girl or I will slay you slowly."

He seemed a little surprised, as anyone would with a threat of dismemberment during the wedding toasts, but he grinned at her and declared he'd try not to 'fook up'.

Cady wobbled back to the head of the table, planting a hot one on Rick as she sat down. He smiled at her, kissing the crown of her head gently as she sobbed on his shoulder. He whispered something in her ear, but she shook her head and carried on crying.

Clearing his throat, he stood up, obviously preferring when his wife-to-be took the limelight.

"Cady and I would like to thank you all for coming tonight," he said, his soft voice only just carrying around the room. "It means a lot to us to have our families and friends here. Mum and Dad, thank you for traveling all this way to watch me marry the woman of my dreams, and I'm really looking forward to you getting to know how wonderful she is. Thank you for being the best parents a man could have—thank you for always supporting me."

And he presented his mother with flowers and his father a pair of first class plane tickets to visit in the summer. He hugged his parents, his gesture saying even more than his loving words.

Ben and Leon received a surprise gift, too—tickets for a helicopter ride over the city the next morning.

Then he turned to his soon-to-be in-laws.

"Nana Dubicki and Grandma Callaghan, thank you both for your advice. It was, um, very interesting. Gerald, Davy, thank you for being here to support Cady—and for not giving me a hard time. Mr. and Mrs. Callaghan—Rachel, Sandy—thank you for allowing me to marry your beautiful daughter and for welcoming me into your family. She means the world to me and I'd give her the moon and stars as well if I could. But please know that I will always treasure her and always look after her—when she lets me."

Rachel had dissolved into quiet sobs, and even Sandy was wiping a stray tear as Rick gifted them with more flowers and season tickets to the New York Giants.

Rachel leapt to her feet and grabbed Rick, kissing his cheek over and over, tears flowing down her own cheeks. Sandy stood and pumped Rick's arm and thumped him heartily on the back.

Finally, he was allowed to continue.

"Grace, thank you so much for being Cady's best friend and our beautiful maid of honor. And maybe I should apologize to you for picking Vince as my best man."

I giggled, because of course that was my first reaction, too. Vince casually scratched his nose with his middle finger to let Rick know what he thought of that comment.

"Vince, mate, you know I'm joking—mostly. But even though you got arrested on my stag night, and even though you lost your trousers, and even though I never got to eat my dinner, it was a truly memorable evening."

Everyone laughed, not entirely sure if Rick was being serious. I could have told them: Rick was *definitely* serious.

"But I do have to thank you for encouraging me to come to the States in the first place—because if I hadn't, I'd never have met this beautiful woman at my side, and I can't imagine living without her. So for that reason alone, Cady and I have been to Walmart and bought you this gift."

He grinned at Vince, pulling a small Tiffany's box from his

pocket. Inside was a pair of cufflinks with diamonds chips in the shape of paw prints.

"Oh, mate, these are epic! Cheers, buddy. Thank you, Cady. I know you chose them and not that loser, because these are class."

Rick punched him in the shoulder, then they hugged tightly

Finally, Rick returned to his seat and it was his father's turn to speak, probably the quietest person at the table.

He cleared his throat several times before he began.

"It's been lovely to meet you all," he began gamely. "And it's been wonderful to see that Rick will be joining such a warm and loving..."

"...and loud!" Cady shouted out, making everyone laugh.

"...and happy family," Mr. Roberts smiled. "Thank you Rachel and Sandy for welcoming us, and for welcoming our son into your family." Then he turned in our direction. "Grace, Vincent, my wife Sheila and I would like to thank you for all your hard work organizing the stag party and hen party for the happy couple, as well as tonight's dinner. It's been lovely getting to know you both, and we wish you every joy in your own journey through life together."

I nearly choked but Vince grinned happily. *What had he been telling them?*

Then Mr. Roberts smiled down at his almost daughter-in-law.

"Cady, most of all we'd like to thank *you*. We Roberts men are not much for talking, as I'm sure you've noticed, but I couldn't let this moment go by without telling you how wonderful it is to see Rick so happy. His mother and I can see it in his eyes and hear it in his voice. Thank you for loving our boy."

By now, all the women at the table were sobbing, Sandy and Mr. Roberts were also wiping their eyes, and Rick was bursting with pride and joy.

Mr. Roberts looked around the table. "Could you all please stand and raise your glasses to our beautiful daughter-in-law ... or you will be tomorrow. To Cady!"

"*Mazel tov!*" yelled Rabbi Buchdahl.

We cheered, we toasted, we bathed in the glow of happiness pouring out of every person, and Vince grabbed my waist and planted a huge kiss on my mouth.

"Oh!" I gasped, kissing him back. "It's such a wonderful evening!"

"Our turn next," he whispered.

Wait, what?

CHAPTER TWENTY

VINCE

Erik the plumber was my designated dog-sitter for the day of Rick and Cady's wedding. There weren't many people I'd trust with the kids for a whole day, but he was one of them—and he was available. All he wanted by way of payment was a couple of slices of wedding cake (cheap) and an Armani cravat like Uncle Sal's (not cheap, but fair enough).

It had rained heavily in the night turning my backyard into a swamp of muddy puddles, but now the sun was breaking through and it promised to be a nice day for early March.

I'd always thought that marriage was a great institution ... if you liked institutions ... but today I felt envious of the commitment that Rick and Cady were about to make.

Shaking off the shadows that followed me, I fed the hounds, then took Tyson out for a quick two mile run. Erik had promised to walk them all later, but Tyson needed more exercise than Tap and Zeus.

Then I sat at the breakfast bar sipping a coffee, with Tap draped over my knees, her eyes closing as I stroked her slowly. I wasn't needed for a couple of hours because Rick was having breakfast with his parents while Ben and Leon were out for their helicopter ride across the city.

I'd texted Gracie an hour ago and she was already with Cady and Rachel, the ladies getting their hair, nails and makeup done. I was looking forward to seeing her all tarted up even though she looked hottest with her hair mussed, wearing my briefs and t-shirt.

Tap sighed in contentment, and I smiled to myself. These moments were precious: Tap on my knee, Tyson snuffling around the garden, and Zeus snoring in his bed. But I wanted to share them with Gracie. For the first time in my life, I wanted intimacy with a woman that came from trust, from love, from being myself and not disappointing anyone.

And maybe I'd get lucky tonight. Weddings made women horny, and wasn't there some sort of rule that the maid of honor had to sleep with the best man? I grinned at the thought. *Lucky, lucky Gracie.*

Glancing at my watch, I realized that I'd zoned out for nearly an hour and only had a couple of minutes before Erik arrived. I checked my list for my best man's emergency kit: two pints of Jack Daniels, mouthwash and mint-flavored chewing gum, Imodium and spare underwear, Aspirin, dental floss, deodorant, glue (in case my tooth dropped out again), tweezers for nasal hair (I'm not saying Rick had a badger's arse growing out of his nose, but it was wise to think of these things). Oh yeah, and eye drops that hid any redness and signs of overdoing it the night before—a tip I'd picked up during my modeling days.

My doorbell buzzed, and the dogs started barking as I welcomed Erik inside. He'd arrived with a pocket full of Milk-Bones. I knew that my pack of hairy hounds would have conned him out of the whole lot by the end of the first hour, but it was a nice gesture.

"You give my regards to Miss Cooper and the happy couple," he said. He sniffed a couple of times. "I love weddings. My wedding, best day of my life. And fashion show—also best day of my life."

I slapped him on the shoulder, gave him instructions for the kids' lunch and supper, and left a hundred bucks so he could order himself take-out during the day.

"What have I forgotten?" I asked out loud, the three dogs staring at me with forlorn eyes when they realized I was leaving them.

"You have wallet?" asked Erik.

"Yep."

"You have condom?"

"Yep," *a new packet.*

"Phone?"

"Yep," I said, patting my pocket.

"You have rings? You have suit?"

"Rick has them." For some reason he didn't trust me to remember them. No fookin' idea why.

"Then I think you're good to go, my friend," said Erik.

I kissed the kids goodbye, picked up my sports bag packed with the emergency kit and strode out to the waiting taxi.

Aw, Erik was standing at the door waving his handkerchief goodbye.

The taxi pulled away when I suddenly realized what Erik was really waving. "Stop!" I yelled.

The driver slammed on the brakes, then swore as I jumped out of the car and ran back to my house.

"You forget best man's speech!" Erik screeched, waving the sheets of paper that I'd so carefully typed with two fingers.

"Mate! You've saved my arse again! I owe you, buddy."

"Two cravats!" Erik bellowed as I ran back to the taxi.

I stuffed the pages in my jeans' pocket as the driver scowled at me in the mirror. I'd broken into a cold sweat at the thought of forgetting the best man's speech.

I'd never been a best man before; I'd never been best anything, unless you counted the time I was voted *Rear of the Year* in the *Gay Times*—Mum had been so proud.

But the point was, even I knew that the best man's speech was a big deal. I wanted to do right by Rick for trusting me with this job, and I wanted to impress Gracie as well. Losing the speech before I arrived at the hotel would not be a good start.

The wedding party had rooms reserved at a dope place named 'The Jewel' opposite Rockerfeller Plaza where Rick and Cady were having their wedding in the famous Rainbow Room. Probably famous if you were a New Yorker, but I'd only lived here a couple of months so I'd never heard of it before.

I found Rick in his hotel room, drinking coffee from an espresso cup.

I leaned forward, staring him in the face and checked his eyeballs.

"What are you doing?" he grumbled, pushing me away.

"Making sure you're not high. All that strong will you have most of the time and it suddenly snaps under stress—I've seen it happen."

"Don't be an idiot if you can possibly help it," he said in irritation. "You know I don't take anything stronger than caffeine. And I'm not stressed."

"Really? I would be. You know, about to stand up in front of 150 people and declare undying love to one woman for the rest of your life, even knowing she'll get wrinkled and old and saggy in a few years. And Cady is..."

"Finish that sentence and I'll toss you out of the window," he said, his eyes glinting in a way that made me think he was serious.

"Right," I grinned quickly so he'd think I was joking.

I wasn't. But he didn't need to know that. Rick's temper was almost non-existent but I'd noticed that he got rather shirty if it was anything to do with Cady, going all caveman, without the wooden club or the pet Saber Tooth.

I dumped my sports bag on the table, narrowly missing the

florist's box containing the boutonnières, and pulled out a bottle of Jack, then looked around for Rick's dad.

"Where's your old man?"

"He just left. I think he's a bit jet lagged and he wanted to take a nap before Mum gets back. She's with Cady, Rachel and Grace.

"Fair enough," I said, brandishing the Jack. "One for the road, buddy?"

Rick grabbed the bottle and took a long pull, looking significantly more relaxed as Tennessee whiskey hit the spot.

"Thanks," he said, passing the bottle back to me. "I needed that," and he sighed.

"Everything alright?" I asked carefully, not wanting to be dangled from the 35th floor, even if the view was fantastic.

"Yeah, yeah, of course. It's just ... I want to marry Cady, but all of *this*," and he waved his arms around at the very nice hotel suite with kitchenette and balcony, the wedding suits hanging in Armani garment bags, and the Tiffany boxes containing the wedding rings. "I don't like crowds," he finished lamely.

I finally realized what the real duty of the best man was: help the groom find his balls.

"Mate, what's the biggest crowd you ever played in front of when you were playing professional rugby?"

He squinted at me as I took a long slug before handing over the bottle of Jack again.

"Um, 16,500 at Gloucester, I think. Why?"

"And you're worried about standing in front of a poxy 150 people? Honestly, mate, when Cady is in the room, you never notice anyone else anyway. I can be standing there talking to you, certain my lips are moving, but you're just staring at her like you've been zombified. Without the peeling skin, but definitely with the drool."

Rick blinked then gave a faint smile. "Zombified?"

I shoved the bottle of Jack toward him again, nodding as I watched him swallow a third of the bottle in one long gulp.

He handed it back to me, his eyes slightly crossed and a soppy smile on his face.

My job was done.

"Right, let's get the suits on and show the women of New York what they'll have to go on missing now we're both off the market," I said.

"You're really into Grace?" he asked, frowning slightly.

"Hook, line and sinker. She's the woman for me."

His eyebrows inched upward. "Are you ... dating?"

"I haven't shagged her yet, if that's what you mean by dating, but it's inevitable at some point. She can't resist my charms forever."

"Sure about that?" he grimaced.

"Mate! You wound me!" I chuckled.

"And then what?" Rick asked, folding his arms across his chest as his gaze narrowed.

"Then we get hitched, and ride off into the sunset with Tap, Tyson and Zeus."

His mouth dropped open and he gave me a weird look. "You want to marry her?"

"Yep," I grinned.

"Um, not wanting to rain on your parade, but does Grace know this?"

I nodded. "She's been fairly warned."

Rick scratched his head. "Eh, that's not quite the same as getting down on one knee and promising to love her forever."

"Is that what you did?" I asked, eyeing him curiously while I pulled out my phone and opened the Notes app.

He sighed. "Vin, mate, you don't *tell* a woman to marry you; you have to *ask* them. Beg if you have to."

I nodded, tapping his advice into my phone.

"Right, gotcha. Ask her first ... one knee ... then shag her. Yeah?"

He pulled a face and reached for the bottle of Jack. "Close enough."

Then he weaved his way to the bedroom with the garment bag draped over his arm. He'd taken the bottle with him. Good thing I'd brought two. I glanced at my watch. T-minus-30 minutes and counting.

I peeled off my shirt, dropped my keks on the floor, then used the large mirror to flex. I stood there in my navy blue briefs (the ones I'd designed with gold paw prints), plus matching socks, and grinned. Yup. Fookin' irresistible. Gracie didn't stand a chance.

Unzipping the bag with my bespoke Armani suit, I stared in awe. That wasn't a suit, it was a piece of art with over 120 man hours to make it. Uncle Sal had played a blinder. I'd have to think of something very special to thank him for all his team's hard work.

Everything was a perfect fit, and I'd expected nothing less. Fook me! I looked great!

I fastened the navy blue cummerbund but left the bow tie hanging around my collar. Plenty of time to be trussed up like a turkey. Poor turkey.

Then I peered down at the one item of clothing that I'd never worn before: a navy blue yarmulke. Rick and I were wearing them out of respect for Cady's religion and Rabbi Lisa who was officiating the marriage service.

I plopped it on my head, then frowned as it slid off. I tried again, but after taking one quick stride, it was back on the floor. I stared at it, puzzled, wondering how other blokes kept it on. My hair was short and spiky, and the bloomin' thing kept springing off no matter how much I tried to squash it down.

I nipped into Rick's bathroom, making him jump while he was shaving, but luckily he didn't cut himself. He was so cack-handed, poor sod.

Squirting a blob of his hair gel onto my hands, I tried to tame my hair, but it was like badger bristles and wouldn't lie flat.

In desperation, I grabbed the tube of glue from my emergency kit and squirted a line around the edge of the yarmulke, then slapped it on my head.

Sorted!

Pleased with my improvisation, I checked myself in the mirror. I was ready to make Gracie beg. Then I frowned and checked the notes on my phone. Oh right, it was *me* who had to beg. I'd better get that the right way around or I'd be in the dog house, and it wouldn't be as comfortable as where my mutts slept.

I glanced over to where the two Tiffany boxes with the wedding rings waited on the coffee table. I couldn't help opening them up to have a look. Both were plain gold bands, simple but beautiful, Rick's larger and a little heavier. My best mate, the man I respected more than any other in the world, was about to make this awesome lifelong commitment. A year ago, that would have horrified me. But seeing him with Cady, any fool could tell they were great together, that they loved each other.

I was happy for him, but maybe a little sad for me. Things were changing: time to finally grow up.

I was ready.

CHAPTER TWENTY-ONE

GRACE

We'd spent the last couple of hours being painted, primped and polished by a lovely hairdresser named Nancy, makeup artist Nerissa, and nail technician Naomi from the *3 Hens Makeup Services*.

We'd laughed, we'd cried, we'd shared stories, and I'd been sipping champagne throughout and was slightly tipsy. Rick's mom, Sheila, had left ten minutes ago to change into her mother-of-the-groom outfit and collect her husband. She hadn't seemed entirely sober either as she'd headed back to her room.

Hmm, time to slow the alcohol consumption. I didn't want to faceplant in front of the *chuppah*. And I didn't want Cady to dehydrate either, so I handed her a bottle of water with a straw; that way she wouldn't smudge her lip gloss.

"I'll be peeing all afternoon if I drink this," Cady objected. "We'll be halfway through the vows and I'll be yelling *bathroom break!*"

Rachel giggled then hiccupped loudly, apologized profusely and excused herself. Side-eyeing the mother-of-the-bride, I watched her weave her way to the bathroom, then discreetly left her a bottle of water plus straw by her purse.

"I'll make sure you go potty before the ceremony," I assured Cady.

"Did you factor it into your schedule?" she teased.

"As a matter of fact I did, except I wrote it down as Powder Room and makeup check, because I'm classy like that."

Cady grinned. "You are an epic wedding planner! I'm going to hire you for all my weddings." Then she winced when she realized what she'd said. "Oh fart! Don't tell Rick I said that—he's sensitive."

"My lips are sealed. What happens in the bride's dressing room, stays in the bride's dressing room."

Cady closed her eyes and blew out a long breath. "I didn't think I'd be nervous, but my hands are shaking."

I'd rarely seen Cady so vulnerable, but I knew my friend was making the right decision in marrying Rick. I took hold of her hands, smiling at our matching navy blue nails, the gloss bright and shiny.

"Cady, you're marrying the man you love today—the sweetest, kindest, most loyal guy you've ever dated who happens to be head-over-heels in love with you, too. I'm so darned happy for you both. You're in love; truly and deeply in love. This wedding will last just a few hours—your marriage will last a lifetime."

"Bitch!" Cady sniffed. "You've made me cry! Ugh, pass me a tissue, quick!"

We both had to touch up our makeup after the almost-crying catastrophe.

"Do you think the guys are doing shots?" she asked, still sniffing slightly.

"Rick chose Vince as his best man. What do you think?"

"Good point. Please tell me you have a bottle of tequila with you for Mom?" she asked hopefully.

"Would you at least get her to finish a bottle of water first?"

She pouted at me and fluttered her eyelashes.

"Fine," I sighed. "Mini bottles are in the fridge, but just one and don't let your mom see the rest. She's definitely had enough to drink."

Cady winked at me. In the past, I was staggered how she managed to stay upright after all the champagne she could drink in one evening. The woman was an Amazon. I was in awe. But then again, I always had been, and I loved her to bits.

"Come on, time to get ready."

We both turned to look at the gorgeous Sophia Tolli wedding dress hanging at the front of the closet. It wasn't an ordinary white wedding dress, of course, because there was nothing ordinary about Cady. My friend was larger than life, with the biggest heart.

The Australian designer specialized in dressing voluptuous women like Cady and we'd both fallen in love with her incredible creation.

It was made from a column of delicate navy blue lace over a contrasting French ivory base of misty tulle bodice, a flared gown with seed pearls lightly scattered throughout, a plunging sweetheart neckline that showcased Cady's awesome boobs, a semi-sheer low cut back, with a tulle and lace accented chapel train that would froth out behind her. It was also detachable, because Cady planned to do a lot of dancing at her wedding.

As I helped her into the gown and fastened the tiny pearl buttons at her back, I could feel myself welling up again.

"Don't," Cady whispered hoarsely.

"I'm trying not to," I whispered back.

But then Rachel returned from the bathroom, and we both heard her gasp.

She rushed forward and hugged Cady tightly.

"You are so beautiful," she cried, her voice breaking. "My beautiful, beautiful daughter. I'm so proud of you: not just today but every day. Every day of my life I thank God for giving me you.

You're the best daughter a mother could want. Rick is a very, very lucky man."

I stepped away to give them a moment, and honestly, I needed one, too. I was feeling incredibly emotional at the thought of my best friend getting married.

I slipped into the bathroom and carefully dabbed cold water onto my neck. Today was a good day and I was happy for her, and maybe just a little sad for me. Just a little.

My maid of honor dress had color accents that matched Cady's dress. It was a gorgeous, knee-length, one-shoulder gown with the navy silk chiffon draping softly, and it was accessorized by a wide belt in ivory with a rose-shaped bow. It was simple and elegant, and I couldn't wait for Vince to see me in it.

Yes, I'd tripped over to the dark side: I wanted Vincent 'the Canine Crusader' Azzo to find me attractive. I prayed he wouldn't let me down. There were going to be several celebrities at Cady and Rick's wedding—young and attractive. In my heart of hearts, I knew that I'd be devastated if he flirted with one of them.

I took a deep breath: in this dress, I felt beautiful.

I stepped out of the bathroom to find Cady's mom drinking a mini bottle of tequila and Cady laughing. I snapped a photo on my phone.

"One for Instagram!" I laughed.

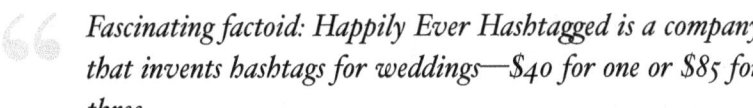 *Fascinating factoid: Happily Ever Hashtagged is a company that invents hashtags for weddings—$40 for one or $85 for three.*

Then I made sure that Rachel had her boutonnière in place, and Cady pinned mine to my dress and we all looked at each other.

"Everyone ready?" I asked softly.

Cady took a deep breath. "Never been readier."

There was a gentle tap at the door and I opened it to find

Cady's father standing there in his tux, looking handsome and nervous.

When he saw Cady, he gasped, his eyes wide, then his face crumpled and Cady ran into his arms.

"Don't cry, Dad," she sobbed.

His shoulders shook silently as he hugged his daughter, and I glanced at Rachel as her own eyes glittered with tears.

"Sandy," she whispered after a minute had passed. "Darling, you'll spoil her dress."

Mr. Callaghan unpeeled himself from his daughter and blew his nose loudly. I helped Cady dry her own tears and dabbed on loose powder the way Nerissa had showed me. I was so glad that she and Nancy were waiting for us in the ladies powder room outside the Rainbow Room. We were all going to need their help.

Mr. Callaghan gave Cady a watery smile and then held out his arm.

"Let's get you to the ball, princess."

I checked that Rachel had Cady's train, and I carried her bouquet of white roses tied with blue silk, and my own, slightly smaller bouquet.

We left the hotel suite and found that a member of staff held the elevator just for our party, congratulating Cady discreetly, and at the lobby, all the reception staff stopped what they were doing and applauded Cady who was beaming happily.

Several guests joined in and others filmed us on their phones.

The doorman escorted Cady and her father to the waiting vintage Rolls Royce and helped her inside without creasing her dress.

Thirty Rockefeller Plaza was opposite our hotel, but still not walking distance: not in heels and definitely not in a very beautiful wedding dress.

"See you there!" I called to her.

"You'd better be!" she laughed.

"Right behind you, sister!"

Pedestrians stared at the Roller with its white wedding ribbon fluttering on the front, and Cady smiled and waved.

Rachel and I had a very comfortable town car to ourselves, following behind the bride and her father.

The other members of Cady's family and the rest of the wedding party should already be in place. I pulled out my phone and checked a few things off the schedule until Rachel took my hand and made me put my phone away.

"Everything's fine, Grace. You've done an amazing job and it's going to be a beautiful wedding. The Rainbow Room events coordinator will take care of everything now. It's time to enjoy yourself."

"Sorry, I can't help it," I said sheepishly. "I just want everything to be perfect."

"I know, sweetheart, and it will be as near perfect as possible because pleasure in the job puts perfection in the work, and you have put your heart and soul into this for Cady. Whatever happens next, all the rest is just life, so enjoy every moment of it."

CHAPTER TWENTY-TWO

VINCE

I stood outside the Rainbow Room with Rick while he swallowed nervously.

"Have you got the rings?" he asked for the hundredth time.

"Of course, mate, right here," I said, patting my pocket.

He was so tightly wound I could hear him ticking. I couldn't bring myself to pretend I'd left the rings in the hotel room or dropped them down the bog.

He nodded distractedly and glanced down at the crumpled sheet where he'd written his wedding vows. I knew this because I'd heard him practice them at least fifty times this morning, and they were only three lines long.

"Mate," I said gently. "It's time to go inside. The woman of your dreams will be arriving in a minute and it wouldn't be a great start if Cady caught you out here looking shiftier than the gearstick on a boy racer's Ford Fiesta."

Rick blinked, then nodded and straightened his shoulders.

"Have you got the rings?" he asked for the hundredth-and-first time.

"Yep, still got 'em, right here in my pocket and safer than a squirrel's nuts."

He frowned. "What does that mean?"

"It means, you tosser, that it's time to get married," and I opened the doors to the Rainbow Room and pushed him inside. Then pulled him back out when I remembered that at a Jewish-Interfaith wedding, Rick had to walk in a procession with all the parentals.

"Just checking everyone's there," I said casually, leading him toward the waiting room where Rabbi Lisa was already chatting to the four *chuppah* bearers: Ben, Leon, Cady's Uncle Gerald, and her friend from work, a dude named Oliver who was also the producer on her radio show.

"Hello, Rick," said Rabbi Lisa, greeting him warmly and shaking his hand. "And Vincent! How lovely to see you again."

"Looking foxy, Rabbi," I said, winking at her.

She gave me a strange look, but was distracted by Rick's parents arriving, as well as Cady's mum.

"Cady and her dad are outside," said Rachel with a huge smile, "but she doesn't want Rick to see her before the wedding."

"Well, okay then. Everyone else here?" asked Rabbi Lisa. "Ready to go?"

She led the way with the four *chuppah* bearers carrying the tent-like structure. Apparently it represented the Garden of Eden—and I'd gone through 35 years of life and never known that Adam and Eve had invented camping.

We were next in the procession with Rick's parents and Cady's mum behind us. Because it was an interfaith marriage, Rick and Cady had taken pieces from both Jewish and Christian wedding services. It was a good thing we'd had the rehearsal yesterday, because the British contingent were all over the place. None of us had a clue where we were supposed to be, and Sandy and Rachel had to keep prodding us into the right positions.

Rick stood at the front of the room under the *chuppah*, his face unmoving and I wasn't entirely sure he was breathing either. I poked him in the ribs.

"What?" he hissed out of the side of his mouth.

"Smile, you twat!"

He grimaced, but then the doors to the Rainbow Room opened again with the wedding march music, and Cady entered on her father's arm—then Rick couldn't stop grinning. She looked really nice, but not as hot as my Gracie walking behind her holding a small bouquet of white roses.

She looked like a goddess and way out of my league. But then she saw me and smiled. I was so proud, I felt like the first Martian to walk on the moon.

Rabbi Lisa raised her hands and everyone behind us sat down.

Sandy handed Cady over to Rick, and they smiled at each other like there was no one else in the room. I was really happy for them, the soppy pair.

"Dear friends and family, on behalf of Cady and Rick, welcome and thank you for being here," said Rabbi Lisa. "They are thrilled that you can share their joy during this wonderful moment in their lives. The greatest happiness of life is knowing that we are loved, loved for who we are."

My mouth dropped open. That was fookin' awesome! And true —*to be loved for who we are*. I felt those words in every part of me. I was definitely going to hire Rabbi Lisa for my wedding.

The rest of the ceremony, I was in a daze, wishing that it was me and Gracie standing in front of our friends and making that commitment. I drifted off in a fookin' awesome daydream, then woke up when Rick started speaking.

"I, Rick, take you, Cady, to be my wife through all the years. I will honor you, protect you, help and support you, and I will never let the cookie jar be empty. I promise to always love you. This is my solemn vow."

I sniggered softly, but Rick was staring into Cady's eyes, both of them wearing the daftest matching smiles.

"I, Cady, take you, Rick, to be my husband. I will honor you, protect you, help and support you, I will train with you, make you laugh every day, and always share my lemon-glazed donuts with you. I promise to always love you. This is my solemn vow."

Rabbi Lisa smiled at them both. "You have declared your consent before this gathering. May the Lord strengthen this consent and fill you both with his blessings. Do you have the rings?"

We all stood there silently until Rick turned around and glared at me.

"Rings! Right! Sorry, got completely caught up in the moment. Nice vows, mate!"

And I placed the rings onto the velvet cushion.

Rabbi Lisa blessed the rings, then Rick and Cady did their thing, and we were at the candle-lighting part.

The two mums stepped up and each lit a candle, and Rick and Cady lit the third together. I liked these Jewish traditions—they were well cool.

Rabbi Lisa stepped forward and said the magic words, "I now pronounce you man and wife, and you may seal your vows with a kiss."

Rick scooped Cady into a real, old fashioned Hollywood smoocheroo. It was epic! I didn't know he had it in him. He must have picked up a few tips from me over the years after all. I cheered louder than anyone.

And then Rick smashed a glass on the floor and Cady stomped it into smithereens.

"*Mazel tov!*" we all yelled.

I'd been to weddings where there had been breakages before, but not where it was deliberate. Still, the night was young.

Then the wedding party signed the *ketubah*, a marriage contract, which spelled out the duties and obligations of the bride and groom, and I was a witness along with Grace. I liked seeing our names together. I liked it a lot. Then Rick and Cady signed the official marriage register.

I'd planned to tell Grace how beautiful she looked, but the words got caught on my tongue and didn't make it out of my mouth. I stood there like a love-struck fool just gazing at her.

"Gracie, Grace," I choked out. "You ... you ... fook me, you're so hot, talk about global warming!"

Her forehead wrinkled before she burst out laughing. "Thank you, Vince. You look great, too."

It hadn't been quite the compliment I'd intended to pay her, but good enough, and we stood there holding hands like a couple of muppets, if muppets had hands and not trotters ... or maybe that was just Miss Piggy. She was hot, too.

After that, we posed for a thousand photos while the photographer made sure everyone in the wedding party was pictured with Rick and Cady.

Finally, we were finished, and everyone was ready for the real party to get started. I'd heard that Jewish weddings could get a bit crazy. I was really looking forward to that because I was loving all of this; I'd even wondered if I had a bit of Jewish in my family tree. And then I wished I hadn't had that thought because I was an orphan and had nobody left to ask. But before I could get too sad, Grace touched my arm gently.

"Are you alright?"

"Never better," I grinned, and kissed the back of her hand.

"You can tell me," she persisted. "You know that, right?"

I shrugged. "Just thinking about my parents," I admitted.

She squeezed my fingers, letting her warmth and kindness flow into me. I lapped it up like a starving dog.

Then the music began and some bloke started warbling *Hava Nagila*. All the men dived into the middle of the room and I started to follow when ... woah! The dancefloor was spinning! That was wicked! I sidled over to the events coordinator who'd introduced herself when we'd arrived; Jenna, I think her name was.

"This is great!" I said, nodding at the slowly rotating floor.

"Yes, we're very proud of it here in the Rainbow Room—it was first installed in 1934."

"Can it go any faster?" I asked. "That would be a laugh."

She gave me a chilly look before she walked away, stating, "It's not a carnival ride, sir."

Huh. No sense of fun, some people.

I sprinted back to the circle in the middle and pushed my way in next to Rick as we danced around the room.

"This is brilliant!" I yelled above the noise.

Rick grinned widely, but his eyes were on Cady who was being hoisted up in a chair by the *chuppah* bearers, and as they heaved her up and down, it looked like the chair was dancing. Four more of us hoisted Rick up, and he was no lightweight either. My mate was 200 pounds of muscle, the bastard.

The chair dipped up and down, and I broke into a sweat as we danced around the room. I saw Gracie laughing and cheering, and I managed a quick smile as we staggered past. Then Cady started waving her hanky in the air and I remembered that Rick had to grab it so they could jig about joined together.

We danced over there, sweating like politicians with a polygraph test. Every time Rick tried to grab Cady's hanky, he lurched forward and nearly fell off his chair, then leaned back gripping onto the seat, wild-eyed and desperate.

Cady laughed like a blocked drain, waving her hanky at him furiously.

And then she leaned too far toward Rick, flailing that damned hanky.

I could see that she was going; I could see her falling, so I ditched Rick to the three losers staggering along without me, and dived toward Cady.

It was like something out of a Tarantino film—the slo-mo bit before everyone gets iced in gory detail.

I caught Cady in my arms but got splatted on the floor as she landed on top of me, knocking the air from my lungs.

Rick came racing over, scooping her up as she laughed helplessly. I was glad someone was having a good time.

I was left on the floor like yesterday's laundry, wheezing louder than a pair of rusty bellows.

Suddenly, an angel descended from heaven and passed me a glass of champagne.

"Vince! Are you alive down there?" asked Gracie, half laughing, half serious.

"Oomph," I huffed, sitting up without spilling a drop.

"You've got some smooth moves, mister!" she laughed.

"Yeah?" I asked, wobbling to my feet. "You ain't seen nothing yet. I'm culturally aware! Watch this!"

And I downed the champagne, leapt into the middle of the revolving dancefloor and started doing the Jewish dance that I'd learned off of YouTube.

"What's he doing?" Cady yelled to Gracie who shook her head.

"Um, it looks like Riverdance," Rick shouted over the music.

I kicked my legs up again, wondering if I'd watched the wrong video.

"Did he hurt his head, too?" Cady sniggered.

"You're doing *Irish* dancing!" Gracie shouted out, as Rick and Cady laughed their arses off.

It looked like I might have made a small snafu, but since I had an audience, I finished my dance and got a round of applause anyway.

"What did you think?" I asked Gracie, as I wiped the sweat off my forehead.

"You're crazy!" she laughed. "And absolutely wonderful!"

And because I agreed, I kissed her soundly until I got another round of applause.

Then I offered her my arm, and had the extreme pleasure of escorting her to the top table where we were sitting with Rick, Cady, and their parents, so the meal could be served.

"Shall we chuck these plates on the floor before or after we eat?" I asked. "I guess after makes more sense."

Gracie slapped my arm and rolled her eyes. "You smash plates at Greek weddings. Please try not to break anything—these dishes cost $70 each: I checked."

"Oh, okay. Fair enough. Pity, though. I was look forward to a bit more mayhem."

"You do fine already on that front," she laughed, which I took as a compliment.

And then I kissed her again. Just because.

The room spun away and the only noise I could hear was the rushing of blood in my head and charging through my body. I could feel every strand of her silky hair under my fingers, and I could sense the heat quivering between us.

Eventually, Cady's mum coughed, and Gracie pulled away, her fingers trailing across my cheek.

"Wow," I whispered. "I want to do a lot more of that."

"We'll see," she said, slightly breathless. "You can take your *yarmulke* off now if you want. I'm amazed it's stayed on, to be honest, what with all your cavorting on the dancefloor."

"That was dancing, not cavorting," I winked at her. "I only cavort in bed."

She laughed again but turned pink, too. I loved making her laugh. I loved making her blush even more.

"Anyway," I said, "I glued it on. I'll have to cut it off later."

She gaped at me, then snorted inelegantly. "Only you, Vincent. Only you."

The servers started bringing out the meal, which was great because I was starving. But I lost my appetite a little when I saw the mini lamb cutlets that were being placed in front of everyone else.

I tried not to squint, but Gracie promised me that a vegan menu had been made especially for me, and something with beetroot and tofu was placed down in front of me. It wasn't bad.

Rabbi Lisa said a blessing, then we all started noshing as the serious drinking began. Gracie laid a gentle hand on my arm as I emptied my champagne glass in one go because I was so thirsty.

"Better go easy on that, champ; we both have speeches to give during the meal—you don't want to be too slurred!"

I grinned at her. "Nah, I'll be fine. I've been practicing," and I patted my pocket. Then I patted it again as my stomach dropped through my stylish vegan shoes.

"What's wrong?" Gracie asked as the MC asked for silence.

"I left my speech in the back pocket of my jeans!" I admitted, horror making me hoarse.

"Is this a joke?" she hissed.

I shook my head, paralyzed with shame as the MC turned to grin at me.

"And now the best man's speech," he announced.

"You'll have to wing it," Gracie whispered, pushing me to my feet. "Just ... oh God ... just be yourself, but not too much!"

"You go first," I begged, pleading with my eyes, "and I'll nip back to the hotel and get it."

"My speech isn't that long!"

I groaned. "Please, Gracie. Just give me a few minutes and I'll ... I'll try to remember what I was going to say. I'll write it on the tablecloth."

I cleared my throat as everyone turned to stare at me.

"Because I'm a gentleman—or that's what my mum told me once after drinking a bottle of Cinzano—I'm going to let the gorgeous maid of honor, Gracie Cooper, go first."

Rick was frowning and Cady was staring at me questioningly. I gave her a weak smile.

Standing gracefully, my girl smiled at the audience and began speaking without missing a beat—she was brilliant.

"I've known Cady since I was 18 years old, a freshman in college. She was loud, funny, confident, daring, adventurous and challenging —and none of that's changed. What I didn't know that first day but have since learned, is that she's also kind, caring, unfailingly loyal and an all-around amazing woman. She took pity on a gawky, awkward kid, and allowed me to hang out with her for the next twenty years. I was welcomed into her family, too, with Rachel, Sandy and Davy, and Cady became the sister I'd never had. But she has two weaknesses—or maybe that's three, now she's marrying Rick!" and she smiled at him.

Thankfully, Rick was no longer glaring at me like I'd be sleeping with the fishes. Which was good, because I had plans for tonight.

"Cady's first weakness is that you can dare her to do anything and she'll do it. Whether it's to eat three-dozen donuts at a single sitting before dancing the twist on a table in a restaurant, or swimming with sharks, or talking live on air to seven million people every morning! Anything. Last year she was dared to run the New York marathon. She had to endure months of people laughing and saying she'd never do it, but they didn't know our girl. Not only did she finish the marathon but she raised over a quarter of a million dollars for veterans charities. Pretty amazing, right?"

I clapped along with everyone else because holy shit! Thirty-six donuts in one go? The woman was a legend.

"Cady's second weakness is lemon-glazed donuts, which you may have guessed by now. Cady, hon, I don't think I'm giving away secrets here!" and Gracie pointed at the wedding cake which was chocolate, perched on a massive mound of multi-colored donuts, and with two little figures in icing laying on a giant donut-shaped double bed.

Cady laughed and shrugged.

"And of course now we all know that Cady's biggest weakness is for a certain Manhattan gym owner who also happens to run marathons, and has been inducted into the lemon-donut appreciation society."

I wondered if that was a real thing, because it sounded fun.

Gracie drew a deep breath and turned to talk directly to the bride.

"Cady, thank you for the privilege of being your maid of honor, but most of all, thank you for the privilege of being your friend for so many years. Love you, hon."

The two women hugged and whispered tearfully to each other as the crowd applauded. I wanted to grab Gracie and hug her too, but I knew that she had more to say.

Wiping her tears but still smiling, she turned back to the wedding guests.

"And thanks to all of you for being here today to celebrate with Cady and Rick. I think we can all agree that we have awesome taste in friends." Then she turned to the happy couple again with more tears in her eyes and a hitch in her voice. "Cady, Rick, when I look at the two of you I see the love you have for each other; I see the joy you share in so many ordinary moments in each day; and I see a long and happy future for you as husband and wife. Ladies and gentlemen, please raise your glasses to toast the bride and groom, Cady and Rick. *Mazel Tov!*"

Everyone stood and roared their names. The two grandmas had to be helped to their feet by Ben and Leon because they were completely sloshed.

"You were brilliant," I said kissing the tears off her cheeks as Gracie sat down.

She smiled and kissed me back.

CHAPTER TWENTY-THREE

GRACE

Finally, with nothing left to say, I leaned back in my chair, watching helplessly as Vince lurched to his feet and stood motionless in front of the wedding guests. I prayed that his natural exuberance and showmanship would save the day, and it hadn't escaped my attention that half the wedding party had been talking about the Canine Crusader as a modern urban legend, but right now, the legend wasn't moving ... unless you counted the wobble and loud hiccup, like a man who'd been up all night partying and drinking all day ... which he pretty much had.

Vince blinked, opened his mouth and hiccupped again.

"You can do it," I whispered encouragingly as I stared up at his frozen face.

He glanced down at me, then gave a huge smile.

"Ladies and gentlemen, family, friends and freeloaders..."

He was off, unstoppable, on a roll, and I relaxed into my seat, taking deep breaths to calm my jangled nerves and collect my scattered emotions.

"We are gathered here today..."

"Oh man! It's the Canine Crusader!" yelped one of the wedding guests. "You're awesome, dude!"

Vince looked over at his fan, gave his trademark smirk and raised his champagne glass.

"Yep, that's me! Cheers!"

Everyone raised their glasses with him as Vince took another gulp of champagne. I rubbed my forehead.

"Fook it! What was I saying? Fook it! Um, sorry, did I say that out loud? Shit! Sorry! Oh, bugger, I might as well be honest as I recognize a few faces among the guests from last night's shenanigans at the rehearsal dinner. Nana Dubicki, what were you doing with that bottle of brandy in your purse? Grandma Callaghan, I'm sorry I couldn't escort you home last night—I have my reputation to think about. But what a night ... totally mental! The Canine Crusader likes to party—all the grandmothers say so—totally hardcore! And it's true, I had all the good intentions of writing a well thought out speech last night as any best man would, and I did. Had it in me hand this morning, but one thing led to another and I ended up getting completely pissed as a fart instead, and yes you're right in thinking I haven't been to sleep ... straight through no brew! That's how the Canine Crusader rolls!" and he howled like a wolf.

Half the guests were shaking with laughter, and the other half looked utterly nonplussed.

Rick dropped his head into his hands, muttering, "Oh my God, somebody stop him."

"No way," laughed, Cady. "Your nutso friend is totally out of control. I love it!"

Vince slapped Rick across the back of the head, "But let me tell you about this guy. To look at him, butter wouldn't melt in his mouth, he's soooo cool, but let me tell you about the time I helped him clean his apartment after a chocolate-fetish-sex party with the bride..."

Cady choked then raised her hands as if to say, *Yep, you got me there, it's all true.*

"Charlie and the chocolate factory would have been impressed with this little spectacle, that's all I'm saying," continued Vince, a runaway juggernaut crashing through this upscale wedding, wearing a smile that would make the angels weep. "Chocolate and random fruit everywhere—bed sheets, walls, floor." He lowered his voice as if speaking confidentially to the assembled guests. "Now, the Canine Crusader likes to party, but the clean up on this one, blimey! Two days we were cleaning that apartment. A little tip, guys, plastic sheets for the next one, you horny chocosexaholics."

Vince winked at Cady who stood up and took a bow, as applause and laughter thundered around her. Rick still had his head in his hands, moaning softly.

"If their first baby's name is Cocoa, we'll all know why ... 'cause chocosexaholic is too long!"

He chuckled at his own joke while Rick's parents looked on in bemused confusion.

"More champagne please, buddy!" Vince held up his glass to a passing waiter. "Thank you, sir," he said, taking another long gulp and emptying half the glass in one go. "And keep it coming. Umm, where was I? We are gathered here today to celebrate Cady and Rick's wedding, aka, the chocosexaholics. But I'm sure everyone will agree with me, how beautiful Cady looks. Raise a glass to the sexy bride."

Half the guests toasted, *the Sexy Bride*, and the rest just said, *the Bride*, either because they didn't think Cady looked sexy, or more probably because they'd known her since she was in diapers, and it didn't seem appropriate.

"And don't forget Rick's mum!" Vince bellowed. "Sheila, you're looking as beautiful as ever, and if I was 40 years older, Rick, my boy, you could be my son. Please raise a glass to the bride and groom's parents."

Once again, the guests obeyed, although several were shaking their heads disapprovingly. The rest were helpless with laughter, and I saw several dabbing at tears in their eyes and choking on bubbles.

"Thank you for all turning up for the free meal and champagne, you cheapskates," Vince grinned at his audience. "Just kidding! Now, let's squash the elephant in the room or should I say lion? Rick's stag night was eventful: strip joints, booze, Broadway shows, lions ... but for the record, we didn't steal the lion. Honest!"

Vince signaled to the waiter to open the doors, and a fully grown male lion padded into the room, pausing to yawn and shake its mane.

Rick and Cady sat with their mouths hanging open, much like mine, as Vince walked over and gave the creature a big hug, stroking his fur and speaking to him in a low voice. Then he turned back to the top table.

"Rick, mate! I couldn't let this momentous occasion pass without inviting *all* your stag night buddies. Meet, Jabari, everybody!"

I wasn't the only one who nearly peed their pants when the lion let out a roar that shook the panes of glass in the windows. The wedding guests nearest were falling out of their chairs to get away from the enormous wild animal, but Vince just kneeled down and put his face against the thick fur, and I watched with amazement as the massive lion nuzzled him, buffeting Vince with his heavy head.

Thankfully, the lion's trainer appeared and led the beast away, but not before Vince had hand-fed him three cooked chicken legs.

Vince walked back to his seat with a huge smile on his face.

"As my gift to the beautiful couple, who, all jokes aside I love like family, the Canine Crusader has arranged for the award-winning *Lion King* musical team to perform a special song, *We are One,* in honour of Cady and Rick's wedding."

Music poured out as singers and dancers from the famous Broadway show burst into the room, dazzling us with their voices, and everyone oohed and ah'ed at the surprise.

Quietly, Vince sang along, and it felt like he was singing to me when he turned and smiled.

"We are one, you and I
We are like the earth and sky,
One family under the sun..."

Cady was singing along, too, gazing into Rick's eyes, and I knew that she'd loved every minute of Vince's crazy best man's speech.

When the singers and dancers took a bow and left the room to heartfelt applause, Vince rose to his feet once more.

"I'm glad you enjoyed that, ladies and gents. Now, let's all raise one more glass and toast to the beautiful couple, to Mr. and Mrs. Roberts!"

He took a bow as everyone cheered and joined in the toast. Then he whispered to Rick, "I've gotta take a piss, mate," and hurried off.

Rick was speechless, but Cady just shrugged and smiled ... right up until the moment when Vince tripped over the cable for the microphone, and fell face first into the chocolate fountain.

There was a shocked silence as he emerged, dripping. My hands flew to my mouth and I held my breath. But Vince just wiped his face on a napkin, picked up the mike and said, "I guess I just joined the chocosexaholic club!"

Everyone burst out laughing, clapping and cheering at a grinning Vince. He'd totally pulled it out of the bag when it mattered. I marveled again at his ability to bring triumph from disaster.

He took another bow and left the room, presumably to wash off the chocolate that dripped from his face.

I knew that I could never be like him: impulsive, disorganized, with a seat-of-my-pants attitude to life, but I envied him too, I really did. And somehow, some way, this complex clown, this warm-hearted jerk, this sensitive soul had staggered, tumbled, tripped and fallen into my life, and I was happier for it. The world was a better place because he was in it: the world according to Vince.

As I pondered this imponderable revelation, he slid back into his seat, his face slightly pink, and his shirt damp.

"I would have let you lick it off me," he whispered, "but then I'd have wanted to get laid on the buffet, and Cady would have punched me in the nuts."

I laughed and shook my head. Just a little smudge marred his collar, but what's a smudge of chocolate between friends?

The speeches continued, and as Cady's father spoke movingly about his daughter, I held hands with Vince, watching his face as he smiled, laughed, and nodded in appreciation for Sandy's words.

He was still crazy, he could still be annoying, he could still stumble into more disasters than anyone else in the history of the world, but he was real and he was loving, and after his trial was over, I hoped he'd be mine.

Rick and Cady stood together and thanked Rabbi Lisa and all their guests, then the MC announced the father/daughter and mother/son dance.

The beautiful lyrics of Carole King's *Child of Mine* rang out from the band at the other end of the room.

> *Fascinating Factoid: The most popular wedding song is Christina Perri's 'A Thousand Years', bumping Elvis' 'Can't Help Falling In Love' off of the top spot.*

My heart started to gallop as I realized that the maid of honor/best man dance came next, but we still hadn't discussed what we were going to do. Well, I'd tried to discuss it with Vince, but each time he'd told me not to worry and that it would be easier than falling off a log. I did *not* want to fall in front of all these people. I tried not to panic even though I always planned things in advance. Always.

But then Vince took my hand, squeezing it reassuringly, so I forced myself to focus on the dancers. Cady smiled lovingly at her father when his eyes became damp, and Rick held his tiny mother in his arms as she laughed softly at something he said. The two couples swayed to the music, and tears came to my eyes. I wasn't the only one.

"I'm nobody's child," Vince sighed as he watched our friends circle the room, Rick smiling down at his mom, and Cady leaning her head against her dad's shoulder. "I haven't been since Mum died last year." Then he turned to look at me. "You're lucky."

"I know," I whispered. "I'm a very lucky woman," and I hoped that my words conveyed several layers of meaning.

Vince smiled sadly and turned his eyes back to the two couples on the dancefloor.

"Fook me," he sighed. "Half the guests are in tears. We're really going to have to work to bring the fun back."

My eye twitched.

"Are you going to tell me what you have in mind?" I asked nervously.

He turned and grinned at me. "Nope!"

"But Vince!" I gasped. "I'm not joking about—*I really can't dance!*"

He kissed my cheek, trying to soothe me. It wasn't working.

"It'll be fine," he said. "Just follow my lead."

"Please don't humiliate me in front of all these people," I whispered, with desperate tears pricking my eyes. "I couldn't take it."

His expression softened. "Never, Gracie. I'd never do that to you. I promise it'll be fine."

And that was going to have to be good enough because Rick and Cady were walking towards us expectantly.

Vince led me onto the dancefloor as all eyes turned to us. Cold sweat broke out across my skin, and my face was frozen in a rictus grin of fear. Then Vince nodded at the band and took my right hand, pulling me in firmly so his arm was around my waist.

"Smile," he whispered against my cheek. "It's going to be brilliant. Hold on tight!"

I closed my eyes and licked my dry lips.

"Okay," I croaked as I clamped my left hand to his shoulder in a classic ballroom hold. "I trust you."

But then I nearly puked as the famous opening violin and accordion notes rang out for La Cumparista, *ta-ram pam pam pa...*

"Let's tango!" Vince grinned.

He started to promenade me across the dancefloor in long, smooth steps, dragging me with him, my stiff body working in my favor for once. As the music dipped and dived, ebbed and flowed, Vince matched it step for step. I shuffled along with him, doing my best not to tread on his toes: left foot, right foot, left foot right foot—I could do that. Was I dancing?

We strode around with Vince dominating the room and me doing my best to keep up, but I didn't look too awful. I didn't fall, I didn't trip, and you know what? I started to thoroughly enjoy myself. I was dancing!

Vince dipped me low to the floor then pulled me up slowly, staring into my eyes with stark passion. Holy cow, it was hot on this dancefloor! Then he swooped past the chocolate fountain, dipped his finger into the flow of melted chocolate and offered it to me. My cheeks flaming, I sucked his finger into my mouth and watched his pupils dilate with desire.

The wedding guests whistled and clapped and stamped their feet, and some smart alec plucked a red rose out of a vase and tossed it onto the dancefloor. Vince scooped it up and put it between his teeth, winking at the wedding guests who howled with laughter.

And I understood—he'd rather play the clown and be laughed at than make *me* look like a fool.

Another part of my heart tiptoed over to #TeamVince.

We tangoed around that dancefloor as if we'd been doing it our whole lives, and when Vince threw his rose to Nana Dubicki, she nearly swooned. Of course, Grandma Callaghan looked madder than a box of snakes, so Vince stole another rose from a vase and presented it to her on bended knee as the music played its last notes.

Honors even for the competitive grandmas.

Honor preserved for me.

I sat down with the biggest smile on my face.

Cady leaned across the table and grabbed my hand.

"Woah! What was that? You've been holding out, girl. You *can* dance!" She squeezed my fingers. "You looked amazing out there."

I beamed like the Montauk lighthouse.

After that, all the guests poured onto the dancefloor, shimmying, shaking, twirling and even tangoing. Maybe we'd started a trend. Vince dragged me back onto the dancefloor, more willingly this time, and we shuffled and swayed to the music as my hands gripped the back of his neck and he rested his on my waist.

"I don't want tonight to end," he whispered.

I looked into his eyes and smiled, truly wishing it wouldn't.

"Me, either. But..."

He didn't let me finish, grinning like he'd won the Lottery. "It'll have to be my place," he went on confidently as I shook my head, "because of the kids."

"I hope they're behaving for their Uncle Erik."

Vince chuckled. "They'll have played him for every Milk-Bone in the house and are probably pinning him to the sofa; Tyson loves Erik, but it makes him think he's a lapdog and he'll try to sit on his knee."

I laughed at the image as warmth filled my chest.

The MC interrupted our moment by announcing that it was time for the bride and groom to cut the cake.

We all turned to face the side of the room where the wedding cake stood resplendent on a hill of donuts in all its chocolately glory.

Cady and Rick picked up a shiny silver knife together to cut a slice through the cake as the wedding guests smiled, clapped and took photos.

"I'm not going to moosh this into Rick's face," Cady announced, "because good cake shouldn't be wasted ... and because I spent two hours getting my makeup done!"

I heartily approved—I hated mess.

"No cake mooshing?" Vince said sadly. "I love that part in American weddings."

"You would," I laughed. "But hasn't there been enough of that already?"

We toasted the happy couple with more champagne, then to raucous cheers, Cady tossed her bouquet into the air. Several women leaped towards it, but Vince jumped higher, and being 6'4", beat them all.

"The bouquet toss is for women only!" I giggled.

"Yeah, but I wanted you to have it," Vince smiled, presenting me with Cady's bouquet. "You know what this means, don't you?"

"Yes, I'll have to find a vase to put it in."

Vince leaned closer. "It means you're getting married next."

"Hmm, we'll see!"

As the evening reached its peak, with many couples getting hot and sweaty on the dancefloor, and Cady's brother making out rather publicly with one of the celebrity guests, the MC announced that the bride and groom would be leaving.

It took twenty minutes to get all the guests down to the lobby and I lost Vince in the crowd.

But when I heard loud laughter and Cady swearing fit to be tied, I guessed that Vince had one last joke to play.

Yes, there was the bride and groom's wedding vehicle, covered in white ribbons, rattling with cans and horseshoes ... attached to a Pedicab that Vince was pedaling.

Rick gave him a stern look but couldn't stop a smile from spilling out.

"No! No way and hell no!" Cady said emphatically. "I'm not getting in that thing, Vincent. Think again. Fast."

"Go on!" he teased. "It's brilliant fun. Rick loved it on our stag night, didn't you, mate?"

Rick had been married eight hours and already knew better than to contradict Cady on something like this.

He shook his head and folded his arms across his chest.

Vince sighed heavily, then stuck two fingers in his mouth and whistled so loudly, dogs two blocks away started barking.

And pulling up to the curb was a gorgeous vintage Aston Martin, just like James Bond would drive, complete with wedding ribbons.

Rick's eyes lit up and Cady sighed with happiness.

"*Much* better, Vince," she smiled. "I'll let you live after all."

The happy couple turned to their guests, smiled, waved, hugged and kissed, then finally peeled themselves free to climb into the car.

"Love you!" I yelled at Cady.

She blew kisses out of the window as the car pulled away.

I looked at Vince and smiled. "That was a great idea."

"The Pedicab or the Aston Martin?"

"Both!" I grinned. "Definitely inspired."

I must have given the right answer because he kissed me soundly before escorting me back inside.

I would willingly have gone home then in a stupor of happy exhaustion, but part of the best man and maid of honor's duty was to make sure the rest of the evening ran smoothly. Besides, I was also Cady's wedding planner, so I felt responsible.

We went around talking to everyone, organizing taxis with Jenna, the Rainbow Room's events coordinator, until there was no one left but us.

"One last dance?" Vince asked.

"The band went home," I pointed out.

"But when I look at you, I hear music," he smiled.

"That is such a cheesy line!"

"Doesn't make it any less true." And he held out his hand. "May I have the extreme fookin' pleasure of the last dance?" he said.

"Such sweet words," I smiled, accepting his hand.

As the servers quietly cleared the tables, Vince and I clung together, swaying to a tune that no one but us could hear.

Then in a soft voice, Vince started to sing:

When I need you,
I just close my eyes and I'm with you,
And all that I so want to give you, babe,
Is only a heartbeat away.

I listened carefully to the moving lyrics but had to admit that I didn't know the song.

Vince shrugged, his thoughts half lost in the past, half fixed in the present.

"It's a song from the seventies by a British singer called Leo Sayer. Mum loved him."

As Vince hummed the tune, the lights dimmed one by one, and we were left alone in the darkness, only the neon glow of Manhattan casting soft shadows across the empty dancefloor.

"Time to go," Vince sighed.

"Thank you for a magical evening," I said softly.

"I fooked up with the Irish dancing."

"You were fantastic."

"And I fooked up again by forgetting to bring my speech."

"You were amazing and everybody loved what you said."

"I fell in the chocolate fountain."

"Highlight of the evening."

"And I brought a lion."

"Definitely memorable."

"And I'm sorry that—"

I reached up to press my fingers over his lips. "Vince, it was perfect. You were perfect."

He smiled, then kissed the palm of my hand. "Will you come home with me?"

"Ask me again after the court case."

He frowned. "I thought that was all sorted. A plea bargain or something?"

That made me grimace. I really hadn't meant to say anything to spoil tonight.

"That was the plan, yes, but the DA is hinting that he wants to take it to trial. He's afraid vigilantes will copy you. Well, that's what he says—I think he just wants some free publicity, and you're very popular."

"Well, that's a bit shite."

"More than a bit," I agreed. "It's not definite, but it's a possibility that we have to be ready for."

He rubbed his hand over his cheeks. "What if we don't tell anyone you came home with me tonight?"

I couldn't help laughing. "Is that all you're worried about?"

"Well, yeah," he grinned. "What else?"

"That's my Vince," I smiled. "One track mind."

"You're really going to make me go home to my kids without their Mummy Gracie?"

I smiled as I stepped away. "I really am."

"Wow, tough love. But I can wait."

We rode the elevator in silence, the quiet that came with a promise for the future.

Vince let me take the first cab that arrived and kissed me sweetly.

"Look after this one," he said to the driver. "She's precious cargo."

The driver grunted and didn't reply, but I smiled up at Vince. "I'll call you."

"I'll be waiting."

"Night, Vince. Kiss the kids for me!" but the driver was already pulling away and my words were lost in the New York night.

I arrived back to my empty apartment, already missing Vince, missing the dogs, missing our easy companionship and the electricity that had been sparking between us all evening.

With a sigh, I hung up my beautiful dress and put my two beautiful bouquets in vases, then cleaned off all my makeup.

I fell into bed with a smile on my face, then ground my teeth when I remembered that I hadn't checked my messages; I hadn't even looked at my phone all evening. I rummaged in the bottom of my tiny wedding purse and pulled it out. I was tagged in a ton of posts from Cady's wedding, and I was already feeling nostalgic about it, but then I checked my voicemail.

There was a message from District Attorney Randolph Barclay —he was denying a plea bargain and taking us to trial. And the smug bastard added a postscript:

"The judge was able to find a space in her schedule to move the trial date forward as that's in the public's best interests to curb the spate of copycat vigilante behaviour that we've been experiencing across the State. I hope you're ready, Counselor."

I felt all the blood rush from my body.

I had one week to prepare for Vince's trial. .

CHAPTER TWENTY-FOUR

VINCE

"Free the Canine Crusader! No walls for four paws! Justice for the dogs' best friend!"

Cady laughed as I chanted, then stopped abruptly when she saw the stern look on Grace's stony face.

"Sorry," she grimaced. "It was quite funny."

"Hilarious," Grace said stiffly. "Am I the only person here who understands that Vince could go to prison?"

"Sorry," Cady muttered again.

"Eh, it's not that bad," I smiled at her. "They're not going to send the Canine Crusader to the clink. They wouldn't dare!"

Grace turned to me with a pained expression. "Vincent, this is what I'm trying to explain—they *want* to make an example of you. They *want* you to go to prison because they think it will stop the rash of copycat crimes that are taking place all along the eastern seaboard."

"No one wants a nasty rash," I winked at her.

She stood up with a frustrated huff. "Will you please take this seriously? I'm worried! You should be worried, too. And I really think it's time to call in an experienced criminal lawyer—I'm a specialist in mergers and acquisitions, for Pete's sake! I've never tried a criminal case in my life! I can't..."

I shook my head, serious for once. "No, it has to be you, Gracie. No one knows me like you do; no one gets me like you do. It *has* to be you. And I know you'll be brilliant."

"I agree with Vince," said Cady. "Words I never thought I'd utter. But he's right. You *do* know him better than anyone, God help you. And you're a great lawyer, Grace. You don't give yourself enough credit. You've been researching this since Vince was arrested and you've got a plan—don't lose your balls now, hon."

Grace's face turned red. "This is not a joke!" she yelled, flailing her arms and losing her cool in a very un-Gracie way. "This is not a game where Vince wins a 'get-out-of-jail-free card'. If a person is found guilty of burglary in the third degree, it's a class D felony, punishable by one to seven years in prison and a fine up to $5,000."

Her nostrils flared. She was really turning me on.

"Then there's the charge of larceny," she said with gritted teeth, chewing the words and spitting them out. "Larceny is when a person wrongfully takes, obtains or withholds property from its rightful owner, with the intent to deprive the owner of such property."

"But they were rescue dogs," I piped up. "They didn't belong to no one."

"They were the property of the shelter," Grace gritted out. "If the loss to the shelter is worth less than $500, you might get away with a misdemeanor, while anything worth $500 or more is a felony."

She sighed, and her voice became quieter.

"I'm confident that we'll be able to dismiss the larceny charge on the technicality that you hadn't left the building, so it's supposition that you were planning to steal the dogs ... even though you had six puppies in your pockets."

"I wasn't stealing them," I insisted. "I was rehoming them,

which is what the shelter was supposed to do anyway. And I can't believe those tossers are pressing charges after everything I've done for them."

"Yeah," said Rick from the sofa where Tyson was sitting on him. "Tossers."

"Cheers, mate!" I grinned at him.

Grace's mouth twisted. "I know," she said quietly. "I think they've been leaned on. I heard a rumor—completely unsubstantiated but probably true—that they've been threatened with closure on some B.S. zoning code. The DA is playing hardball. That's why I'm so worried, Vince. They're not going to play fair because they intend to find you guilty."

"Bloody hell," said Rick, summing up the situation for all of us.

For the first time since I'd been arrested a two months ago, I felt a nervous twitch in my gut. I still didn't believe that I'd done anything wrong, but the law seemed to say otherwise. And I didn't like to see Gracie looking so stressed either—I wanted to make her life easier, better, not worse. It was a kick up the arse to realize that I was fooking up her life ... again.

"Will it be a trial by jury?" Cady asked.

Grace nodded uncertainly. "Yes. Vince had the option to be judged by a jury or by a judge. I thought that his popularity and, um, charm, would work in our favor. When we have jury selection, I'll be asking who has pets, and I'll try to select women ... for obvious reasons..."

I had to grin at the look on her face when she said that.

"And you're worried because...?" Cady prompted.

"Because Randolph Barclay will be asking the same questions and crossing out anyone who might look favorably on the Canine Crusader's capers."

"That sounds like a TV show," I said, wondering if I could pitch the idea to a network.

Grace speared me with one of her sexy-as-fook glares.

"And my concern is," she said sharply, ignoring me and speaking directly to Cady, "is that we'll end up with a jury of twelve straight men who were bitten by dogs as a child and hate animals."

We all fell silent as I contemplated my future wearing a prison suit and wondering if the arrows would make my arse look fat.

"Okay," I said, defeated and deflated, "what's the plan? I'm sure you have one."

Grace nodded jerkily. "We're going to rehearse every possible question and every possible answer, and you're going to learn them off by heart so there's no ad libbing. I'm going to write it all down, and Rick and Cady will practice with you."

"Sounds good. What are you going to do?"

"I'm going to think like a prosecutor—I'm going to find every precedent that could send you to jail ... and I'm going to think about how to argue it out of court. That's what I'm going to do."

"Sounds like fighting talk to me," I grinned.

Grace stood up and put her hands on her hips. "I'm only just getting started," she said sternly. "No one messes with *my* boyfriend!"

"Boyfriend?" I repeated hopefully.

"When this case is over, you're going to owe me breakfast, lunch and dinner fifty times over," she said. "And I *will* collect. So as we'll be doing all that, I think you'd better be my boyfriend, too, or people will talk," she smirked.

I stood up to pull her into a hug and give her the kissing she so deserved, but she held up her hand like a traffic cop.

"No kissing until the case is over," she insisted.

"But Gracie..."

"No!" she said firmly. "It's too ... distracting."

I grinned at her. I really liked her being distracted by my kissing.

"But Gracie..."

"No!" she yelled, burning me with her laser stare, so that I sat down again. "No kissing, no touching, no canoodling of any kind."

Cady snorted in the background and rapidly turned it into a hacking cough as Grace gave her a good glaring at.

"That goes for you two, as well," she said, pointing a finger at Cady and Rick. "While you're here, you work on the case. The focus is on keeping Vince out of the dog pound. No mistakes, no excuses, and absolutely no kissing."

"We're supposed to be on our honeymoon," Rick muttered.

"And your point is?" Gracie said stonily as Rick recoiled.

I waved my arm in the air.

"Yes, Vincent?"

"What about holding hands?"

"No."

"What about a foot rub after a long day?"

"Certainly not."

"Well, can I think about kissing you while I'm in the shower?"

Grace rubbed her forehead. "I'm going to work at my apartment. Cady, I'll email the list of questions and answers later. Vincent, I expect you to be word perfect by tomorrow morning." The she glowered at all of us. "We're running out of time."

Zeus jumped into my lap and Tap nuzzled my ankle, looking as worried as the rest of my friends.

After Grace left, all the energy went out of the room.

CHAPTER TWENTY-FIVE

GRACE

I was nervous. Actually, I was terrified. I'd researched the hell out of Vince's case and knew that there was a good chance of dismissing the larceny charge, but I also knew that wasn't enough. This trial wasn't going to be won on points of law, it wasn't even about justice: it was about the DA needing positive publicity to be re-elected—and using Vince to get it, ironic as that seemed. He wanted to be the DA who was 'tough on crime; tough on the causes of crime' with zero tolerance for pretty much everything. You'd think that wouldn't go down well in hip NYC but he was winning a lot of votes.

So even though my defense had merit, I also knew that I was the weak link in Vince's case: I simply didn't have the charisma needed by a great trial lawyer. Vince's lawyer needed to be liked and trusted by the jury, and I knew that I came over as cold and emotionless, and I couldn't help that. If, for one second, I let my emotions rule me, I'd fall apart ... because I cared too much.

I'd done the best preparation I possibly could, but it still might not be enough. Vince would go to prison, and the world would be less colorful because of it. As for me, I'd lose my best chance at happiness.

Even the selection of judge was against us and it seemed as if Fate hated us: Judge Herschel had been given the job—the woman who'd already been inflicted with a dose of Vince at his arraignment and his most inept. It would be harder to convince her that he was a sober, upstanding and useful member of society than someone who'd never met him.

I stared in the mirror, thin-lipped and haggard, with more makeup than I'd normally wear in court, trying to mask the dark circles under my eyes. But nothing could hide the six pounds in weight I'd dropped this week, leaving me looking ill and drawn. I'd barely eaten at all until Cady and Rick had come over and force-fed me a nutritious veggie omelet yesterday, before my first day in court, and again today.

Jury selection had been a grisly affair. DA Randolph Barclay and his deputy, Judge Herschel and myself had spent four, miserable hours questioning potential jurors, hoping to detect bias either in our favor or not. Both Barclay and I knew that getting the right jurors during *voir dire* could increase one's chances in predicting individual verdicts by as much as 78%. But instead of the pet-friendly, animal-loving jurors I'd hoped for, it seemed we'd gotten Cruella De Vil's meaner, extended family—all the tree-hugging Vince fans had been rooted out and sent home. I wanted to cry. But everyone was counting on me, most especially Tap, Zeus and Tyson.

I took a deep breath and forced myself to woman-up for the first day of trial.

Today would be the opening statements, giving a general overview of the case. The prosecution always went first, so I'd have to sit and listen to Barclay grandstanding, but it was my chance to analyze how the DA was planning to play this. It also meant that I'd have a brief chance to alter my plan of defense accordingly.

I'd been given a list of the prosecution's witnesses in discovery, and had practiced the questions I'd be asking them. Vince had been determined to speak in his own defense, although I still wasn't sure that was a good idea, given his history of going off-script, but he'd promised me that he wouldn't. So, reluctantly, I'd be calling him as a witness. My last witness. The very last. God help us.

~

The bailiff, clerk and court reporter were already seated when I entered Courtroom Five of the Supreme Court with Vince, and the jury were lined up on one side.

Ten men in well-pressed clothes, only two elderly women. That wasn't the odds I'd wanted. I'd hoped for lots of straight women and gay men, all with memberships to the ASPCA.

> *Fascinating factoid: the American Society for the Prevention of Cruelty to Animals began in 1866 in New York City. It is the oldest animal welfare organization in the United States, and inspired by the RSPCA which was set up in the UK in 1824.*

Cady, Rick, Erik the plumber and a number of Vince's supporters were sitting in the public seating area, along with what looked like several members of the press who were busy scribbling notes.

Vince grinned and was about to wave at his friends when I gripped his sleeve.

"Don't!" I hissed.

"Sorry," Vince muttered. "Fookin' forgot."

"Well, don't forget again!" I shot back. "You only have one chance to make a good first impression. Serious, sober, sensible—remember?"

"The judge isn't here yet," he said.

"You have to impress the jury, too. Don't forget that either."

"Fook," he sighed.

Randolph Barclay overheard us and smirked, stroking his tie the way a Bond villain would stroke his cat. He looked poised, polished and unbearably smug.

I ushered Vince into his seat and plopped down beside him, trying to look cool, calm and collected instead of hot, sweaty and flustered.

The Bailiff stood and instructed us all to rise as Judge Herschel entered the room. If anything, she looked even more severe than when I'd seen her ten weeks previously.

She arranged her robes and sat, frowning at the shuffling of feet as everyone else took their places.

"Good morning, ladies and gentlemen. Calling the case of the People of the State of New York versus Vincent Alexander Azzo on charges of burglary and larceny. Mr. Azzo is represented by Grace Cooper, and the State of New York is represented by District Attorney Randolph Barclay. Are both sides ready?"

DA Barclay gave her a blinding smile as he stood, looking as if he was auditioning for a toothpaste commercial, bowing his head slightly in deference. "Ready for the People, your Honor."

Taking a deep breath and giving a small, professional smile, I stood and spoke clearly. "Ready for the defense, your Honor."

Judge Herschel gazed at me over her half-moon spectacles, then flicked those all-seeing eyes across her courtroom.

"Will the clerk please swear in the jury."

The clerk leapt to his feet obediently. "Will the jury please stand and raise your right hand? Do each of you swear that you will fairly try the case before this court, and that you will return a true verdict according to the evidence and the instructions of the court, so help you, God? Please say 'I do'."

They all spoke, some mumbling, some clearer, and the clerk nodded.

"You may be seated."

As they re-took their places, I leaned closer to Vince, speaking out of the corner of my mouth.

"Whatever Barclay says, don't say a word, don't respond at all. You'll hear things you won't like or that you'll disagree with. But Vince, keep it zipped."

He mimed zipping his lips and my heart sank. Could he really keep his mouth shut? It seemed unlikely.

Barclay rose to his feet and faced the jury, the smugness gone from his face, replaced by a sincere and earnest expression.

"Your Honor, ladies and gentlemen of the jury: the defendant has been charged with two serious crimes..." Barclay swept his arm towards Vince, his face stern and lawyerly, punctuating each charge for emphasis. "Burglary of a charitable institution..." he paused dramatically. "Larceny, theft. The evidence will show that the defendant deliberately, calculatingly and violently broke into a charitable institution, a charity, ladies and gentlemen! Breaking two doors, two sets of locks, and damaging a third—a charity that can ill afford to pay for repairs; a charity that is supported by tax payer donations—that's *your* donations and, of course, the generosity of strangers. Further, on the night of January 4th, the defendant attempted to steal 17 valuable animals and was arrested with six of the animals about his person, with a clear intent to remove another 11 without the owner's permission. The defendant's fingerprints were on all three doors, the two locks and 11 leashes, and as I must reiterate—he was arrested at the scene of the crime, red-handed. The evidence I present will prove to you that the defendant is guilty as charged.

"And I must add, the defendant's grossly negligent and self-aggrandizing behavior since his arrest, his utter disrespect for the law, has led to a significant increase of copycat crimes—a crime wave across the whole State and beyond—that must not be condoned, and indeed must be punished to the full extent permitted by law."

Barclay adjusted his tie, staring at Vince, who watched him with a slight frown, then turned to the jury.

"Notoriety, celebrity, it's a curious thing in the modern world—curious that they can be so closely linked as to appear to be inseparable, but ladies and gentlemen, they are *not* the same thing. The defendant has sought to sway opinions on his crimes by his antics, but imagine for one moment that a young person was swayed to attempt a similar stunt—to climb a high wall, trespassing and risking serious injury, for example. That would be unforgiveable. But the truth is much worse—all across New York State and, in fact, the whole eastern seaboard, other criminals have sought to copy these dangerous crimes along with the use of violence to emulate the man you see before you, the man arrested at the scene of his crimes.

"This is a court of law, not a popularity contest. I will bring witnesses to bear testimony against him, and you will hear indisputable evidence from experts in their field to prove the defendant's guilt, and I fully expect you to do your duty as responsible citizens and find Mr. Azzo guilty as charged. Thank you."

It sounded bad and Barclay was doing exactly what he'd accused Vince of—inciting a popularity contest between himself and Vince. He was seeking to influence the jury's opinion against Vince because of the so-called copycat 'crimes' of rescuing more animals from shelters, when he knew full well that it would be impossible to bring that to Vince's door. He was playing to the audience, and I'd expected nothing less. I'd prepared for nothing less.

I gave Vince an encouraging smile as I rose to my feet.

"Your Honor, and ladies and gentlemen of the jury: under the law the defendant is presumed innocent until proven guilty. Counsel is correct: this is a court of law, and yet you will hear no real evidence against the defendant. You will come to know the truth: that Vincent Azzo is a man of strong principles and unassailable ethics. The so-called 'crime' that he is being accused of is that of having a kind heart; he is a man who loves animals, a man who cares for those who cannot care for themselves, for those creatures who have no voice. He simply wished to save the lives of innocent animals who had been listed to be euthanized; in his eyes, to be murdered for being homeless. He wished to save them."

I glared theatrically at Barclay.

"And since Counselor Barclay has claimed that the defendant has courted publicity, I would remind him that this passionate animal-lover has worked tirelessly to raise over half a million dollars for animal shelters in the State." I turned to the jury. "Half a million dollars to…"

"Objection!" Barclay snapped, leaping to his feet. "Repetition and relevance. Fundraising efforts undertaken to make himself look good after the fact, does not erase the original crime and furthermore…"

"Objection sustained. Please continue carefully, Ms. Cooper."

Two spots of color flared in my cheeks. It was traditional for opening statements to be delivered without interruption. Barclay had seriously pissed me off—and Judge Herschel had seemingly condoned his rudeness.

Barclay gave a small, pleased smile as he sat down.

"I will prove," I said, speaking as calmly as possible, as if his interruption meant nothing, "through evidence and witness testimony that the defendant is innocent of all charges, and I'm confident that you will find him so."

I returned to my seat next to Vince.

"The guy's a twat," he whispered. "And you were fook hot."

I suppressed my smile and nodded sagely. It was all about the performance.

Judge Herschel glared at Vince. "The prosecution may call its first witness."

Barclay rose smoothly to his feet. "The People call Benson Luft."

The bailiff took the witness to the witness stand, and the clerk spoke next.

"Raise your right hand. Do you promise that the testimony you shall give in the case before this court shall be the truth, the whole truth, and nothing but the truth, so help you God?"

"I do," said Benson Luft in a squeaky, nervous voice.

Barclay strode toward his witness with a reassuring smile. "Thank you for coming, Mr. Luft. Please tell the ladies and gentlemen of the jury your job title and role."

"I, um, I'm the director of Barkalaureate Animal Shelter. We take in upwards of 6,000 stray and homeless animals every year that have been found or brought to us. On any single day, we can have between 20 and 40 animals waiting to be re-homed. I have one full-time and two part-time staff, but we rely on our team of volunteers to feed and exercise our animals. We do our best for each and every one of them, but the truth is that there's never enough time or money, especially for veterinary bills. Every penny is spent on making the animals' lives better. We have no budget for marketing. A volunteer runs our website. Every penny counts."

"A very worthwhile, interesting and difficult task, no doubt," said Barclay, patting Benson Luft on his shoulder in a warm and fraternal way.

Barf.

"Please tell the court, Mr. Luft, what happened the night of January 4th."

"I'd had dinner with my wife, and was putting our son, Oscar, to bed. He likes a bedtime story. Um..."

"And you were interrupted in this homey scene, were you not?"

"Yes, the phone rang and Sylvia, my wife, said it was the police."

"And when you talked to the officer, what did he say?"

"That someone had broken into the shelter and was stealing our dogs!"

"Stealing your dogs," repeated Barclay, staring significantly at the jury.

"Yes! It was him! The Canine Crusader!"

"You mean the defendant, Mr. Vincent Azzo," Barclay chastised gently, a flare of irritation in his eyes.

"Yes, him."

"I see. And when you arrived at the shelter, can you tell me what you found?"

"The place was a mess! There was police tape everywhere, and two of the doors looked like they'd been kicked in, the locks were hanging off. The dogs were barking and all out of their cages. There was shi—, um, dog feces and urine everywhere. Someone had stepped in it and trodden it into the carpet. My office chair had been chewed!"

He looked like he was about to cry.

"And what were your feelings on seeing the extensive damage?"

"I felt hopeless," said Luft. "I didn't know where we'd find the money to make the repairs."

Vince hung his head, and I had to give him a nudge to remind him to look positive at all times.

"And have you since had a bill for the repairs required?"

"Yes, around $500."

"A substantial amount of money for your charitable shelter."

"Yes."

Barclay looked at the jury significantly before continuing.

"And could you tell the court what happened the following morning?"

"I didn't get home until 3am because I had to call an emergency repair service to secure the shelter. I returned at 8am and..."

"And?"

"Later that morning, I started receiving death threats from animal rights people! As if I'd *wanted* to euthanize those stray dogs. I didn't! I hate that part, but we had *no room*, and elderly or sick dogs—no one wants to re-home those. Even the larger ones can be difficult to re-home, waiting months and months for their forever families. We do our best."

"Death threats for a hard-working family man running an animal shelter," Barclay sighed, shaking his head, more in pity than anger. "No further questions."

"Cross-examine?" Judge Herschel asked me.

"Yes, your Honor," I said, standing up and walking towards the witness, summoning the confidence I needed. "Mr. Luft, on the night of January 4th you had three dogs that were planned for euthanasia the following day, is that correct?"

"Yes."

"And how long had those dogs been with you?"

"I ... I don't remember exactly. I'd have to look at our records and..."

"Well, let me refresh your memory since I appear to have studied those records more recently than you." Judge Herschel gave me a warning look but I carried on. "A nine year-old chocolate Labrador named Peanut had been with you ten days; a one year-old Akita-Alsatian-cross named Monty had been with you 14 days; and Bronco, a seven year-old Bull Terrier had been with you three weeks. Does that sound right?"

Luft nodded his head unhappily.

"Please speak clearly for the court reporter," Judge Herschel intoned.

"Yes, that sounds right," Luft coughed.

"Thank you," I said coolly. "Is it usual to euthanize dogs who've been with you for such a short space of time?"

Luft flushed a dirty red as he tugged at his tie. "Older dogs and bigger dogs are really hard to re-home; Akitas are banned in five states and..."

"Mr. Luft," I interrupted. "The question is whether it was usual to euthanize dogs after such a short time."

He cleared his throat nervously, glancing at Barclay repeatedly. "It's a question of room and knowing which dogs we can best help..."

"Please answer the question, Mr. Luft," Judge Herschel instructed.

"No," said Luft at last. "It's not unusual."

"Thank you," I said crisply. "And since Mr. Azzo's intervention, how many of those dogs are still waiting to be re-homed?"

I paused in what I hoped was a dramatic fashion, waiting for the answer.

"None," he said quietly.

"None!" I repeated loudly. "Isn't it true that in the ten weeks since Mr. Azzo's help, you don't have a single animal waiting to be re-homed?"

"Objection!" snorted Barclay, leaping to his feet. "The defendant is accused of a serious crime, not 'helping'!"

"Please re-phrase your question, Ms. Cooper," Judge Herschel ordered.

"Of course, your Honor. Mr. Luft, how many animals are currently waiting to be re-homed in your shelter?"

"None."

"None! Good gracious! When was the last time that happened?" Luft was silent. "Is it true, Mr. Luft, this is the first time in your four years' tenure that you don't have a single animal to re-home?"

"Objection!" Barclay said, standing once again. "Relevance! Mr. Luft is not on trial. Mr. Azzo is the one who was arrested for burglary and larceny."

"Sustained," intoned Judge Herschel, cutting off my best line of questioning.

And so it went for the rest of the day. Every time I tried to bring up the good that Vince had done, Barclay was after me faster than Tyson after a bacon sandwich. Judge Herschel sided with him every single time.

He then called a fingerprint expert who confirmed that Vince's prints were found inside the shelter in a number of places; I had no questions for him. Then Barclay called the police officer who had arrested Vince at the scene, and after several minutes, I had the opportunity to cross-examine her. I had her pegged for a Vince fan, so I was hopeful.

"Officer Sharon Tomás, you arrested the defendant at Barkalaureate Animal Shelter on the night for January 4th, is that correct?"

"Yes, ma'am," said the officer, studying her notebook although it was obvious that she had no need of it, the unusual events being clear in her mind, especially when Vince couldn't help himself and winked at her.

The officer smiled back then remembered that she was in court and her expression hardened.

"Let me be clear, Officer Tomás, you arrested the defendant *inside* Barkalaureate Animal Shelter."

"Yes, ma'am."

"Had any of the dogs been removed onto the street outside the shelter?"

"No, ma'am."

"Had any of the dogs been removed from the offices inside the shelter?"

"No, ma'am."

"No more questions."

Barclay stood at once.

"Officer Tomás, had any of the shelter's dogs been removed from their kennels when you arrested the accused?"

"Yes, sir."

"How many had been removed from their kennels, Officer?"

"Seventeen, sir."

"Seventeen! And was that not, in fact, *all* of the dogs at the shelter?"

"Yes, sir."

"And how many of the dogs were puppies?"

"Six, I believe, sir."

"And how many puppies did the defendant have about his person at the time of his arrest?"

"All of them, sir. All six."

"Thank you, Officer," Barclay said with a smug look at me.

I cursed Barclay. I'd hoped to establish that none of the dogs had been removed from the shelter and therefore no theft had taken place; now he had completely demolished my line of questioning.

"Re-direct, Counselor?" Judge Herschel asked me.

"No, your Honor. No further questions for this witness."

I could almost hear the prison door slamming behind Vince.

CHAPTER TWENTY-SIX

VINCE

We all sat in silence at the breakfast bar as I watched Tyson racing laps around my tiny backyard. I'd taken him for a run first thing this morning before court, but he was long overdue for another walk.

I glanced over to see Cady leaning against Rick's shoulder and him with his arm around her. They'd postponed their honeymoon to be at court every day—I had fookin' awesome friends. But I wished I didn't keep screwing things up for them; I just couldn't seem to help it.

My eyes were drawn to Gracie, and she was never far from my thoughts. At this moment, she was furiously scribbling notes and frowning, pausing only to push up her glasses when they slid down her nose. She was dressed in a pair of my old sweatpants and an NYU t-shirt, having changed out of her power suit as soon as we'd all arrived home. Her hair was pulled back in a no-nonsense ponytail which I found sexy as fook, but that frown was now permanently etched between her tired eyes.

I stroked Tap absentmindedly while Zeus snored loudly on the sofa. I couldn't help smiling at the racket he made. My dogs had always been there for me during my darkest hours, and now was no exception. If you've never been comforted by a warm ball of fur curled up on your lap, or a heavy furry head resting on your knee, trust me, you're missing out on one of the greatest sources of comfort since the first wolf decided that bunking down with a well-fed human seemed like a smart move.

But I was worried about Gracie. She looked worn-out, and worse than that, I could tell that she hadn't been eating, and that was a punch in the gut. I'd done that to her, and I knew better than most people that once someone who suffered from anorexia stopped eating, it could become a dangerous habit and hard to re-start a healthy relationship with food again.

Determined that she wouldn't go any longer without something nutritious, I pulled up the website for my favorite vegan restaurant on my phone and ordered pretty much everything on the menu. I'd make sure Gracie ate even if there wasn't anything else I could do to help her.

Tomorrow, she was calling Greg Pinter, the Central Park Zoo Director, to be a witness. She'd already warned me that Barclay would be yelling, 'objection' and 'relevance', leaping up and down like a kid who'd dropped a turd in his pants. I didn't dislike many people because it's a waste of energy, but that smug bastard had definitely made it onto my shortlist.

The food arrived in a mountain of steaming boxes and spicy aromas that made my mouth water before they even reached the coffee table. The dogs all looked hopefully at Cady and Rick as they started unpacking the food immediately, and I walked to the breakfast bar, taking the opportunity to massage Grace's shoulders.

She moaned softly and my Johnny-cum-lately stood up and paid attention. I shrugged. He was lonely and lacking the touch of a good woman. Well, he had the choice of my left hand or my right hand until Gracie decided to make an honest man of me. I hoped it wouldn't be too long. Could I die from blue balls? Or maybe the question I should be asking was: Could I get married in prison?

"Oh, that feels wonderful," she sighed.

"You've got knots in there like a brickie's biceps," I murmured, pushing my thumbs into the tight muscles at the base of her neck.

"I'm not sure what that means but don't stop."

I kneaded those tight muscles until Cady and Rick had unpacked all the food, and Grace was soft and relaxed, leaning backwards against my chest.

I kissed her cheek.

"Grub's up! Time to eat."

Her muscles went rigid again, and she shook her head while grabbing her notebook and pen.

"No, I have to work."

At which point, I didn't bother arguing, but picked her up bodily and carried her into the living room, chucking her on the sofa and narrowly missing Zeus whose wounded eyes haunted me as I apologized to him.

"Vincent! What the hell?" Grace shrieked, as she untangled herself from a pile of dog blankets.

"You have to eat, Gracie," I said gently. "You need protein and carbs and just some fookin' food. I don't want me lawyer fainting on the floor."

She grumbled a bit but I ignored her while I put tiny portions of a little of everything on her plate. I knew from experience that anorexics can't stand to stare at a full plate of food—it has to look manageable.

We all tucked in while Rick inhaled his food, and Cady looked pretty enthusiastic, too. Gracie picked at hers but I didn't comment because at least she was eating. I tried not to watch her either, because that can cause performance anxiety in anorexics, and I didn't want her to think I was judging what she ate (or didn't eat). I wouldn't let food be a battleground.

"I need to make the jury aware that Pinter wanted to recruit you as the zoo's animal advocate," she said, making a note with one hand as she pushed food around with the other. She glanced up. "He still wants to, right?"

"Yeah, don't worry," I said. "He thinks I'm the dog's bollocks." I paused as she gaped at me. "He thinks I'm the mustard, the sliced bread in the supermarket, the sparkle in a tart's vajazzle."

"Riiiight," she said slowly. "Vincent, promise me you won't mention a dog's, um, bollocks anywhere in front of the judge or jury."

"Oh, gotcha," I grinned at her. "Be Saint Vin. Yup, I can do that."

My grin became wider as she shook her head. But if I was being honest with myself, I wondered what tomorrow would bring.

And I'd never tell Gracie, but I was worried, too.

CHAPTER TWENTY-SEVEN

GRACE

"It's not going well, is it?" Vince said quietly, not looking up as he stroked Tap.

Understatement. Day three of the trial had been a disaster.

Barclay had yelled 'objection' and 'relevance' so frequently during my questioning of Zoo Director Greg Pinter, that my planned narrative had lacked coherence, and the jury became confused and bored. I had just about managed to get across the two important facts: that Vince had been offered a role (unpaid) as the animals' advocate, and that he'd returned Jabari to the zoo.

Barclay had been quick to point out that Vince hadn't yet accepted the advocacy role, and dismissed the second point as 'a cheap publicity stunt'. I wished he could have seen the way Vince had been with Jabari at Cady and Rick's wedding.

I could tell that Vince had been furious, but all credit to him, he kept his peace in the courtroom just like he'd promised me.

Cady had gone home in a towering rage, swearing to turn her radio show into a 'free Vince' show, if the worst happened. I wasn't sure if I was supposed to thank her for her support for Vince or suck up the knowledge that she thought I was going to lose the case.

I watched Vince stroking Tap, with Zeus asleep next to him and Tyson laying on his feet, drawing comfort from his dogs

"No," I admitted with a soft sigh. "It's not going well."

He nodded, but didn't look up.

"If I don't make it home from court tomorrow, you'll take care of me dogs, won't you, Gracie?"

He looked so sad and defeated, and I felt like the worst lawyer in the history of the world, the worst friend, the worst almost-girlfriend ever.

He raised his head, meeting my eyes, then gave a wry smile and squeezed my hand, not an ounce of blame in his deep blue gaze.

We sat hand in hand as tears gathered in my eyes.

It was just plain wrong that this amazing human being, this crazy, kind, generous man could be facing prison. It was *wrong!* It wasn't justice, even if it was the law. How could someone so sweet and genuine end up behind bars? Someone who only wanted to do good? A man that others had named the Canine Crusader?

How could he...

Wait...

WAIT!

Just wait a doggone minute! I was having an idea...

No, not an idea, a genuine epiphany ... a revelation—not the kind with choirs of angels and baby cherubs shooting me with arrows of love—but an honest-to-goodness belief that we could still win this case.

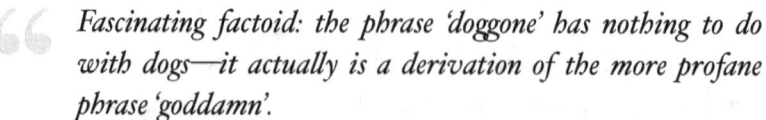

Fascinating factoid: the phrase 'doggone' has nothing to do with dogs—it actually is a derivation of the more profane phrase 'goddamn'.

"No!" I yelped, shooting up from the sofa and pacing the room.

"No?" Vince stared as his furry trio watched me with worried eyes. "You won't look after me dogs?"

"No!" I laughed out loud. "No, I won't look after them because *you're* going to look after them!"

"I am?"

"You are!"

"I am!" he yelled, standing up with Tap under one arm and Zeus under the other as Tyson barked with surprise and joy.

For several minutes it was adorable mayhem with Vince chasing the dogs, catching them and kissing them, and receiving a thousand licks in the process, while I jumped up and down on the sofa, yelling like a Banshee, yelling like we'd already won.

Vince lifted me off the sofa, whirled me around and planted a firm kiss on my lips that turned soft and sweet and far too sensual.

"Put me down," I said in a muffled voice, and he obligingly dropped me back onto the sofa, laughing as I bounced.

Then his beaming smile slipped slightly. "So, eh, a minute ago you thought we were going to lose, and now you think we're going to win?" he asked carefully. "I know I'm not the sharpest mallet in the kitchen drawer, but how's that work?"

"I know how we're going to win," I grinned at him. "I have a secret weapon!"

"You do?"

"I do."

"Fookin' fab!" he grinned at me, while I continued to laugh like a lunatic. "Okay, are you going to tell me what it is?"

"You," I said with a wide smile.

"Me, what?" he asked, a puzzled frown marring his handsome face.

"You!" I laughed. "You're my secret weapon! I've been doing this trial all wrong! I've told you to behave, be quiet, be a sensible and sober citizen. It's all wrong!"

"Hang on a minute, being sensible and sober ain't cutting the French mustard?"

"No! Because you're *not* sensible and sober! You're the kind of ... of ... adorable tosser ... who breaks into animal shelters to save dogs from being euthanized! You're the kind of hero who donates half a million dollars to help re-home dogs across the whole state of New York! You're the giant jerk who breaks into Central Park Zoo to help an elderly lion find his way home! You're completely crazy, and half of Manhattan is in love with the Canine Crusader!"

"Does that include you?" he asked with a hopeful grin.

"I refuse to answer that on the grounds that I could incriminate myself," I said primly. "I'm pleading the Fifth. But ask me next week."

"You can bet your bra and knickers on that!" he smirked. "So, what's the big plan to win the case?"

I took a deep breath. "Be yourself."

He blinked, a look of confusion that was completely adorable. "Be meself?"

"Yes! Be your own wonderful, crazy self in court. Let the jurors see the real Vincent Azzo, the real Canine Crusader. Let them see your passion; let them see the man who puts his own freedom on the line to ensure that unwanted dogs, scrapheap dogs, are wanted by *him*. Show them the real you, Vince."

"Are you sure?"

"One hundred per cent."

He scratched his head, his smile starting slow and growing bigger. "Be meself. I can do that," he grinned. "I can definitely do that!"

"And wear your Canine Crusader suit."

"Really?"

"Truly."

"With the cape?"

"Yep."

"And the tail?"

"Definitely."

"And the floppy ears?"

"Heck, yeah!"

Then he swept me into his arms and we kissed passionately, happily, lovingly, while the dogs barked their approval.

CHAPTER TWENTY-EIGHT

VINCE

"Are you completely crazy?!" shrieked Cady. "Are you certifiably nuts? Maybe the stress of the case has gotten to you at last. Or maybe alien bodysnatchers have taken over your mind!"

She grabbed Grace's shoulders and shook her.

Grace laughed and turned to smile at me. "I think Vince looks wonderful."

I stood tall, glowing with pride in my Canine Crusader costume of gold Lycra body suit with my logo on the chest, the long green and red cape that flowed behind me, and a furry tail that peeked out below the cape. I wasn't wearing the hood right now, but I had a thing for those floppy dog ears. So did Gracie, just sayin'.

"Do you *want* him to go to jail?" Cady cried, her hands still clamped on Grace's shoulders, still shaking her until Rick peeled her off.

"Of course not," Grace snapped, her eyes flashing. "But so far the jury have only heard words, so much hot air from the witnesses, from me, and from Barclay—I need them to *see* Vince; they have to understand that he's not like the rest of us," and she swept her hand in front of me the way P.T. Barnum introduced a new elephant-on-a-bicycle act.

"Yeah, I'm unique," I grinned. "They broke the mold when they made me."

"I always wondered if the mold was broken before they made you," Rick mumbled in the background.

"Oh, man! And what the freakin' hell did you do to your hair?" Cady wailed.

I glanced in the mirror at the tufts of hair left on my bald head that showed two interlocking letter 'C's and a paw print, my Canine Crusader logo.

"Cool, innit?"

"I helped," Gracie said proudly. "The paw print was the trickiest part."

"But, why?" Cady groaned.

"I told him to be himself and he wanted to have his head shaved with the logo, so..." Grace shrugged.

"But, why are you listening to Vince?" Cady groaned even louder. "He's a giant jerk! He's a knob-head idiot! No offense."

"None taken," I laughed.

"Exactly," Grace said calmly. "I've been trying to portray Vince as a sane and sober citizen when in fact he's adorably nuts. So far, it's just been another case for the judge and jury—they need to see who Vincent really is."

Rick scratched his beard. "Could work."

"Or Vince could end up going to jail!" Cady yelled.

"Aw, I didn't know you cared," I teased.

"Not that much, jerkoff," she growled. "But Grace is my best friend and I care about *her*. She'll be devastated if she loses."

Grace took her hand. "Thank you for saying 'if'; I love you too, hon. Now, we need a favor. Who's sitting in for you on your radio show this week?"

"Dude named Ragin' Rob. He's pretty good."

"Can you gatecrash his show for ten minutes before court this morning?"

Cady perked up. "I sure can," she said, her eyes gleaming.

"Great! Talk up the case. I want as many Canine Crusader fans as possible outside the Supreme Court. Use your contacts to get TV and press there, too."

Cady barely waited to hear the end of Grace's sentence before she was ordering an Uber to take her to the radio station.

"Vince, get on social media and put a call out for your fans to come to the Supreme Court—banners and placards preferred. If they can't be there in person, I want them tweeting and posting, using the hashtag #Justice4CanineCrusader."

"On it!" I grinned, grabbing my phone and sending out an SOS to my 500,000 followers.

"Rick, you have some high profile gym members, would you send out an email to them asking for their support?"

Rick nodded and pulled out his phone, concentrating on typing.

"What have I forgotten?" Grace muttered to herself, peering at her notes.

"You forgot to kiss me," I whispered in her ear, making her jump.

"Later!" she laughed.

"Now," I insisted.

I won that argument. I knew there wouldn't be many that I won with my sexy Counselor, but today was a good day, I could feel it in me water.

By the time we arrived at the Supreme Court, I knew that my fans had come through for me. Not only were they out in their thousands, but a large number had come wearing doggie-style onesies, and at least fifty were wearing their own Canine Crusader costumes (which I'd been retailing online for $74.29 including tail, ears, cape and delivery).

But that wasn't the best part—many had brought their beautiful mutts with them: big, small, hairy, smooth-coated, rough-coated, young, old and all amazing in their own special way, giving love to their hoomans as they milled around the entrance to the Supreme Court, held back by a thin blue line of two startled-looking police officers and a roll of incident tape. As we watched, a second patrol car screeched to a halt with four more officers leaping out to help with crowd control as my followers surged forwards.

"This is your moment, Vince," Gracie said, nudging me gently. "Go meet your adoring fans."

I shrugged humbly and grinned at her. "They're just dog lovers, like me."

The Uber driver was shaking his head.

"I cain't get through, man. There's some crazy shit going on out there. Those your people?"

I nodded happily. "Yup, they're my tribe."

As soon as I climbed out of the car, the chants grew louder and the noise was incredible as hundreds of dogs all started barking at the same time. I threw back my head and howled like a wolf, laughing like fook as a thousand of my followers did the same.

The TV presenters on the news crews were trying to speak to camera but had to give up and just film the fookin' fabulous mayhem that was happening as I moved through the crowd, shaking hands, shaking paws, stroking furry friends, and giving out hundreds of dog biscuits until my treat bag was empty.

"Sorry, buddy," I said to a pit bull who smiled and showed me all his teeth.

I gave him a pat instead, and only left when Gracie grabbed my arm and tapped her wrist watch.

I climbed the steps to the Supreme Court and turned to face my fans.

"No walls for four paws!" I shouted.

I listened, awestruck, as the words were yelled back by the crowd, and I punched the air in triumph. I may not be good at much, but I recognized fellow animal lovers when I saw them.

A microphone was thrust in my face as a reporter with a bad quiff pushed his way through the crowd.

"Vince Azzo, the Canine Crusader, are you worried about the possibility that you'll go to prison today? Do you have anything to say to your fans?"

I nodded and grinned. "I'm not worried about prison because this is America, land of the free, and although it's been an epic struggle between the forces of darkness and true justice, I know that the jury will make the right decision. No dog deserves to be put in prison—they all deserve to have a home—and every animal lover knows I did the right thing. And besides," I smiled, winking at Grace, "This is me lawyer, Gracie Cooper, and when we win this case, she's promised to be me girlfriend, too."

The crowd roared, and a thousand wolf howls echoed through the Manhattan morning.

Gracie's cheeks were pink and she had the biggest smile on her face.

"Couldn't have gone better," she said, squeezing my arm. "Now let's go and crush this case under the heel of justice!"

"Fook, you're hot when you go all lawyer on me!"

Gracie gave me a sly smile. "I'll take that under advisement," and she winked.

I couldn't get over the change in her from 24 hours ago. Yesterday, she'd been down and defeated, but now she was coming back fighting. For me. It had been a long time since anyone had fought that hard for Vince Azzo.

When I walked into the courtroom, my supporters in the audience cheered, and the press were busy making notes. The bailiff looked worried and spoke to the two security guards on the door.

I took my seat next to Gracie and pulled up my hood, shaking my head so my ears flopped around my face, causing people around us to laugh.

Except son of Satan, Randolph Barclay, who had a face like a smacked bottom. As usual.

Gracie held back a grin as the court was ordered to rise for the arrival of Judge Herschel.

As soon as the judge saw me, her eyes narrowed and her lips thinned. She looked like the kind of woman who would give Barclay a smacked bottom and tell him he liked it, too.

"Counsel, please approach the bench," she barked.

Grace strode forward confidently. "Your Honor?"

"Give me one good reason why I shouldn't charge the defendant with contempt of court. Be careful with your answer, Ms. Cooper, because I'm also considering charging *you* with contempt of court!"

I held my breath.

"Of course, your Honor," Grace said, her voice clear and self-assured. "I requested that Mr. Azzo be himself today—it's as simple as that. The jury hasn't truly seen how passionate he is about saving animals, they've only heard it second-hand; and I might add it wasn't Mr. Azzo who named himself 'the Canine Crusader' but his supporters. District Attorney Barclay is correct when he says that his case has much wider repercussions than the events of January 4th—much wider. It was never about trying to steal dogs but to rescue them. *This* is what Mr. Azzo does; *this* is who he is."

The judge stared down at Gracie for so long, I started sweating in the Lycra suit, my groin becoming very damp, and not in a fun way.

"Very well, Ms. Cooper," the judge said at last. "I'll allow the defendant to wear his costume, but I warn you, do *not* try my patience further."

"No, your Honor," said Gracie, crossing her fingers as she turned to walk back to her seat, a small smile of triumph on her face as Barclay turned the color of a pickled beet.

He probably whiffed like one, as well, vinegar-faced arsehole.

Gracie took a deep breath and pulled her shoulders back, her eyes glowing at me with belief.

"The defense calls Vincent Alexander Azzo."

She looked so hot in her dark gray pant suit and cerise blouse with a pussycat-bow that I was still staring at her when she cleared her throat and gave me a pointed look.

"Oh, right! That's me. Sorry, Gracie."

People in the audience chuckled, but the judge threw them a very frosty look. Blimey, had she found her knickers in the fridge this morning?

I strode to the witness stand, giving a quick twirl of my cape on the way, took the oath, then lowered my hood so I could hear better.

"The defendant would like to plead 'not guilty' on the grounds of inhumanity," Gracie said loudly.

"The defendant has already pleaded, and surely, you mean 'insanity', Ms. Cooper?" Judge Herschel asked.

"Definitely debatable, but not today, your Honor," Gracie smiled. "He is not guilty on the grounds of inhumanity because the way animals are treated is not humane."

"Objection!" yelped Barclay. "That's not a real plea! She's grandstanding!"

"Sustained," said the judge, looking grim. "Ask your first question, Ms. Cooper."

"Of course, your Honor." Grace turned to me. "Mr. Azzo, in your own words, please tell the ladies and gentlemen of the jury what happened the night of January 4th."

"Well, I'd been polishing me knob, your Honor," I began confidently.

"Excuse me?" Judge Herschel interrupted.

I was going to say it again, but Gracie jumped in first.

"Ah, um, he'd been doing some housework, hadn't you, Mr Azzo?," she said pointedly. "Before going out for dinner

Right. Don't mention my Tinder date!

"Leading the witness," Barclay spoke sullenly.

"Overruled. Please continue, Mr. Azzo."

"Right! So, after I'd, um, done me housework, I went out to meet a friend and then go for dinner. I left Roxy's hotel at 9pm and asked Alf, the doorman, if he knew of any good vegan restaurants nearby. He tipped me the wink and I gave him a score so..."

"Mr. Azzo is British, as the court will know by now," Gracie said with an artificial laugh. "I believe Mr. Azzo is saying that he was given the information required and tipped the doorman twenty dollars."

"Objection!" Barclay whined. "He's not even speaking English!"

"He's speaking what they speak in England," Gracie said coolly, "which I believe is English. I'm merely interpreting a few colloquialisms for the benefit of the court, but I can desist."

"Please continue," Judge Herschel sighed.

"Right! So I was on my way to this Thai vegan place when I heard dogs crying. Not just barking or howling, but really crying like their little hearts were breaking. It was the most terrible sound," I said, choking on the words as I remembered that night. "I thought one of them must be hurt, but when I got closer, I realized the crying wasn't coming from a street dog but from an animal shelter."

"Objection!" Barclay snapped. "Dogs can't cry."

"Were you bitten on your bony arse as a kid?" I snapped back. "Dogs cry. It's a sound that if you ever hear it, you'll never forget."

"Overruled," Judge Herschel said again.

"I rang the doorbell and knocked loud enough to wake the dead," I continued, "but nobody came. Blimey! What kind of animal shelter doesn't have a night nurse in case one of the beasties gets sick? So, I, um, climbed over the wall—which was easy, crappy security—then kept pounding on the office door and it, um, gave way. I nearly fell face first. Flimsy locks. Very unsafe." I cleared my throat at the way I'd stretched the truth, knowing full well that I'd climbed over a nine-foot wall then booted open the inner door.

"There were 11 adult dogs in cages, and another cage that held six puppies with no mum. They looked hungry and they were trying to get out of their cage to reach me. I thought I might be able to find them some food."

"Objection!" Barclay yelled. "Mr. Azzo's fingerprints weren't found on the dogs' bags of food, but on the door handles and those of the animals' cages. The puppies were found about his person—clearly he was intending to steal them."

Grace stood up.

"Objection, your Honor! District Attorney Barclay is stopping the witness from making his statement—and the defendant wasn't trying to steal the dogs, just cuddle them. He's a great dog-lover and has three rescue dogs of his own. He felt sorry for them, all alone, in the dark, surrounded by other strange dogs and..."

"Yes, thank you, Counselor. I get the picture," Judge Herschel said acidly. "Please return to your seats, Counselors, both of you. I wish to hear what Mr. Azzo has to say." Then she muttered to herself so only I could hear her, "This should be entertaining."

"Right, so there was no one there to feed the puppies. They're like babies—they need milk every few hours—I didn't think that was right. And then three of the adult dogs were scheduled to be euthanized, put down by lethal injection. That's murder! They were all healthy, friendly as foo—, and I couldn't stand by and let that happen. All me own dogs are rescue dogs, me Lud, I mean Judge Hershey..."

"It's Judge Herschel, not Hershey!"

I grinned at her. "Right, right! 'Cause you're sweet enough already."

CHAPTER TWENTY-NINE

GRACE

Did he really just say that? Oh my God, he did!

Vince had named the judge after one of Cady's favorite chocolate brands then called the judge 'sweet'.

> *Fascinating factoid: Milton S. Hershey founded his famous chocolate company in 1894. It's one of the biggest chocolate manufacturers in the world.*

I gulped. Oh well, I had told him to be himself.

Judge Herschel looked Vince up and down as he continued to grin at her.

"I'll pretend you didn't say that, Mr. Azzo," she intoned as people in the audience sniggered behind their hands, and I noticed that several of the jurors were hiding smiles. Then the judge's voice dropped to a mutter that only the defense table could hear, "But it'll definitely be going in my autobiography."

She liked him! The judge was being won over by Vince's unique and peculiar charms.

I'd taken a huge gamble telling Vince to be himself, but I'd needed to do something to shake up the trial because dry and dusty evidence wasn't cutting the French mustard, as Vince would say.

It seemed like the gamble was paying off, although I couldn't count my penguins before they'd hatched just yet. *Oh my God! I was starting to talk like Vince, too!*

"Thank you, Mr. Azzo," I said, restarting my questioning. "And then what happened?"

"The police arrived and carted me off to the clink, and that's where you came and saved me bacon! Vegan bacon, that is."

"And the following day, did you re-visit the animal shelter?"

"Yep."

"Why was that?"

"I wanted to see how the puppies were. And if they were still planning to euthanize those three dogs, I was going to adopt them."

"Even though you already have three rescue dogs of your own?" I pressed.

"Yeah, definitely." Vince's face was serious. "I couldn't allow those dogs to be murdered. It's not right, killing healthy dogs. Aren't we supposed to be the civilized ones?"

I left his words hanging in the air before I asked my next question.

"I see," I said, sending a look to the jurors that was laden with significance. "So you returned to adopt the three most desperate dogs, but what did you find when you arrived at the shelter?"

Vince grinned. "They'd already been adopted! Every single one of them. Every dog in the shelter! It was foo— freakin' fab! There was a crowd out front, and when they saw me, they started calling me the Canine Crusader! It was well epic."

I smiled at the jurors. "The Canine Crusader? And why do you think they chose that title for you?"

Vince shrugged. "Because I was trying to save dogs. I dunno really; I just thought it was cool."

"Yes, very cool," I said with a dry smile. "And you say that all the dogs had suddenly been adopted, even the ones scheduled for euthanasia? Why do you think that was?"

"Uh, well, the shelter's director, Benson something, he said that word had got out about what I'd done and that they'd been getting calls all morning from people wanting to adopt dogs. He said all the shelters in the city were emptying faster than a fart in a vegan restaurant! It was fantastic!"

"Let me clarify," I said, slowly and clearly, while trying not to laugh. "Mr. Luft, the director of Barkalaureate Animal Shelter said that *you* were responsible for *all* of the dogs being legally rehomed? Not just in his shelter, but across the whole of New York City?"

"Yes," Vince said, pure joy shining in his eyes. "He said it was because of me."

"So, you were happy with that state of affairs?"

"Well, bloomin' happy with that part, yeah. I was happy that all the dogs had got homes, but Benson said they were skint—none of the shelters had any money: they'd got no money to make the upgrades for the shelter, and sweet FA for marketing or fundraising. Which means they can't afford to publicize when there are dogs needing a new home. That's when I came up with the idea of the Canine Crusader dog fashion show fundraiser. We ended up raising over half a million dollars, and it all went to shelters across the city. Foo— freakin' fab!"

"Did you make any money personally from this fundraiser, Mr. Azzo?"

"No, and everyone involved gave their time for free. Uh, but I sell S&M dog-inspired leisure wear on my Instagram. Does that count?"

"No," I said hastily. "Defense rests, your Honor."

Barclay rose with a sour look on his face.

"What a fascinating fairytale, Mr. Azzo, almost believable in places."

"It definitely had a happy ever after ending," Vince agreed, and several people chuckled quietly.

"It seems an extraordinary coincidence that you decided to fundraise for the shelter only *after* being arrested for burglary and larceny, only *after* needing some positive publicity to rehabilitate your image."

"Not really," Vince said calmly. "I'd only been in New York City for a few weeks—I didn't know that the shelters had money problems. I've done fundraising for animal shelters in other places I've lived. What I don't get is why no one else did anything about it in New York before."

Barclay dismissed the answer with a sneer. "How noble. And what did you intend to do with six puppies and 11 adult dogs that you'd released from their cages?"

Vince looked puzzled. "Take 'em home."

"All of them?"

"Well, yeah! No man or dog left behind, right?"

"And what were you planning to do with them once you got them home?" he asked.

"Feed 'em, cuddle 'em, and then find them their forever homes."

"And why did you think you were equipped to do that when the shelter had been unable to?" he pressed. "Surely you intended to sell them?"

Vince shrugged. "Nope. All me friends are dog lovers—I'm good at publicity and the shelter doesn't have any budget for marketing. I'd have found them homes."

"You certainly are good at publicity," Barclay said snidely. "Self-serving publicity, one might say."

"Objection!" I snapped, jumping up.

"Sustained," intoned the judge.

"And I suppose you would have accepted money for this re-homing service?" Barclay pressed on.

"No!" Vince snorted. "I wasn't going to *sell* them! I just wanted them to find families to love them."

"How noble."

"You said that before—I'm deducting points for repetition, mate—but loving a dog isn't noble, and it isn't a one-way street because they return that love tenfold and..."

"Thank you, Mr. Azzo."

"You're welcome, but dogs love unconditionally. And I can talk to them."

"Excuse me?" said Barclay, raising his eyebrows.

"Yeah, I can talk to animals. Like Dr. Doolittle."

"You ... have conversations with animals?"

Barclay looked like he couldn't believe his luck, and I wasn't sure how this would play out. But I'd told Vince to be himself...

"Yeah. I'm an animal whisperer."

"Do the dogs tell you their feelings?" Barclay jeered.

"Of course," Vince scoffed. "It's not hard to know what they're feeling when you listen. But if you're asking me if they help with the crossword, I'm more of a bingo man."

The audience exploded with laughter, and some of the jurors were chuckling.

Even Barclay had to turn away from the jury to hide a smile.

"Did you know that vigilantes are copying your actions across the whole state, causing damage and mayhem, egged on by *you* and your inappropriate social media comments?" he pretended to huff as if he was personally affronted.

"They're my people," said Vince at the same time I leaped to my feet yelling, "Objection!" and trying to drown out Vince's comment.

"Overruled," said Judge Herschel. "I'd like to hear the answer to this question, but be careful, Counselor."

"Mr. Azzo," Barclay intoned, "did you know that vigilantes have been copying you?"

"I've become aware that other dog lovers are working to save dogs in shelters," Vince said with a shrug. "No walls for four paws!" he shouted suddenly making me jump, then did his iconic wolf howl, and several people in the audience copied him. "Free Milk-Bones for every dog!"

Judge Herschel banged her gavel several times. "Order! Order! Bailiff, anymore outbursts like that and I'll clear the public area. And you, Mr. Azzo, are wearing my patience very thin. No more antics!"

"I'll try, Me Lud, but sometimes I just open me mouth to change feet. Ask Gracie, she'll tell you."

This time, I was the one trying not to laugh, but Judge Herschel banged her gavel for silence again. Vince winked at her, and gave me a look so scorching that I thought I'd melt.

"Court will recess one hour for lunch," the judge said, somewhat wearily, rubbing her forehead.

Vince had probably given her a headache. I used to feel like that.

I sat with Vince, Rick and Cady in a small café near the Supreme Court. We'd had to use a back entrance to avoid Vince's fans, and I'd insisted that he cover his costume with sweatpants and a shirt, no floppy ears allowed, no matter how cute.

I watched as he munched through a PBJ sandwich.

"Weird combination that you Americans have invented if I'm being honest," he frowned around a mouthful, "but I'm getting quite a taste for it."

Cady had ordered half a dozen apple and blueberry blintzes, offering them around, keeping two for herself.

"I'm stressed," she mumbled between bites. "I eat when I'm stressed."

"I wish I could," I sighed, nibbling on a banana that seemed to take forever to eat.

"Don't matter," Vince said, polishing off the last bite of sandwich and brushing the crumbs from his Lycra suit while he reached for a fruit blintze, "I'm taking you for a celebratory dinner tonight." He paused. "Aren't I?"

"It's going better today," I admitted, "but it's not a done deal. Barclay is no fool, so don't underestimate him. He's mauled more than few lawyers in his closing statement."

Vince stared at me, then leaned forward. "Say that again."

"About Barclay? I'm just saying that he..."

"No, the other part. It's given me an idea."

And then Vince told me his idea and I felt all the blood drain from my body.

"Vince, no!" I whispered, utterly horrified. "Even for you, that's crazy! It's dangerous! Cady, Rick, back me up on this!"

"Yeah, completely certifiable," Cady coughed, brandishing a blintze at Vince. "No way you can do that!"

We all turned to stare at Rick, the quiet man who weighed his words.

"I know it sounds crazy," Rick said slowly, "but I've seen it in action, we all have. It's unbelievable ... it might be just what this case needs."

I shook my head, hardly able to take in that sensible, reliable Rick was agreeing with Vince.

"Yeah!" yelled Vince. "Let's do it!"

I shook my head again and dropped it into my hands.

"What's the worst that could happen?" Vince laughed happily.

"Other than lose the case and you go to jail? I could be disbarred!" I sighed. "Then again, I've never liked being a lawyer that much."

"You're kidding!" said Cady. "You've worked so hard! I thought you planned on making partner any time now?"

"Oh, I did. I have," I admitted. "They offered me a partnership with a salary increase and percentage of the profits. I turned them down and gave them my two weeks' notice."

"What?" Cady gasped. "Why would you do that? *When* did you do that?"

I shrugged and smiled at Vince. "Two days ago. I've decided to become an events planner instead. Someone told me that life's too short not to enjoy your job, and planning Canine Crusader fashion shows is much more fun than mergers and acquisitions. So, what the hell—I'm going to go with Vince's crazy idea."

Vince gave a happy howl and kissed me.

That sealed the deal.

CHAPTER THIRTY

Vince

Grace threw me a scathing look and I glared back at her, then she faced to the judge, her body stiff and hostile. She still turned me on, but I couldn't help that. It didn't make me a bad person just because I was fantasizing about her spanking me. Grace, not the judge, although she definitely looked she knew her way around a feather flogger.

"Your Honor, do I have permission to treat Mr. Azzo as a hostile witness?" Grace cracked out, her words like a whip.

"But he's your client, Ms. Cooper!" Judge Herschel coughed.

"Unfortunately, yes."

"Uh, well, this is rather unusual."

"He's an unusual client," Gracie spat.

Pencil-dick Barclay looked happier than a camel on hump day when he saw that me and Gracie were fighting.

"I wish to call new a witness," Grace declared coldly.

"Objection! I have no prior notice about anyone who wasn't on the witness list during discovery," the tadpole tosser griped.

"Counsel, approach the bench," Judge Herschel ordered. "Please explain yourself, Ms. Cooper."

Both lawyers strode up to stand in front of the judge, a mulish expression on Barclay's face; a furious one on Grace.

"Your Honor, we didn't know that we'd need this witness, but their appearance can provide testimony critical to the case, although I'm not sure he ... well, he might not ... um..."

She tried to appear uncertain and hesitant, and Barclay took the bait, looking very pleased with Grace's apparent lack of confidence in the new witness.

The judge peered over her glasses, her eyes narrowed. Either she had a squint, or she was pissed off.

"Very well, Ms. Cooper. As District Attorney Barclay has no objection, I will rule on this and allow your new witness."

Grace kept her face blank. "Thank you, your Honor. Defense calls Jabari."

I punched the air and waited expectantly.

The bailiff looked scared stiff (or probably scared limp) when a giant lion, me old pal Jabari, strolled into the courtroom, shaking his mane and yawning. The jurors gasped and scrambled over each other to get away from him, huddled together and squawking like ducks in a feather factory. The people in the audience made a right racket, yelling and shouting, and even Jabari heard them, despite being mostly deaf. I think he read my lips when I talked to him.

Barclay looked like he was about to wet himself, and even Grace seemed apprehensive despite having seen Jabari at Rick and Cady's wedding. Judge Herschel stared without speaking, her mouth moving but nothing coming out.

"It's alright," I said, nodding to Jabari's keeper, "you're an old mate, aren't you, Jabari?"

I knelt down and that ole lion buffeted me with his heavy head, knocking me on my arse, then yawned in my face and lay down next to me with a heavy sigh. I sat up, slinging my arm around his neck and whispering in his ear. That bit was mostly for show, but I knew

Jabari liked it because it tickled. He flicked his ear and closed his eyes, smiling blissfully, then rolled onto his back for a belly rub.

"I am the Canine Crusader," I announced, standing up and facing the jury who were suddenly silent. "I'm an animal whisperer and can talk to animals. That other lawyer," and I pointed at Barclay, "says I'm a liar and that helping Jabari home after he'd had a night on the town was a publicity stunt. Well, he's welcome to tell Jabari to go home. Come on, Burk-ly! Come and tell Jabari to clear off. No? The truth is that I was out on me best mate's stag night, um, bachelor party, when we saw Jabari wandering through Central Park all by himself, right, Rick?" I turned to Rick and he nodded, grinning widely while Cady seemed to have climbed into his lap. "He looked lost, so I decided to take him back to Central Park Zoo where he lives. But when I got there, the gates were locked. I had to climb over the wall to open the gates and let him back in. Saved him from being shot in the backside with a tranquilizer gun. The zoo people were grateful and so was Jabari, weren't you, mate?"

Then I did my Crocodile Dundee thang, and sent Jabari to sleep. Unfortunately it worked on half the jury, too.

"Remove that animal!" the judge said in a croaky voice. "Get it out of my courtroom! Now!"

I'd said what I needed to say, and the jury had seen me with Jabari—the ones who were still awake—so I didn't mind that the judge looked like she was about to do a Mount St. Helena.

"Right-o, Judge," I winked at her.

I prodded Jabari awake and held onto his mane while I walked him back to his keeper, then gave him a kiss, got a lick like being sandpapered in return, and promised to visit him soon. Jabari, not his keeper. Although he seemed like a nice bloke too, but I just shook his hand.

As soon as Jabari had gone, the courtroom erupted.

"Order! Order!" The judge slammed her gavel so hard, the hammer flew out of her hand and bopped Barclay on his conk.

"Nice shot, Judge!" I laughed as Barclay moaned loudly.

It would have been worth being sent to the cells for contempt of court. Unfortunately, it was Gracie who was sent down.

"Um, yeah, maybe not my best idea," I admitted, as she sat in the stinking concrete box with bars on the door, and one bog that didn't look it had seen a toilet cleaner since Prince sang *1999*.

Oddly, she didn't seem too mad, and just shrugged as I stood on the other side of the bars. It was nice of the bailiff to let me go and talk to her, and he said it was the most fun he'd ever had in court. It made everything that happened in the courtroom seem a bit more human somehow.

"I knew it was a risk," said Gracie, taking my hand through the bars and giving me a slow smile. "But it was worth it, if only to see the look on Barclay's face."

"Yeah, that's one ugly mug he's got," I said sagely.

Gracie stood up and hugged me as well as she could through the bars, her hair standing on end from the static caused by my Lycra outfit.

"He's just doing his job."

That made my hackles rise and I ground my teeth. "He's a pencil-dick!"

Gracie laughed. "If you say so. You were amazing with that lion, by the way. I didn't think ... well, I've never seen anything like it. I mean, I know you did at the wedding, but I'd had all that champagne so I wasn't sure if I'd imagined half of it. But you really are an animal whisperer! They'll do anything you say!"

"If I whisper to you, will it work?" I asked hopefully.

"Well," said Gracie carefully, "I'm not promising I'll roll on my back with my legs in the air ... but then again, I might."

I groaned at the image and got a full-on chubby that the Lycra couldn't hide or contain.

Grace's eyes bulged. "I think we'd better talk about something else," she said breathlessly.

"Um, yeah, we should," I said, shifting around uncomfortably, the bars pressed between us. "So what happens next?"

"Cady uses my credit card to pay my fine and we all go back to court to finish the case. Usually, the judge would keep me in overnight to encourage me to think on the error of my ways," Gracie smirked, "although I'm quite enjoying being the one who's a bad influence, but I'm sure that Judge Herschel wants to get this case over and done with today. I heard on the grapevine that she's got a vacation coming up and she doesn't want this to run over."

Thirty minutes later, we were back in court, and Gracie had to look sorry.

"I apologize to the court and jury and to you, your Honor," she said, sounding sincere. "I recognize that I behaved in an improper way. At the time, I believed it was the best way to demonstrate the defendant's expertise and special bond with animals. I realize that I caused distress, and that was not my intention."

"No more stunts, Counselor," Judge Herschel said firmly, "or you will be spending more than an hour in the cells for contempt of court. You may continue. Are you ready for your closing arguments?"

"Yes, your Honor."

"District Attorney Barclay?"

"Ready, your Honor."

So this was it—final roll of the dice, and Barclay went first.

"Ladies and gentlemen of the jury, you have a very clear case in front of you: the law is the law, not the law according to Vincent Azzo. He broke the law. This isn't a popularity contest."

"Just as well for you, mate," I interrupted with a grin, "because you'd lose, you mad muppet."

The judge pointed a finger at me and I mimed zipping my lips.

But it didn't count, because I'd crossed my fingers.

"He's not a hero," Barclay went on. "He's an out-of-control vigilante who has shown no remorse for his actions."

Yeah, well that part was probably true.

"He revels in his role as a rule-breaker."

Also true.

"He has no respect for the law."

Eh, that was going a bit far. It depended on which law.

Barclay blathered on, the boring fart, telling the jurors that I was an unsalvageable rebel, which I rather liked. I wondered how that would look on a t-shirt as a new Canine Crusader slogan.

Finally, he sat down with his arms crossed, as pleased as a pig in shit.

Then Gracie faced the jury, looking as serious as she was fookin' fabulous.

"Laws were created to serve justice; laws were created to serve the people, to protect the weakest and most vulnerable in our society. Vincent Azzo fights for justice for animals; he gives a voice to those who have none. He is loud and flashy and stands out in a crowd; he is also kind and thoughtful and a savior to unwanted, unloved, scrapheap animals in this city, across the whole state and beyond. He did what he thought was right; he fought for justice for dogs who would have been euthanized, dogs who, thanks to him, now have loving homes. Ladies and gentlemen of the jury, ask yourselves why we are here today: is it to follow the letter of the law, or is it to serve true justice? I ask you now to make the *just* decision for Vincent Azzo and for the animals he saves."

My throat burned. Is that how Gracie thought about me? Gracie. My Gracie.

Her eyes met mine and she didn't look away. I saw love. I saw so much love. And I knew then that there'd never be another woman for me but her. She held my heart.

My Gracie.

She sat down next to me, and up close, I could see the pulse beating rapidly in her neck, the drop of sweat at her temple, the tremor in her hands.

Then the judge spoke.

"Ladies and gentlemen of the jury, now that you have heard all of the evidence, and the arguments of counsel, it is my duty to give you the instructions of the court concerning the law which governs this case. It is your duty as jurors to follow the law as I state it to you, and to apply that law to the facts as you find them from the evidence presented in court. Regardless of any opinion you may have as to what the law is or ought to be, it would be a violation of your sworn duty to base a verdict upon any view of the law other than that given in the instructions of the court, just as it would also be a violation of your sworn duty, as judges of the facts, to base a verdict upon anything other than the evidence presented during the trial."

She took a deep breath and stared at the jurors purposefully, and I found my palms growing damp.

"You must consider all of the evidence. This does not mean, however, that you must accept all of the evidence as true or accurate. You are the sole judges of the credibility of each witness. The jury will now retire to consider their verdict." She banged her gavel and we all stood as she swept out of the courtroom, her face grave.

"Oh, shit," I said softly. "I'm going to jail."

"I'll start working on your appeal tonight," said Grace, and when I turned to face her, she was wiping a tear from her cheek.

I held her hand, squeezing gently when I really wanted to take her in my arms and stop her looking so sad, but I'd done enough damage in this courtroom, to her, to me, to our future. So I just held her hand, but the words I wanted to say tumbled out regardless.

"Uh, it's probably not the time, but I just wanted to say something."

She turned to look at me, her eyes glazed with sadness and tears.

"So, what I wanted to say is this: I love you, Gracie Cooper."

Her head shot up, shock on her face. Then she smiled through her tears.

"I love you, too."

CHAPTER THIRTY-ONE

GRACE

I'd fallen in love with Vincent Azzo, something I never would have believed possible when I first met him, something I found hard to believe even now. But I did. I loved every crazy part of him. I loved his strength and his softness, his humor and his pranks, the voice he gave to those who needed it, his belief that the world was a good place but could be even better. I loved his impulsiveness, his headlong assault on life; I loved his loyalty and his kindness. I loved the world according to Vince.

Cady interrupted the happy turmoil of my thoughts.

"Is it a good sign that the jury are taking so long to deliberate?" she asked, anxiously eating a lemon-glazed donut that Rick had bought for her.

> *Fascinating factoid: The longest U.S. jury deliberation took place in a 1992 California trial. The case had taken eleven years to get to trial, and the jury sat through six months of testimony. They then deliberated for four and a half months before reaching a verdict.*

"Yes, I think so. It suggests that they're finding it difficult to reach an agreement, which means at least some of the jury are on Vince's side. I hope."

I spoke quietly while Vince answered messages on his phone and put out new posts to his fans. I'd peeked outside the courthouse window and the crowd of his followers had increased. There was a greater police presence now, as well, and I could see at least half-a-dozen news crews, all waiting for the verdict. I wasn't generally a nail-chewer, but now seemed like a good time to start.

"So there's hope?" Cady asked quietly.

I smiled stiffly, my mouth arcing upwards with reluctance. "We're talking about Vince, king of the comebacks. Yes, there's always hope."

"You know we'll do anything for that crazy dude, right?" Cady whispered urgently. "I mean anything: you name it, you got it. You're my best friend, Grace, and what hurts you hurts me. I'd do anything to keep King Klutz out of jail. I'll do anything for you. Rick and I, *we'll* do anything for you and Vince."

"I know," I said, feeling the warmth of her love and support. "I know you will. You're an awesome best friend. Love you, Cady Callaghan. Or is it Cady Roberts now, you never said?"

"Meh, I've been Cady Callaghan my whole life; it would feel weird to change my name now. But I gotta say, I did get a kick out of the hotel staff saying 'Mrs. Roberts' on our wedding day."

I smiled a little sadly. That wonderful day had ended with news of the trial. Why was good news always chased by bad?

I was just about to have a wallow in self-pity when we were informed that the jury had reached a verdict.

"Here we go," I said, taking a deep breath and trying to look positive.

The four of us had a group hug, then Vince gave me a long, sweet kiss, before we hurried back to the courtroom.

Judge Herschel looked her usual severe self, and I wondered what she was thinking.

"Ladies and gentlemen of the jury, have you reached a decision?"

"We have, your Honor," said the foreman.

The judge nodded slowly, then turned to Vince.

"Will the defendant please rise."

Vince stood, his chin lifted, refusing to be beaten, even now. I stood next to him in silence.

"On the charge of burglary, how does the jury find the defendant?"

"Guilty, your Honor."

I heard Vince suck in a breath, while I stopped breathing altogether.

"On the charge of larceny, how does the jury find the defendant?"

"Not guilty, your Honor."

Not guilty! What did this mixed verdict mean for us?

Judge Herschel turned to face Vince.

"Vincent Alexander Azzo, you have been found guilty of burglary at the Barkalaureate Animal Shelter on the night of January 4th. This has been an unusual case with significant public interest. The court recognizes that you are passionate about animal welfare, but cannot condone breaking the law to support your beliefs. You have been found guilty by a jury of your peers. Ordinarily, there would be a pre-sentence report, however, after hearing testimony of the circumstances, it is the judgment of the court to move forward, and I therefore sentence you to eight weeks' community service, to be served at Barkalaureate, and a fine of $100. Court is dismissed."

Vince let out a loud whoop and scooped me up into a hug before kissing me full on the lips while Cady and Rick, and Vince's fans in the audience cheered loudly.

Barclay looked astonished, then irritated, then gave me a wry smile and a salute for Vince. He really wasn't a bad guy.

Judge Herschel stood to leave the courtroom, but Vince yelled out.

"Judge Hershey, will you marry us?"

Time stopped as I stared at Vince. I wasn't the only one staring; every man and woman in the courtroom had their eyes riveted on him.

The judge pinned him with a long, searching look.

"I'll remind you for the last time that it's Judge Herschel. And this is highly irregular, Mr Azzo." Then she swung her piercing gaze to me. "Do you *want* to marry this ... person, Counselor?"

"Course she does!" Vince interrupted with a laugh.

"I'm asking Ms. Cooper."

"She'll say yes."

"Ms. Cooper, please restrain your client."

"I haven't had much luck with that, your Honor," I said honestly.

Judge Herschel sighed. "You're very annoying, Mr. Azzo."

"In a cute way, right, Judge?"

"No, in an annoying way. Have you even asked your lawyer if she wishes to marry you? She seems like an intelligent woman so she might say no."

"Ah, good point," said Vince, dropping to one knee and opening his arms. "Gracie, babe, wanna marry me? Let's get hitched ... the ole ball and chain. Let's do it!"

"Is this a joke?" I asked feebly, struggling to find enough air in my lungs to speak.

"Ah come on," he grinned, his blue eyes twinkling. "I know you do really. Give a man a break and lower your standards. You're the love of me life. Marry me?"

"Okay," I said, as he walked forward on his knees and wrapped his arms around my hips, mushing his face into my stomach. "Stand up!" I hissed.

"I'm going to kiss you now," said Vince, squeezing my hips harder. "Fair warning, Gracie. After this, I'm never letting you go again. I'll even make you a matching Canine Crusader costume— you'd look fookin' hot in that!"

I laughed out loud. "Sure, why not? If I'm crazy enough to marry you, I guess I'm crazy enough to have my own Canine Crusader costume."

Vince stood up and turned to Judge Herschel. "Will you marry us now, Judge?"

"Very well, if that's what you both want. If you're sure, Counselor?" and she gave me a piercing look.

"I'm sure," I smiled, shaking my head at the bizarre turn of events.

Judge Herschel sighed heavily. "Vincent Alexander Azzo, do you take this woman Grace...?"

"Grace Beatrice Cooper," I whispered.

"Do you take this woman Grace Beatrice Cooper to be your lawful wedded wife, to have and to hold, in sickness and in health, so long as you both shall live?"

"Is the goat kidding around?"

"Say yes," I hissed.

"Yeah, yes! I do!" Vince said loudly.

"And do you, Grace Beatrice Cooper, take this man Vincent Alexander Azzo to be your lawful wedded husband, to have and to hold, in sickness and in health, so long as you both shall live?"

"I do!"

"By the authority vested in me by the State of New York, I now pronounce you husband and wife. You may kiss the bride. Again."

The courtroom exploded into cheers and applause, but all I could hear was the rushing of blood through my body as Vince kissed me and I kissed him, our mouths and bodies meeting and melding.

"Ahem," said Judge Herschel interrupting us, a smile on her normally severe face. "I do hope that I'll be able to forgo the pleasure of having you in my courtroom again, Mr. Azzo."

"Yeah, you bet, Judge!" Vince grinned at her. "I have faith that Gracie will keep me out of trouble."

Judge Herschel shook her head as she turned and walked back

to her chambers. "Even Our Lord Almighty hasn't seen fit to perform that miracle."

As Vince stood at the top of the steps to the Supreme Court, he punched the air and gave his trademark wolf howl. I had to cover my ears when a thousand people and dogs howled back at him.

"Justice has been done!" he shouted, his voice carrying to the crowd as a tangle of microphones bristled in front of him. "The Canine Crusader is walking out as a free man ... with a lifetime sentence to Gracie Cooper, me lawyer and now me wife!"

Howls filled the air like, almost deafening us, and Vince pulled me to his side, gripping my hand tightly.

"The fight goes on!" he yelled. "I'll carry on, I'll keep fighting for the rights of dogs, of all animals to have a home. Are you with me?"

"YES!" the crowd yelled back.

"Yee-ha!" Vince crowed. "I love America!"

Then Rick hustled us into a taxi and from there, we dropped by Tiffany's to buy our wedding rings, then stopped at the nearest bar to drink champagne with Cady and Rick, and then with more and more of Vince's fans who'd tracked us down—which wasn't hard, considering he was still wearing his gold Lycra costume and updating his Instagram every few minutes.

We celebrated life and liberty and the pursuit of happiness. We celebrated our love and our crazy, impulsive decision to get married. My parents were going to kill me for getting married without them being there, but I'd make it up to them. Vince was going to love Minnesota. So would Tap, Tyson and Zeus.

Our home would be full of life, full of love, and full of dogs.

When we finally headed back to Brooklyn Heights—Vince's home, my home, our home—we traveled in silence, an undercurrent of electricity sparking between us. We held hands and gazed out of the window, occasionally turning to look at each other and sharing secret smiles.

We were both tired and emotional and not entirely sober. At Vince's apartment, we entered as silently as possible, our quiet footsteps masked by Erik's rumbling snores. He'd offered to dog sit and had spent the day with the kids.

When we peeked into the living room, he was laying on the settee with Tyson sprawled across him, his heavy head resting on Erik's chest. Tap was curled up in the armchair and raised her liquid eyes to ours, and I swear she smiled. Zeus had taken himself off to bed and was curled up on Vince's pillow in the bedroom.

I coughed discreetly but it took Vince holding Erik's nose to wake him up.

He sat up yawning as we pretended we'd just walked in.

"Vincenzo! Miss Cooper! You home free! All happy people?"

"Yes, very good, thank you," I replied at the same time Vince said, "Fookin' awesome. We got hitched, too!"

Erik started to cry, slapping Vince on the back, and kissing my hand many times. All the dogs woke up and came charging in, demanding pats and strokes and furry kisses.

"You will need more Milk-Bones," Erik said sheepishly. "I buy them for you as wedding gift!"

Vince just grinned and saw him out to the waiting cab.

And then we were alone, with three furry family members, which was slightly unnerving as they watched us with interest.

"Uh, I'm not sure about the audience," I said as Vince approached me with a hot look in his eyes.

He turned to glance at the dogs. "Right, you lot! Time for a piss then bed. And don't ask for any more Milk-Bones because they're all gone."

And he let them out to do their business while I sat on Vince's bed feeling slightly more sober and a lot more nervous. It had been quite a while since I'd liked a guy enough to get to this stage.

When Vince came back in, he quickly carried all the dog beds into the living room.

"They're too young to watch live porn," he said with a grin.

Then he peeled off his bodysuit and dropped his briefs faster than a hot potato. I scooted right across the bed and over the other side.

"Wow! Um, that's a lot to bite off!"

Vince cringed and edged away with both hands covering his considerable manhood.

"Gracie! You wouldn't?!"

"What? Oh! I didn't mean it like that! Well, maybe just a little nibble."

"Don't tease," he whined, eyeing me warily.

"I have no intent to wound," I said, crossing myself and bringing a worried smile to Vince's face. "Although accidents do happen."

And then I jumped into his arms, knocking him backwards onto the bed.

"Mind the meat and veg, Mrs. Azzo," he said, spinning me onto my back.

Oh, my sweet man with his sweet words.

"I have every intention of taking *very* good care of your meat and veg," I smiled. "You've been found guilty of being completely adorable, Vincent Alexander Azzo, and it's a lifelong sentence."

EPILOGUE

VINCE

Grace was pissed off. Not the way I'd wanted to start our four-week trip. It had been bad enough leaving the kids with Rick and Cady for a month, but now my wife of 72 hours was glaring at me. Although to be fair, that was nothing new...

"Seriously, Vince? We have a film crew coming with us on our honeymoon?!"

She folded her arms which pushed out her sweet little tits. I grinned to myself. I'd been up close and personal with those last night. And the night before. And the night before that, as well as at lunchtime, after breakfast, before- during- and after our morning shower, and again when ... you get the picture.

Right now, she was staring at me with an expression that said I'd never get laid again. Then I glanced down at the simple gold band on the fourth finger of my left hand. Yep, she'd gone and married me, so she'd have to relent eventually. Besides, she was hot for my studliness. Smart woman.

"Yeah, well, it's like this. I got offered a load of cash."

"And?" she said frostily.

"And it means I can think about opening my own non-profit shelter when we get back. And it could be just the start! If the series is popular, the Canine Crusader could be going global!"

She shook her head, a reluctant smile fighting to get out.

"Fine, but the camera crew is *not* allowed in our hotel room."

"Um, yeah, no problem. Um, Gracie, we won't be staying in a hotel."

I grinned at her, but her cool expression wasn't encouraging.

"Why not? Did you rent a house?"

I shook my head.

"An apartment?"

"Nope."

"An RV?"

"Not exactly..."

"Vincent! Where the heck am I staying on my honeymoon?" Gracie yelped.

"It's more of a *money*moon," I quipped, then moved on quickly when she didn't smile back. "We'll be camping while we're on safari. In tents. Big tents. The best tents—with, um, zips ... er ... zippers and everything."

Gracie closed her eyes, then blinked a few times before her voice came out in a whisper.

"Showers?

"At the end of filming, yeah!"

"But ... but the film crew said they have a month-long shooting schedule?"

"Yeah! Innit fab?!"

"No showers for a month?" she said faintly, then smiled. "Bring it on."

"That's me girl!"

Grace

We stood by the Chobe River in northern Botswana as the

setting sun turned the water blood red, and the sky blazed orange and gold while we stared down at the herd of elephants, silent and awed as the massive animals sank their enormous feet into the dark, gluey mud of the riverbank.

The producer nudged Vince, reminding him that he had a job to do.

Vince walked over to our guide, Baruti, a gnarled old man with wiry white hair and a ready smile, dressed in his uniform of khaki shorts and shirt. He'd worked with the wild elephants in Botswana for over 40 years, and there was nothing he didn't know about these magnificent creatures.

He led Vince toward a female who was standing by herself, watching the two men and swishing her stubby tail.

"This is Nkechi," said Baruti. "Her name means 'loyal'. Her mother was killed by poachers when she was just a month old. I helped to hand-rear her until she was old enough to return to her herd. She is very friendly. She likes you. See? She is wagging her tail, just like a dog."

"That's a bloody big dog," Vince laughed. "Imagine cleaning up that shit!"

"We'll have to cut that bit," the cameraman mumbled, but the producer disagreed.

"TV gold," he said.

Vince and Baruti walked right up to the large female, and even after all this time and knowing he really was an animal whisperer, my nerves jangled as Vince ran his hand down the ridged skin of the four-ton animal.

Vince stroked her a few more times, then turned to do his piece to camera.

"Elephants love me, don't you, baby," he said to Nkechi, making me smile nervously. "I can talk to them. All animals understand me —we have a thing. How's it going, beautiful? You ready for your close up?"

I don't know why I should have been surprised, but Vince's TV show had been a huge hit as the weekly program was broadcast on the internet, and several hours of live footage streamed every week. Millions of people were watching *Azzo in Africa—Walking and Talking with Elephants*. He had more work offers and endorsements than he knew what to do with, and it quickly became clear that my idea of becoming an events planner would have to go on hold while I filled the role of his manager and sorted through the dozens of offers he was getting every day.

My crazy goof of a husband was becoming one of the most popular wildlife presenters since Sir David Attenborough and only just behind Bindi Irwin. Who would have thought it? But that was Vince's world, and he was great at it.

My heart was filled with love as I watched him. Vince had taught me so much: he'd taught me to plan less and enjoy life more, to value the sheer joy of taking what life threw at us, together. He'd taught me to open my heart, and he'd taught me to hope. Most of all, he'd taught me to seek the sunshine, to look for the positives, even when life seemed dark and dreary. He'd taught me that being happy was a choice we had to make every day, finding the smallest thing to smile about.

I'd smiled a lot on our safari, even managing to forget that the camera crew followed our every step.

The production company were already talking about a follow up series, *Azzo in the Arctic—Walking and Talking with Penguins*, which I greatly preferred to their original idea of walking and talking with polar bears, which would have been a lot more dangerous. Vince was even planning to get a Canine Crusader suit made in penguin colors.

Vince was smiling happily as he continued to stroke the enormous elephant.

"Me mate here, Baruti, has told me that many elephants mate for life, which is just like me and Gracie," Vince grinned. "But I might see if I can steal a kiss from Nkechi while Gracie is over there. Give us a kiss, Nkechi!"

The elephant ran her trunk lovingly over Vince's head, making him laugh as his eyes sparkled with happiness.

Then Nkechi sprayed a trunkful of water right over his head, and I swear she laughed as Vince howled like a wolf.

That's my guy, I thought to myself. Life will never be dull, not while Vince is in my world.

> *Fascinating Factoid: elephants purr like cats when they're happy. They also have a sense of humor.*

THE END

Swipe the page to read an extract about what happens next to our crazy couple in *The Baby Game*

EXTRACT FROM BOOK 3 IN THE GYM OR CHOCOLATE SERIES

THE BABY GAME

Best friends Rick Roberts and Vince Azzo have given up the single life and are happily married: Rick to radio host, Cady Callaghan; and Vince to event organizer and lawyer, Grace Cooper. But when both wives become pregnant within weeks of each other, are the guys up to the challenge of hormones on parade, Lamaze classes, and lots of shopping trips for two tiny humans who are months from making an appearance?

When the babies *are* born, all four adults have a steep learning curve, and when Cady wants a night off from mom-hood to celebrate her 40th birthday with her bff, Grace, the guys are left in charge.

After all, how hard can it be?

THE BABY GAME

The Lasses

The following conversation takes place at Katz's Deli, 205 E Houston Street, NYC

"There's something I've been meaning to tell you," said Grace, twisting her serviette into a tight knot.

"Ooh, a secret!" smiled Cady, her eyes lighting up. "I've got one for you, too. I would have said my secret is bigger, but you're the one who ran away to court and ended up married to Vince."

She'd expected Grace to laugh, but all her best friend could manage was a weak and watery smile.

"Oh, honey, I'm sorry! I'm being a terrible friend. I think it's my hormones—they're going a little crazy right now."

"Because you're pregnant," Grace sighed.

Cady's mouth dropped open. "How did you know? I mean, I was going to tell you today, but ... well, I got sidetracked. I've been wanting to tell you for ages, but there was so much going on, what with Vince getting arrested, the whole Canine Crusader thang, his court case, and then *pow!* You go and marry him. It never seemed like the right time."

Grace nodded. "I'm not mad at you, Cady. I guessed the night of Rick's bachelor party when you were so upset. It wasn't like you to..."

"...completely lose it in a loud, dramatic and very shouty way?"

Finally, Grace smiled. "Yes, all of that. I suspected then that hormones were the culprit. But like you say, it's been a crazy few months."

Cady laughed. "You can say that again! But I'm so glad that you know. I'm totally relying on you to organize my baby shower and ... honestly, Grace, I'm really excited about the baby but I'm kinda freaking out, too, ya know? It's such a massive responsibility, not to mention the whole unmentionable prospect of pushing a tiny human out through my vagina. I've got to keep the kid alive, sane and sober until he or she is at least 18. Thank God I'm married to Mr. Responsible."

She didn't notice that Grace winced when she said that.

"Bringing a baby into the world, into *this* world with terrorism, pandemics and politicians, I don't know if that's the right thing to do, but I already love him or her. It's weird."

"I know," Grace nodded fervently.

"I mean, Rick is so calm about everything. He's already started a list at *buybuy Baby*, and on the scratchpad by his desk, he's been doodling names for girls."

"You know that already?" Grace asked.

"No, we don't! That's exactly my point. He's so super organized, he's not leaving much for me to do, except have it, of course. *Oy vey!* I'm so excited! You'll be Aunty Gracie!" Her smile faltered. "And then there's Uncle Vince. But, ya know, I'm not leaving my kid alone with him till they've passed puberty—Vince, as well," and she laughed. "He'll probably put the baby in one of the dog beds by mistake, and I'll find the small pooch..."

"Zeus."

"Yeah, I'll find Zeus in the stroller! I mean, can you imagine? Uncle Vince! Oh, my God, what a disaster!"

Cady laughed again loudly, and it was several seconds before she realized that Grace wasn't laughing and that possibly, probably, she'd offended her best friend.

"Oh, wow, I'm sorry, Grace. I open my mouth these days and so much crap falls out. I know he's your husband and I do love him. I didn't mean all of that about Vince."

"Yes, you did," Grace said tiredly. "But it's okay—it's probably true."

Cady thought she ought to change the subject before her next trick was to swallow her other foot.

"So, what was it you wanted to tell me? You said you had some news, too?"

Grace looked up slowly and met Cady's eyes.

"I'm pregnant," she said. "Vince and I are having a baby."

The Lads

Meanwhile, two miles north in Rick's central Manhattan gym...

"Hey, guess what?" said Vince as lifted 250 pounds above his head.

Rick didn't answer until his friend had safely landed the huge dumbbell back on the floor with a thud.

"What?" he asked, economical as ever with his words.

"Me and Grace are pregnant! I knocked her up on our wedding night. I've got super sperm, me. She didn't stand a chance. The Canine Crusader's super sperm broke through the rubber and swam to freedom. The docs say she's due on Christmas Day. If it's a boy, I want to call him Jesus."

Rick stared at his friend, trying to take in the rapid flurry of his words. Then he blinked and slapped a grinning Vince on the shoulder.

"Congratulations, buddy! That's awesome. Especially 'cause the thing is that Cady and me..."

"I know, she's up the duff, too, right?" Vince said with a wink.

Rick frowned. "How did you know?"

"Well, Gracie guessed—we were just waiting for you to tell us. It's going to be epic! You and me with a pair of rugrats running around. When's Cady calving down?"

Rick cringed. "Don't ever say 'calving down' in front of Cady. In fact, don't ever say it in front of me. Or Grace, if you want to keep on living."

Vince laughed. It was hard to make him mad. The only thing that really wound him up was seeing mistreated animals.

"Yeah, whatever. Did the docs give you a due date?"

Rick smiled, a smile that told of a deep contentment, a happiness that filled every part of him.

"First of December," he said.

Vince held out his hand, and the two friends shook hands, grinning like loons, then pounding each other on the back.

"It's going to be such a rush being a dad," said Vince. "I can't wait."

"Me neither," said Rick, still smiling. "It's going to be an epic journey."

"Yeah, we'll have a laugh," said Vince. "You, me, our lasses and the baby game."

Read The Baby Game

REVIEWS

We love reviews! Other readers do, too, because it helps them decide that our book is as awesome as you say it is (we hope!). So please leave a review—it would be totally appreciated. Thank you!

MORE ABOUT STU REARDON & JANE HARVEY-BERRICK

Sometimes you meet people, and sometimes you meet people and they become friends. That's our story. From first contact at a book event in Edinburgh, then again in Dublin, we've gone on to travel to Rio de Janeiro, Paris, São Paolo, Lille, London and Denver with our books. We've written together, laughed together, and even done a sky dive together #teamdare

Stu is a great cook. Jane isn't. Jane has cooked for Stu and his fiancée, Emma; babysat their son Phoenix Rai and Rocket the French bulldog—there's trust.

VINCE'S ENGLISH-AMERICAN GLOSSARY

Arse – ass

Birds – women

Bloody hell – oh dear

Bog – slang word for a toilet

Bopped – hit (in this context; sometimes it means danced like a dork)

Brickie – brick layer/construction worker

Burk – idiot (when Vince calls the district attorney 'Burk-ly', he's being a bit cheeky!)

Cack handed -- clumsy

Char – tea, made with boiling water on tea leaves, steeped for five minutes, then milk added to taste. (Lemon is only acceptable with Earl Grey tea, just sayin'.)

Conk – nose

Dead sensitive – very sensitive

the Dog's Bollocks – very good

Doing me head in – giving me a headache

Feel it in me water – feel it deep inside, bone-deep

Fook, Fooker, Fookin' – a term of affection, in a northern (British) accent, or possibly a term of derision: context is all

Git – jerk

Grotty – dirty

Grub – food

Hen party – bachelorette party

Innit – isn't it

Keks – trousers, pants

Knob-head – jerk, idiot

Lad – boy

Lass – girl

Little bugs / beasties – dogs, animals that you like

Me Lud – My Lord, a term used in a British courtroom when speaking to a male judge

Mate – friend

Me – My

Naff – dumb, stupid

Nippy around the nethers – chilly around the groin area

Nowt – nothing

Nuff said – enough said

Played a blinder – done a good job (cricketing or rugby term)

Plonker – jerk (affectionate)

Polishing one's knob – having sex

Poxy – small or small and unpleasant

Shagged – slept with

Shite – shit

Shirty – irritable

Skint - broke, without money

Soppy – silly

Sorted – Job done

Snuffed it – died

Stag party – bachelor party

Tart – prostitute eg. 'the tart with a heart'

Tarted up – dressed nicely with makeup on; *or* dressed like a hooker – go figure!

Todger – penis

Tosser/wanker – jerk

Totty – an attractive woman

Twat – jerk

ACKNOWLEDGEMENTS

Huge thanks to **Tonya Bass Allen** and her boss **Gary Burbank**, Attorney at Law, for helping with legal questions—although we did play rather fast and loose with the laws and rules according to real life. Luckily, this is the world according to Vince, so the rules don't always count

Tonya was also editor-in-chief for this book.

Aiding and abetting, **Lara Herrera** was proofreader-in-chief.

Here, Lara and I are in a hugging sandwich with the very lovely Gergo Jonas.

Thanks to **Sharon Tomás** for jazzing up my website and lending me her name to Vince's arresting police officer, and to **Elisabetta Finotello** for Uncle Sal's Italian, as well as misappropriation of her surname.

ACKNOWLEDGEMENTS

And finally, thank you to **Rachel Williams** for advising on Rick and Cady's Interfaith wedding – we hope we didn't take too much artistic licence!

VINCENT AZZOPARDI

Against all the odds, Vince is a real person. Stu met him on a photoshoot in the US, then again when he and Jane travelled to Brazil. Much of what you've read about Vince in this book really happened: he really was an Armani catwalk model, he really does model a range of S&M underwear on his IG page, and his tooth really did fall out while he and Stu were sharing a room. It really was ice-white, and they really did struggle to find it on white sheets.

He really does rescue dogs, and Tap is a real beastie, too.

Happily, Vince is not the knob-head portrayed in this book, but a lovely guy who loaned his name and image to the story. Thanks, Vince! (Or possibly, sorry, Vince!)

ROMANCE WITH STUART REARDON

My lovely co-author - our joint titles

Two book series - contemporary romance

*Undefeated

*Model Boyfriend

Three book series - romcom

*Gym Or Chocolate?

*The World According to Vince

*The Baby Game

Standalone

Survivor Love Island *(romcom)*

*Touch My Soul *(novella)*

MORE BOOKS BY JHB

Series Titles
The Education Series
An epic love story spanning the years, through war zones and more...
*The Education of Sebastian (Education series #1)
*The Education of Caroline (Education series #2)
*The Education of Sebastian & Caroline (combined edition, books 1 & 2)
Semper Fi: The Education of Caroline (Education series #3)

The Traveling Series
All the fun of the fair ... and two worlds collide
*The Traveling Man (Traveling series #1)
*The Traveling Woman (Traveling series #2)
*Roustabout (Traveling series #3)
*Carnival (Traveling series #4)
*Gypsy (Traveling series #5)

The Justin Trainer Series

The bodyguard and the billionaire
Guarding the Billionaire (Justin Trainer series #1)
Saving the Billionaire (Justin Trainer series #2)

The EOD Series
Blood, bombs and heartbreak
*Tick Tock (EOD series #1)
* Bombshell (EOD series #2)

The Rhythm Series
Blood, sweat, tears and dance
*Slave to the Rhythm (Rhythm series #1)
*Luka (Rhythm series #2)

Standalone Titles
Contemporary Romance
The Lilac Cadillac
Battle Scars
One Careful Owner
*Lifers
At Your Beck & Call
The New Samurai
Exposure

New Adult
*Dangerous to Know & Love
Dazzled
Summer of Seventeen

Paranormal
*The Dark Detective: Venator (Book #1)
*The Dark Detective: Paukúnnum (Book #2)

Novellas

Playing in the Rain
*Behind the Walls

Anthologies of Short Stories
*The Year Book Volume 1
*The Year Book Volume 2
*The Year Book Volume 3

Audio Books
One Careful Owner
(*narrated by Seth Clayton*)

On the Stage
Later, After: Playscript
Trailer

With Alana Albertson
Father Figure

* These titles are published in languages other than English.
Please check Jane's website for details—and receive **a free short
story every month** when you sign up for her newsletter :)

QR code for Jane's website

WRITING AS BERRICK FORD

Police Thrillers, UK

Dead Water
Dead Man's Dive
Dead Reckoning
Dead Shore

www.berrickford.com

www.ingramcontent.com/pod-product-compliance
Lightning Source LLC
Chambersburg PA
CBHW070832250626
47159CB00003B/740